UNTAMED

LAUREN LANDISH

Edited by
VALORIE CLIFTON
Edited by
STACI ETHERIEDGE

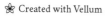 Created with Vellum

INTRODUCTION

Join my mailing list (www.laurenlandish.com) and receive 2 FREE ebooks! You'll also be the first to know of new releases, sales, and giveaways. If you're on Facebook, come join my Reader Group!

Irresistible Bachelor Series (Interconnecting standalones):
Anaconda || Mr. Fiance || Heartstopper
Stud Muffin || Mr. Fixit || Matchmaker
Motorhead || Baby Daddy

———

Everyone has their first love. Mine was Aubrey O'Day.

We were high school sweethearts with our futures planned, together every step of the way.

Then one day, he disappeared.

I was shattered, left with questions and doubts.

I've worked hard to rebuild my future, to create a different life. And I have. Good job, good friends... but something's missing.

A decade later, he's back in my life. But he's changed. Gone is the happy-go-lucky boy I knew, replaced by a brooding, mysterious beast of a man. Gone are the boyish good looks and innocent laughter. His broad chest, rippling arms, and chiseled abs have all exploded until he's literally a mountain of pure muscle.

Still, some things haven't changed. One look from him, and the fire he lit in my belly flares back to life. But where has he been? Why did he leave me?

And can we still have that future we dreamed of so long ago?

PROLOGUE

ANA

I shouldn't be here, lying in bed in a barely-there silk shift, my goosebump-covered thighs half-exposed, waiting for *him*. Not after what happened. Not after what he did. If I were smart, I'd leave now.

But I can't help myself. My body wants him, needs him, even if my mind is screaming that this is a bad idea.

I turn my head at the sound of creaking wood and bite my lower lip as our eyes meet. He's standing in the doorway, tall, muscular, and imposing. His mostly-shadowed form nearly fills the space, and only the ethereal light coming through the small window above me lights his face, making his eyes almost glow ferally as they devour my every curve.

A beast-like hunger radiates from him, so palpable the hair on the back of my neck rises and a damp, primal heat starts to warm the space between my thighs.

My pulse quickens and my breathing is heavy as I press my thighs together, my limbs trembling with an almost insatiable craving. Never in my entire life have I seen someone look at me with this much want. This much *need*.

And I need him.

I need him right fucking *now*.

The corner of his lips quirk upward as his burning eyes take in my trembling body. He knows exactly what his greedy stare does to me, and he has me exactly where he wants me.

"Please," I half moan, half whisper, hearing how desperate I sound. It's an alien feeling. I've always been the one in charge, never begging a man for anything.

But in this moment, I don't care.

I want this. I want *him*.

"I need you now," I whimper, sliding one shoulder strap off. It's a silent offer, with no conditions. Just take me, ravage me, give me the animal pleasure that's hiding behind your eyes. Show me what desire brings. "Claim me. After so long, take what's yours."

Grinning like a wolf, he pulls off his red flannel shirt and tosses it to the side, exposing his rippling muscle, hardened by years of hard work. His faded blue jeans are hung low, showing off the rock-hard 'V' at his hips, his happy trail descending to the huge cock imprint that even the sturdy fabric can't fully cloak.

My mouth waters at the sight, my lips parting in a soft moan of desire.

God, he's so fucking sexy, a true mountain of a man. I never thought it was possible to want another human being this much.

His eyes burn into me, tracing down my chest, my hips, before centering on my core. As his gaze brushes along my skin, my nipples harden and my clit begins to throb like a war drum. I'm ready to explode . . . and he hasn't even laid a finger on me yet.

He growls, sniffing the air. "You're already so wet for me."

It's not a question but a statement of fact. There's no denying it. I am beyond wet for him. He can probably smell my arousal, and I know he can see it too, his eyes flashing lust as they come to rest on my soaked panties.

"Yes," I sigh, my hands unconsciously drifting down my stomach toward my dripping mound, my knees parting to show him the near-translucent wispy garment.

"No," he grunts possessively. I freeze instantly, my hand a fraction above my throbbing clit. "Mine."

I watch him, my chest heaving, as he strides across the room, each massive footstep filling the cabin with the sound of creaking wood. Each step he takes is an eternity as every cell within my body awakens and screams in anticipation, electricity carried within my bloodstream itself as he nears.

When he gets to the side of the bed, he drops down, making the steel frame squeak loudly in protest, his almost massive weight settling upon my lower body. He spreads my legs wide before him, his deep voice dropping into a hungry growl that sounds more animal than human as he slips my soaked panties down my thighs.

I can't take it. The sight of him a breath's width away from my soaking wet pussy is too much to take. I can feel my inner walls clenching even though there's nothing there yet. "Fuck, you smell fucking delicious and sweet . . . like wild honey," he rumbles, licking his lips. "And finally, I get the taste I've dreamed of for so long."

His words have me bucking my hips toward his face, wanting what he's about to give me so badly I fear I'll break in two. "Yes . . . get your fill. Take what's yours."

"*All* mine," he says as he inhales my scent, looking as if he's preparing to devour an all-you-can-eat buffet. I realize the truth

3

of his words as my clit throbs in tandem with my raging heart-beat. I'm too scared to say it, but it's the truth.

My heart . . . it's his. Always has been. Though it might kill me if he breaks it again.

My body . . . all his. Every *fucking* part of it.

CHAPTER 1

AUBREY

*W*ork and pain. It's my entire existence. I wake up, wash under a flood of cold water, do chores around my cabin, go outside, hunt or chop fire wood if I'm running low, and then return when the sun goes down to eat and sleep in a bed that's more steel tubing and springs than mattress. Rinse, repeat.

It's a monotonous cycle. Some might even think of it as hell.

But for me, though, it's peace. It's a hard sort of heaven.

The work and strain keep my mind occupied, freeing it from the demons that torment me and the ghosts of my past.

But not today. Today's agenda is a different kind of hell. From far away, like the buzzing of an annoying fly, I vaguely hear . . .

"Fresh crisp air, sweeping views of Great Falls, magical nights spent looking up at the twinkling stars. Enjoy it all while staying at our amazing cabin, featuring all the amenities you need. So what are you waiting for? Book your trip to Bear Mountain now. How's that sound?"

"What?" I grunt absently, sitting back in my great oak chair. It's handmade, like most of the furniture in my cabin, but there aren't too many chairs that can take a man who stands six five and is built like a Strongman contestant.

Seated at a large wooden table near the window in a chair that makes her look not much bigger than a child, Carlotta Lawson, my fiery-haired second cousin and sales and marketing consultant, looks up from her laptop and scowls murder at me. "Have you been listening to me at all?"

A lock of red hair falls in front of her green eyes and she brushes it back in annoyance to continue her glare. She's been working for the past hour to create a presentable brochure, and my lack of attention to detail has her on edge. I know I should be helping out more. She's just about the only member of my family . . . hell, nearly the only *person*, I have contact with anymore.

But to be honest, I haven't been listening for the past ten minutes, though I should be. I need this sales pitch to be a hit with potential customers. Rising taxes on my fifty acres of land have been brutal, and if I want to hang onto my mountaintop paradise without dipping into my savings, I need to raise some cash.

Luckily, there's an extra little cabin on the property that will make a great seasonal Airbnb rental to help pay the bills. I won't even need to do any face-to-face contact with guests. I can hire a cleaning person when I need it, or just clean it when they're not around. But I'm not the marketing genius she is, so I need Carlotta to come up with the perfect vision . . . with as little input from me as possible.

I'm not the creative type, but give me an axe and I'll impress anyone with how fast I can send a tree crashing down before I lug it through the woods to turn it into firewood.

Carlotta continues to glare daggers at me as the silence drags out. "Well?" she finally says. "I'm waiting!"

I scratch at my beard, reminding myself I need to trim it. "Sure, I have," I finally say. "I've been paying attention."

Carlotta huffs, unconvinced. "Then what did I say?"

I think for a moment and say an approximation of what I think I heard. "Something about twinkling stars and gorgeous bears. And maybe crisp apples, but I don't know where you got that shit from."

Carlotta snorts in disgust. "See, that's my point exactly!" she says, ignoring her laptop to stare at me. Before I know it, she's slipped off into one of her epic rants about how I'm an inconsiderate, 'grunty' bastard who might as well be a caveman. She gets out of her chair, stomping back and forth and waving her arms around as she explains all of my shortcomings, behavioral, physical, and maybe genetic, in excruciating detail. It'd hurt if I still had feelings, or if they weren't all things I've heard before. Reality is . . . she's right, though, so not much I can do but let her get it all off her chest. " . . .always so rude. I'm here to do you a favor and you don't even have the decency to pay attention!"

I let her irritation run its course before replying, knowing if I don't, I run the risk of it starting all over again. "I was thinking, and really, there's not much I can offer. If you think it's good, it's good. I trust you and your skills."

It's about as much of an apology as she'll get out of me, especially after her little tirade. Carlotta shakes her head, crossing her arms and giving me the stink-eye. "If I could fight a man . . ."

I'm barely able to contain my grin at the image of her tiny fists flailing at me as I hold her back with a single finger to her forehead. "Listen, what you have sounds about right. Make it official."

Carlotta throws her hands up in defeat, snapping her laptop shut and climbing to her feet. "I know you're just saying that to get rid of me, but fine. I'll get the brochure printed and sent out to all the local businesses as soon as possible and finalize the online ad so it's live. I'll help, though you don't deserve it."

I rise out of my chair, towering over Carlotta. She doesn't mean it. She knows why I live the way I do, even if she doesn't quite approve. "You do that. I'm sure it will get us some traffic."

It's not quite a compliment, but close enough, especially when partnered with my telling her she's got good skills that I trust. I hand pleasantries like that out about as often as the Bills win the Super Bowl. But truth is, I'm amazed she puts up with my ass at all. Most of the world, and most of my family, stopped trying years back.

Carlotta glares up at me for a moment before her expression softens and she lets out a soft sigh. "Look, I'm sorry, Aubrey. You know I didn't mean to go off on you like that. It's just that I'm worried about you. Everyone is. You've moved up here, practically become a recluse, and haven't talked to your parents in years. You know your mother misses you terribly, right?"

I cross my arms over my chest, jutting my jaw. Carlotta never misses the opportunity to bring that little fact up whenever she's here. Seeing as how she's the only person I've let into my life lately, I don't necessarily blame her for trying to get messages through to me on others' behalf.

It's never worked though. Maybe it will change in the future, but for now, the door is closed. Carlotta doesn't understand the whole picture, even though she's probably seen a side of it.

"Anything else?" I grunt stonily.

Carlotta stares at me for a moment before looking all around, stopping at the logs I keep stored on this side of the cabin. "Yeah, how about getting someone in here to help you keep this place tidy? Or better yet, get a girlfriend? It *has* be lonely up here all by yourself."

The latter question is one she also brings up, and one I have no intention of answering.

"For your second question, none of your business. As for your first," I reply, hooking a thumb at the broom against the wall that I just used yesterday, "you're welcome to help yourself to sweeping and mopping." My voice is hard, dismissive even to my ears.

I fully expect Carlotta to storm out, but she just shakes her head, looking up at me worriedly. "I'm just going to pretend you didn't say that." She leans in closer, her piercing green eyes filled with concern. "In all seriousness, I think it is my business. You can't stay alone forever, Aubrey. You really need to find someone. At least a damn friend. I can't even imagine what it must be like for you."

"I'm fine. It's just the way I like it," I say stubbornly, refusing to budge. Carlotta sure is pushing the envelope more than usual today. If I didn't know better, I'd swear she wants to give me a hug, and I hug about as often as I compliment. "You needn't worry about me."

Carlotta bites her lower lip and then her voice drops low. "I know you're still hurting over . . ." She stops short of bringing up a name that we both avoid saying, "but it's been ten years now. You've got to start moving on. You don't have to keep torturing yourself like this. He wouldn't want you to."

I keep my stone-faced expression, silent and imposing, not letting Carlotta in on the emotions roiling beneath the surface. Instead, I nonchalantly nod at the door. "I'd invite you to stay for dinner, but it seemed you wanted to leave?" It's more order than question and works exactly the way I wanted it to.

Anger flashes in her eyes, and she steps back, turning on a heel. "Fine, be that way. I'll have the proofs to you by tonight."

Snatching her laptop and bag from the table, she leaves. For a few moments, I hear muffled cursing and then the roar of an ATV engine and the sound of tires rolling over snow and gravel as she drives off.

After she's gone, my stony demeanor crumbles a little and my shoulders slump. I usually like Carlotta's visits, and she's right about a little human interaction being a good thing for me. But only a little, and on my terms. I didn't mean to piss her off, but I wasn't about to let her into that side of my brain either. Usually, she knows not to push me, but today, she was bolder than usual.

She'll get over it.

Truth is, I ran Carlotta off for hitting my sore spot. Her only fault lay in reminding me of what I don't have . . . and might *possibly* miss. I'm stubborn as a mule, but even I can see that maybe it's time to test the waters a little bit.

Living up here in the mountains, though, I wouldn't know the first place to start. Hell, maybe this Airbnb idea might be that first step. I could actually say hello to someone every now and then. Work on my terrible fucking social skills.

"Carlotta's right," I mutter as I realize grunting 'good morning' isn't exactly rejoining the world. I was just too prideful and stubborn to admit it in her presence.

Looking around the cabin, it's cozy enough, with caramel hardwood floors and a stone fireplace in the center of the living room. I laid that fireplace with my bare hands, picking the rocks out of the land surrounding my cabin and hauling them in a pack all the way here. It's some piece of work. But the whole place is more functional and minimal than inviting. It looks like exactly what it is . . . a mountain man bachelor pad with no heart, no softness.

Beyond the cleaning, the connection with someone Carlotta talked about would probably do me even more good.

Having a woman around probably would make life easier.

But I haven't been with anyone in a long time . . . and I'm practically a caveman these days. I don't need Carlotta to tell me that.

It's been a while since I've had a woman. And I'd be lying to myself if I said I wasn't as horny as a bull that's been caged up in a pen. There's only so much 'self love' you can do before you're frustrated for something more.

But what would happen if I actually started dating and let the caged beast within me free? I'm almost afraid to find out.

Tap. Tap. Tap. The sound comes from outside, and the pitter patter of furry feet breaks me out of my reverie. The wooden dog door I put in last winter swings in, and I look into the piercing grey-blue eyes of my only companion, Rex, a Siberian husky that's been with me since moving to Bear Mountain.

If dogs are a man's best friend, then Rex is the closest thing to a soulmate that I've had with a non-human. I've raised him from a puppy, taking him from Doc Jones, the vet in town, when Rex was abandoned by his owners. He's always by my side whenever I need him and has proven himself to be of great use, helping me do chores around the property. If anything, he scares the shit out of local bears.

Rex stands in the short entrance hallway, gazing at me, obediently waiting for permission to come all the way in, though I don't mind where he goes. He's my buddy. I snap my fingers and he trots up to me, sitting right at my feet as I squat down, rubbing him behind the ears.

"You hear that conversation between me and Car, boy?" I ask him, finding his secret spot behind his left ear that makes his tail wag extra-fast. "She thinks I need a woman around here to keep things straight. What do you think about that?"

Rex tilts his head to the side, looking curious.

I chuckle at his expression, shaking my head as I walk over to the calendar I use to keep up with my logging schedule. "Yeah, I think she's crazy too."

I quickly scan the jobs I have planned for the rest of today. It's not too much, just an old pine that could fall across the trail off my property in the next snow, but it involves some tedious chopping. Fuck chainsaws. I do this right. But if I want to be done by sunset, I need to start now.

I walk over and grab my favorite axe, an exquisite workhorse with a hickory handle and a hardened steel blade. I'm actually relishing the prospect of a hard afternoon of work. It'll allow me to forget my problems.

At least I hope.

"Come on, boy," I tell Rex, who obediently pads to my side as I shoulder my axe and begin gathering my gear. "We've got a lot of work to do."

I WALK BACK INTO THE CABIN COVERED IN SWEAT, AN IRON ACHE running down my back between my shoulder blades from an afternoon's labor, my booted feet *clunking* across the hardwood floor. Rex obediently pads in behind me, panting, and drops down on his worn and tattered dog bed.

Grinning at him, I fill his water bowl at the kitchen sink and place it in front of him. I watch him lap up the liquid like it's the last drink he'll ever have.

"That's a good boy," I tell him. "You act like you've been running a marathon in the desert."

Grabbing a cold beer out of the fridge, I sit back in my big chair and prop my feet up onto the table, letting out a weary sigh.

"We made good progress today, Rex," I say, looking out the front window. The sun is just now dipping into the horizon, and the surrounding trees and land are bathed in tones of yellow and orange. It's a picturesque scene and the reason I chose here, along with the peace and quiet.

But wouldn't it be better to share the sunsets with someone? the annoying voice in my mind whispers.

I shove the voice to the back edges of my mind, irritated. But it reminds me of something.

Carlotta was supposed to be sending me the final brochure.

I take several more chugs of my beer before getting out my laptop. Besides going down into town for the food I can't get my hands on out here, this cranky old thing is my only link to the outside world. I use it to keep current with world affairs and to handle my limited business matters.

Ironically, an email from Carlotta is the first thing that pops up on my screen.

Dear Stubborn Pain In My Ass,

Aww . . . and here I was thinking she didn't care.

Here is the brochure in its entirety. I hope it fits your liking, but even if it doesn't . . . too late. Using my judgement and your lack of input, I've decided that it conveys the vibe we want perfectly and have gone through with a final version. The online profile's updated, and the order is at the printers.

I should pick up the hard copies by week's end and then I'll get them all sent out. I've included my name and number on the brochure since you said you wanted me to handle all inquiries for booking. By the way, I'm taking a cut from that, so there!

In the meantime, I've included a digital copy that's specifically formatted for email. So if you have any friends who might be interested in a vacation or people who can help you pass it around to get the word out, feel free to share.

Friends? She is being optimistic, isn't she?

By the way, I'm not mad at you for being an ass today. I recognize it's a defense mechanism and I was skating on a touchy subject. I'm sorry. I'm just worried about your wellbeing. I hope you understand.

Love,

Car

I read her letter again before opening the attached document. I have to give the girl a salute with my beer, so I do, lifting my can toward the screen. It's gorgeous, with professional pictures of the rental cabin and the surrounding landscape laid out in a neat collage intertwined with text. There's even a link to a YouTube video, a two-minute overview that Carlotta narrated herself.

There's no way I could have come up with something like this, and it proves I made the right decision in hiring Carlotta to handle the matter.

Still, I look over the finished product several times, looking for any mistakes she might've missed.

One picture in the collage, one that I was adamant that Carlotta include, keeps popping out at me. It's an area I used to frequent a long time ago and one of the reasons I bought the property with the inheritance my grandmother left me.

It's a nighttime shot of a small lake that leads off into a quiet cove, the stars twinkling above. It's a romantic scene if there ever was one.

Seeing it brings back memories, memories I've tried to keep buried. Of the last time I felt romantic. Of the guy I used to be. Of her . . .

Ana Tucker.

Even after all this time, my heart skips a little at the mere thought of her. I don't know why. She probably doesn't even remember who I am. Even if she does, considering what I did, she probably hates my guts.

Unable to resist the melodramatic curiosity, I bring up Google and type her name in the search bar. I hover the mouse pointer over the search button for a moment, filled with indecision. I've never dared search her name before, making a pact with myself to forget her. That's easier if I don't know anything about her.

But after the visit with Carlotta today, and staring at the romantic lake image, I'm feeling a bit vulnerable.

Don't do it. Don't do it.

My mind goes through a million and one reasons it isn't a good idea to search Anabelle. The biggest reason, of course, is that she's probably married and has at least one kid that she's proudly showing off all over social media.

I couldn't handle that. In fact, even thinking of the possibility makes the dark clouds start to push in again and makes my decision easy.

Tapping my touchpad, I close the tab and shut down my laptop.

I'll leave the memory of Ana Tucker in the past where it belongs since we'll never be.

CHAPTER 2

Beep, beep-beep, beep, beep-beep . . . the monitor chirps at slow, even intervals, like a slow waltz. It's a sound that I've grown accustomed to working in Great Falls as a nurse at St. Joseph's Memorial Hospital, so familiar I can tune it out unless it stops.

But in this particular patient's case, someone who had been at death's door just a week ago and a half ago, it's music to my ears. Fighting off severe pneumonia can be hard for anyone, and this patient wasn't the strongest to begin with.

A hacking cough interrupts my thoughts, and my instincts kick in. I can't help it. Even before I was a nurse, I wanted to take care of people.

"You feeling okay, Mrs. Smith?" I ask concernedly, rushing over to check the numbers on the monitors and more importantly, pat her back and comfort her through the coughing fit. "How's the chest?"

Eleanor Smith, a seventy-one-year-old woman with a shock of wiry gray hair who's a total hoot and has taken to giving me unsolicited advice over the week she's been here, waves me away unconcernedly, her bushy brows crinkling her forehead into a patchwork of wrinkles. It takes a moment for her to regain control of her breathing to speak as she shakes her head. "Of course I am, dear. Just a little coughing, that's all. Probably from being cooped up in this dreadful room all day."

She gestures a gaunt arm at the window where I see the clear blue skyline of Great Falls. The air is so crystal-clear I can even see the snow-capped Bear Mountains in the distance. They look so beautiful. A part of me wishes I were there soaking in some sunlight, right up at the ski resort I can just make out on the nearest of the hills. "I understand, Mrs. Smith."

"It's so depressing lying in here when all that is waiting for me out there." She shakes her head, looking rightfully agitated. "A damned shame, really. My garden needs me."

I smile knowingly. It's the beginning of spring, barely past our last frost and while Great Falls thawed quickly this year, the only thing Mrs. Smith's garden is growing is mushy snowmen. "Well, I have some good news for you," I say cheerfully. "Dr. Turner says your condition is stable enough that you'll likely be discharged in a couple of days. He just needs to run some additional tests to make absolutely sure you're all set."

"Well, he'd better hurry the hell up then," Eleanor grumbles. "The radishes can't grow themselves."

I chuckle, knowing her radishes will be just fine even if she's here for another month. "I'm going to change your bedsheets out now, Mrs. Smith, okay?" I ask gently. "Do you want me to roll you over or do you want to get in the chair?"

Eleanor gives a faint nod towards the chair. "Oh, I want to sit up in the chair for a bit. Can you help? Just watch the hip. It's always giving me trouble. Too much rump shaking in my younger days, if you know what I mean."

I can't help but giggle, realizing patients like Eleanor are one of the reasons I love what I do. Sure, it's a little weird to see a woman old enough to be my grandmother talking about booty shaking, but who knows? Maybe she was getting her freak on at Woodstock. And I've always enjoyed meeting new people, getting to know them, their personalities and all their quirks. Helping them get better and sending them on their way in better condition than when they arrived are what drive me to do what I do.

"All set," I say when I'm done helping Eleanor's to the chair and changing her bed. "Is there anything else you'd like to make you more comfortable?"

Mrs. Smith shakes her head, patting my hand. "No, thank you. You're such a sweet girl, Anabelle . . . and a wonderful nurse."

A surge of warmth flows through my chest. I always love to get compliments from my patients, a sign that even if they're stuck in the hospital, something that is by nature depressing, I did something to brighten their day. "Thank you, Mrs. Smith."

Eleanor looks at me, her wise rheum-lined blue eyes searching my face. "But my word, child, you look tired. Are you getting enough sleep?"

I open and close my mouth for a moment, shocked by her blunt statement. "Pardon?"

Eleanor gestures at the mirror over the sink. "Look at yourself, girl. You look like you haven't rested in days."

I begin to protest but stop short when I catch a glimpse of my face in the mirror. With brown sugar eyes, bra-length honey-brown hair, and an hourglass figure, some would say I'm pretty. But with a shock, I realize that Eleanor's right. I do look more haggard than usual, and the dark circles under my eyes are underscored with bags fit to be luggage.

But I can't help it. The flu season this year was a bitch, and a lot of nurses have been calling off with bugs of some type or another. I've been helping, taking overtime shifts on the regular because they needed staff. But I've been so busy lately, I haven't even noticed the subtle changes in my appearance.

"I've been working a little overtime," I admit grudgingly, "but I don't mind."

Mrs. Smith tuts me, and I'm reminded that in her previous life she was a junior high school teacher. "Oh, that's bull, young lady. You're a human, not a robot. How long have you been working hard like this? A year? Two? I think you need a serious break, my dear," Eleanor says, gesturing back at the window. "And a lot of sun. You've been here since they brought me in on what I thought was my last breath. I've seen how hard you work, but you need some down time too. Do it for yourself, but if you won't do that . . . do it for me, an old lady who understands that a day relaxing in the sunshine is just what you need. Trust me. You'll thank me later."

My immediate urge is to brush off Eleanor's suggestion. Yes, I work hard, but I'm used to it, going straight from all-night study sessions to twelve-hour shifts at the hospital. Plus, honestly, I need to work hard. I've still got a stack of student loans roughly as long as my arm. Besides, I truly love what I do, so working a lot doesn't feel like a burden. It gives me focus and keeps my mind off my lack of a social life.

I hold back the dark snort at my 'social life'. My life consists of work and the occasional dinner with my brother, Trey. He seems to think it's my fault I haven't found a man, dramatically bemoaning that I spend most of my time working or with my nose stuck in a book. Of course, it doesn't help that he's found the man of his dreams in Brad, a hair and makeup wizard who is an absolute trip. Falling in love has suddenly made Trey into *Team Love's* biggest cheerleader, and he's decided that I'm missing out.

Worst part is? He might be right. I haven't been looking for love, but lately, nights alone over TV dinners and DVR reruns don't feel the same. I'd like to find that 'special someone' to come home to, but it hasn't happened. I really don't know what's wrong with me. At twenty-eight, I still have time, and my biological clock hasn't started screaming doomsday. Maybe that's been the issue? No sense of urgency, so I've just been coasting along, focused on other things like school, work . . . the past. Nope, not going there. Definitely not.

As if reading my mind, Eleanor pulls me out of my reverie. "And you definitely look like you could use a date," she says, putting a little emphasis on the word 'date' to show she doesn't mean a dinner out on the town. She lowers her voice to a whisper. "How about that Adam fella who comes in here at night? That boy's sure got a nice tush on him."

I start to protest. Adam is definitely not my type, considering his brain is solely focused on gym schedules and new protein shake combos to help bulk up. But to my horror, a giant yawn escapes my lips instead of my explanation.

Eleanor jumps at the opening. "See, what did I tell you? You're about to pass out on the floor."

"Okay," I admit grudgingly. "Maybe I am a little overworked. But it's nothing a good night's rest won't fix." I give Eleanor a gentle smile. "Thank you for your concern, Mrs. Smith, but I'm fine. I'll be back to check on you in a bit, okay?"

She gives me a wise scowl and crosses her bony arms across her chest. "You'll be seeing things my way soon. Watch. Us old bats know these things."

For the rest of the morning, I make my rounds through the floor, checking in on each of my patients. Eleanor's words never leave my mind, and the more I think about it, the more I like the idea of a little vacation—some fresh air, clear blue skies, and sun to keep the pep in my step. The flu 'epidemic' is waning. What harm could it do?

It's not long before I'm daydreaming about all the fun places I can visit. Disneyworld . . . Hawaii . . . okay, those might be a little beyond my means. But there's one place that stands out to me more than others, a place I haven't been to in over ten years but a place I've been yearning to go back to.

Ironically enough, it's local.

You can't go back there. That was a different time, a different space. There's nothing there now but memories. Dead memories.

By the time I make it back to Eleanor's room for a scheduled check-in, I admit to myself that I'm feeling a little bit tired from all the running back and forth between patients. And I've still got med rounds and making sure lunches go out correctly.

"Well look who's back," Eleanor teases, taking her eyes off the TV and fixing them on me. "Ready to switch places with me yet? I've got this bed warm and comfortable for you." She grins and pats the bed next to her.

I laugh and throw my hands up in defeat. "Okay, Mrs. Smith, I'll admit it. You're right. I'm a little tired, and now that you mentioned a getaway, I've been thinking about it all morning."

Eleanor smiles and gives me a thumbs-up. "That's the spirit! Have you thought about where'd you like to go?"

Picking up the clipboard from the end of her bed, I write as I talk. "A little bit. But if I do end up taking off, it has to be somewhere that's worth it." I give Eleanor a wry smile as I fix my eyes on the snow-capped mountains in the distance. "Somewhere special."

I'M HUNGRY BY THE TIME I MAKE IT TO THE BREAK ROOM. Unfortunately, I didn't pack lunch, and I have no desire to walk down to the cafeteria. But I did manage to stuff two of my favorite dudes in the freezer for a snack before my shift.

Ben & Jerry . . . I know you're cheating man-whores who'll put out for any girl who'll wave some money and a spoon in your face, but damn if a mouthful of your cream isn't what hits the spot.

I grin at my own dirty double-entendres and retreat to the corner of the room to enjoy my half-eaten tub of Rocky Road, sinking down on the beaten-up but comfy old couch some doctor donated long before I started working here. While I eat, I watch as some of my co-workers come in and out, chitter-chattering about the latest gossip.

Usually, if a subject interests me, I join in. That's how conversations go around here, just jump in with both feet while you can and drop out when you have to. But today, I'm content to listen from afar. My mind is too busy contemplating an actual vacation.

Throughout the day, I've thought about going to Paris, Barcelona, Greece, a whole bunch of exotic places. But I quickly discarded those ideas. If I can't even do Disney, flying overseas would break the bank, and besides, I definitely don't want to take a trip like that by myself. I try to remember the last vacation I actually took. Maybe when I was a kid, piled up in the backseat with Trey to drive to some rock formation or museum? Shit, has it really been that long?

I'm in the midst of a delicious bite of ice cream, my tongue lightly scraping over a nugget of delicious fudge, when a brochure on the wall catches my eye. I squint, trying to see details from where I'm sitting. It looks like some brochure for a vacation hot spot.

With all the talk of a vacation today, I can't help myself. I get up and walk over to examine it. The headline at the top seems to jump out at me.

Relax and get away. Find peace and beauty you have to see to believe!

It's a gorgeously laid out pamphlet, with pictures of a beautiful cabin and scenery located in the Bear Mountains. The same mountains I saw through Eleanor's window today.

There's one picture in particular that sticks out to me. A nighttime shot of a small lake that feeds into a lagoon, the stars twinkling above. It's so beautiful yet so very familiar. It plays with my mind as I leave the break room and go to get meds ready.

I'm about halfway through Mr. Robinson's twelve pills when I realize, and I'm so shocked that my fingers go numb and the bottle falls out of my hand to clatter to the top of the med cart.

That lake . . . I've been there before.

CHAPTER 3

ANA

*T*wo weeks.

One beautiful cabin.

And a whole lotta *me* time.

It took me a week to get the time off arranged, but just the idea of having plans helped buoy me through the past few days of overtime shifts. Now, vacation time.

I'm excited but a little scared. I've never taken a vacation by myself. What if I get bored? What if I don't? Maybe I'll just hole up in the cabin, pamper myself with spa treatments, and eat junk food. That sounds great, but I do want to get outside a bit too, enjoy that sunshine Mrs. Smith told me I needed.

And I won't be alone the whole time, just for most of it. Trey and Brad are coming for the first few days, a nice weekend getaway for them too, but they can't take that much time off.

I initially insisted that I'd rather go alone, but Trey likes to play big brother. And he wanted to make sure I got settled into the cabin safely and that it wasn't some *Deliverance*-esque trap via vacation brochure. After the past few hours of listening to

Brad's crass jokes and reminiscing about the good times with Trey, I'm kinda glad they've tagged along.

"So I said, girl, I'm a makeup artist, not David Copperfield. I'm nowhere near as old and a whole hell of a lot better looking," Brad quips from the back seat as I round a bend going up Bear Mountain. We're riding in a rented Volkswagen SUV for the trip. No way would my little day to day car make it. "You want a magic act, head yourself to Hollywood for some CGI-action, because I can't make a Hyundai look like a Mercedes without a green screen!"

I chuckle and then give him a scowl. "You know you shouldn't talk about people like that. Especially your customers! That's so wrong," I scold him.

"Me? Wrong? What about her? I might be good, but I ain't *that* good," he laughs, then grows serious. "Relax, girly. Don't get your panties all in a bunch. You know it's a joke . . . but it works better if I say it in first-person, dammit!"

I smile and shake my head, giving an 'I feel for you' look at my big brother, Trey, who's sitting in the passenger seat. "I don't know how you deal with him."

Trey, who's dressed for our trip with dark jeans, a flannel shirt, and a fur cap, returns a tight smile. "With *a lo*t of patience. Besides, I'll take it out on him later."

"Oh, please, would you?" Brad says, little hearts almost visibly shooting from his eyes as he bats his lashes at Trey. "You know I love it when you get all sweaty and primal and just . . . mmpfh." His eyes don't leave Trey, but his next words are to me, "Ana, you're gonna have to take a walk when we get to the cabin. And don't mind the ropes in the back seat. They're just for fun."

Trey rolls his eyes. Their constant banter is a trip, but it can get old after a while. Hopefully, they'll be long gone before either one happens too much.

"Seriously though, Sis, I tell my clients all the time how important it is to take a time-out from work and de-stress, so I'm really happy that you're finally doing something like this for yourself," Trey says a few minutes later as we round another bend. He gently pats my shoulder. "You need this." Trey's a personal trainer by definition, but really his approach to his clients is much more holistic and I frequently tease him that he's more life coach than meathead. He humbly rejects that notion, but the truth is, my big brother is a pretty smart guy and I respect the hell out of him for doing his own thing and making a living at it.

As we come around the side of the mountain, the sun hits the windshield, dazzling me before the road adjusts and everything clears dramatically. I can see we're a thousand feet in the air, in the lower portion of the snowline, Great Falls sprawled out below. It's dramatic, a postcard in itself, and looking at the town below me makes me feel like I've been freed, a great weight lifted off my shoulders for a little while.

"For real," Brad adds as I start to smile. "All jokes aside, Ana, you are the sweetest, most down to earth bitch I know. And you work so hard at that germ-infested hospital, always giving and never taking. Ain't no way in hell I could do that. So if anyone deserves a vacation, it's you."

"Gee, erm, uh, thanks."

"You're welcome, honey."

I come up another curve that leads off to a level road and the GPS dings. We're getting close to our destination and I'm getting excited. Just the thought of being able to lay out, meditate, take a hike, or do whatever I damn well please for the next two weeks sounds so appealing.

It's amazing how I didn't even know I needed a little break from work until a patient pointed it out to me.

I guess sometimes we get in a rut, spinning in the wheel like a hamster but never going anywhere, and it takes someone on the outside to tell us that we need to step off, get help, and try something new.

The good thing is once this is over, I can return to work fresh, able to make even more of a difference in people's lives. The thought makes me feel warm and fuzzy inside.

I turn down a dirt road that goes on for another twenty minutes, narrowing a few times, and I start to worry, double-checking the GPS, but then it opens into a clearing. My breath catches in my throat as I take it all in—a beautiful, lush landscape of gorgeous trees, open land, and two scenic cabins spread about fifty yards apart. Actually, the far cabin is close enough that I wonder where the hell it was on the promo materials.

A light film of snow is on the ground in patches and on the trees, like someone took God's spray can of Christmas frosting and had a party. My tires squeal as I break through the frost, rolling to a stop near the first cabin. I hop out along with Trey and Brad.

"Wow, this place is *so* beautiful." Brad gawks, his mouth open wide and a little wisp of frosty breath trickling out. "Trey, we should've totally booked this place for ourselves! Big campfires, hot cocoa nights, and days of enjoying this alpine winter wonderland? I'm so freaking jealous!"

I have to agree with Brad. The land is breathtaking. Just like in the photos. It's so serene, I feel relaxed just being here.

But I have to wonder . . . what's up with the other cabin? The brochure and the lady who managed the property didn't mention anything about another cabin nearby. I thought I was paying for an exclusive setting.

Trey seems to be thinking the same thing as he starts to ask a question. "The other cabin for rent too?"

"I don't know, maybe—" I reply, but I'm interrupted by a strangled cry and several barks.

"What the hell was that?" Brad demands, but I'm already running toward the direction of the sounds. My booted feet find solid ground as I run.

We're about a hundred yards on the up-mountain side of the other cabin when I find a large man lying there with logs scattered about him, a large husky hovering over him. The dog barks and growls menacingly at me as I approach, and I raise my hands defensively, hoping it doesn't attack.

"Easy, boy," says the man, his voice deep but strained, pain evident in every syllable. "She's harmless."

There's something familiar about the way the man speaks, but the pain's distorting it, and I don't have time to figure it out right now. My main concern is assessing the situation and seeing how injured he is. My eyes are already scanning him, looking for blood, broken bones, anything life-threatening, and I take in his flannel shirt and jeans, along with his sensible boots, so I at least know he's prepared to be up here on the mountain. I try to scan his face, but all I can see are his bearded jaw and the flops of dark hair that drape over his face, hiding his features. The sheer size of him along with the overall effect of mountain man is enough to make me pause, but he needs help and my instincts take over.

"Little help?" I ask, nodding toward the dog, hoping he gets my meaning because he can't see me.

The man hesitates for a moment but then does a sharp whistle. The dog instantly stops and sits back on his haunches but still watches me warily. I crouch next to the man, looking his massive body over for wounds. "What happened?" I ask.

"I chopped a tree down yesterday and was hauling some pieces for my stockpile . . . tripped on something," his deep voice strains out.

"Let me take a look." I start to pull on his pants, but he jerks his leg away, hissing in pain. Well, looks like we've found our problem.

"I'm fine," he grunts. "Just need a minute to shake it off."

"Stay still," I command with authority, not paying him any mind. In the face of serious injury, there's no time to be prideful.

"Really, I'm fine—"

I ignore him and turn to look at Brad and Trey, who've finally caught up with me. "Brad, go get the First-Aid kit out of the trunk."

"Listen, lady, I don't need help," the man protests, trying to sit up.

"Stop moving!" I crack sharply, pushing him back down. Well, trying to push him down, but it's harder than I thought, he's just that fucking big and strong. I think he more gives up against the pressure of my hand on his shoulder than my actually moving him. But he's sitting again, at least. I swear this guy's head must be as hard as a rock.

"No, let me get up and I'll show you—"

"You'll do nothing of the sort," I growl, using the sternest voice I can manage. "I'm a nurse, and you could be seriously injured. Let me take a look. It will only take a minute."

I turn to give him a hard look, letting him know I mean business. Being soft-natured, it's a face I don't like to use, but he's leaving me no choice. The man looks like he's going to continue arguing but then relents, falling back on his elbows and watching me. His brown eyes peek from behind the curtain of hair, and there's a moment of recognition in his eyes, and I wonder if I've treated him before. No time for that right now.

Satisfied that I won't be interrupted, I grab his right leg and pull up his jeans above his ankle. It's swollen and already turning purplish. I suck in a breath instead of hissing in displeasure. Not good.

I gently press on the bruised area, and the man winces as I take his entire foot in my hands. There's no grating feeling and he doesn't scream like a baby, so I'm going to guess there's nothing broken.

"Looks like you have a bad sprain," I announce after my examination, hoping there isn't anything torn. Either way, that's beyond my skills, and if he does need surgery, he's coming off the mountain. "Pretty bad one. You're going to need to rest and stay off it."

"Shit . . ." the man mutters in dismay.

Brad returns just in time with the First-Aid kit. I take it from him and begin rummaging through it for what I need.

I locate the elastic wrap and begin bandaging the man's ankle with Brad, Trey, and the husky looking on. I can feel their eyes on my back, but what's making my hands a bit shaky is the glare of the man I'm helping. I get it, man. *You're all big and burly, probably usually a badass. But right now, you need help, and I can offer that, so quit being so damn grumpy about it.* Of course, I wouldn't say that out loud. He'd probably eat me, and not in the fun way. *Ugh . . . focus, Ana!*

"You know what?" Brad begins to say, "You're lucky Florence Nightingale was here to help." I can hear the fairy-tale tilt to his voice, like he's getting ready to start some wondrous story about the sweet nurse and the growly beast.

"Shh!" Trey says sternly with a scowl. "Ana's trying to work."

31

"Spoilsport." Brad goes silent, but when I peek over at him, he's staring at the man as if he's a scoop of ice cream with caramel bourbon sauce on top.

When I'm done, I sit back with a scowl. It's ugly, but it'll work, and I can do better when we get inside.

"I've got you all bandaged up. You need to stay off the ankle for a bit, probably a week or so—"

"A week?" The man snorts. "I can't do that. Got too much work to do."

Anger sparks in my stomach as I gesture at his ankle. I'm not sure why, maybe because he seems so stubborn and is questioning me, but I swear I've heard that voice before. "You have to if you don't want it to get worse. I mean, you're lucky all you have is a sprain. You could have broken it or ruptured a ligament or worse! And then you'd be fucked from here to Sunday." Nice nurse Ana is gone, a sassy, mouthy version taking her place.

"Here to Sunday . . . Ana?" the man asks suddenly, looking pale.

I freeze as he shoves his thick fingers through his hair and I finally get a good look at his face. Moments before, I was too filled with adrenaline to even pay attention to his features, and he's got a dirty face and his beard needs a little trim, but . . .

My eyes take in his dark hair, longer than it used to be, with his brown eyes that seem to look into my soul. He's definitely rough around the edges, but he's almost too handsome to be real.

He can't be real, can he? a voice says in the back of my head.

Ten years. He was just a boy when he left, though a *big* boy. But now he's a full-grown man. Taller, a hell of a lot more massive, and corded with muscles. His chest and shoulders are about a mile wide and look chiseled like a rock.

Aubrey O'Day.

The boy I thought I would be with forever.

The boy I thought I'd never see again.

The bastard who broke my heart.

"You."

We both gape at each other as the recognition washes over us. Behind me, I can hear Trey and Brad whispering, then Brad gets a little louder. "Ooh, things are about to get good. Wish I had some popcorn for this little showdown."

I ignore Brad and hop to my feet as soon as the shock wears off. "What the hell are you doing here?" I ask, trying to keep the tremble out of my voice. I'm rocked by the range of emotions running through me. Shock. Anger. Attraction. Yeah, that last one really pisses me off, but it's undeniable. Ten years have taken Aubrey from being 'handsome' to being 'holy fucking shit.'

Aubrey grimaces as he sits up, but I refuse the urge to comfort him. "What do you mean? I live here." His voice is a gravel-filled rumble, a soothing balm to the cracks he left in my heart. And that pisses me off even more.

I used to come up to Bear Mountain with Aubrey back in high school, but he didn't live here then. "What do you mean, you *live* here?"

"I bought this place a few years back." He nods at the cabin that's near the one I rented. "I live next door."

The world seems to spin around me as I stare into his face. My mind is whirling, the past and the present colliding inside my brain in an explosion of darkness and sparkles. And isn't that just the perfect image . . . dark for the pain he put me through, but sparkles for all the good times, because we did have them.

I look over at Brad and Trey, who are just as bewildered as I am.

"Ana, I feel like I need to explain some things."

I draw myself up, pull myself together from a pain I thought I'd long ago outgrown, and hold a hand up, silencing him. "Don't bother. I don't know why you're here . . . and I really don't care. That was ten years ago and you don't owe me anything. I don't owe you anything either."

"Ana—"

No stopping me now. I just roll over him like a juggernaut of words and attitude. "I'm here for a much-needed vacation. And since that woman told me my payment was non-refundable, I'm not going to let your presence deter me from enjoying myself."

He's trying to get up, but he shouldn't bother. I'm not going to listen to a word he says.

"Stay off that ankle for at least a week. And please don't come over here. Don't ruin my vacation."

"Ana, wait!" Aubrey tries to call, but I ignore him, trying to get as far away from him as I can. Behind me, I can hear Brad and Trey talking to each other about what to do with the still-wounded man, but I don't care.

Right now, I need to process what just happened.

Aubrey is here. My high school sweetheart. My first love.

Instead of nursing his wound, I should have kicked him right in the balls and screamed at him what a jerk he was. He doesn't deserve any sympathy or help from me. Lord knows, he didn't give me any help when he left me broken.

CHAPTER 4

AUBREY

I watch, mesmerized as Ana stomps away, her curvy hips swaying with each step, her ass looking mighty fine in her Levis. I call for her to come back, but she ignores me like the bastard she thinks I am.

Every part of my body screams at me to go after her and make her listen to me. But I'm frozen, standing on one foot like Bigfoot fucked a flamingo and I'm the result.

That beautiful woman, that gorgeous fucking creature who just bandaged up my ankle, is Anabelle Tucker? Little Ana, who last time I saw her, barely broke five feet and was shy, sweet, and . . .

And the one I let get away. Or should I say more correctly, the one I stupidly ran out on. The one I always thought would be my wife. Sure, we were young as fuck, but I just had that feeling.

Her pretty face still possesses the sweet innocence I remember, but now it has a maturity that comes with being a grown woman . . . and apparently, a nurse.

It doesn't seem humanly possible, but she's even more beautiful than before.

I brush off my momentary shock and try to take a step, putting most of my weight on my left foot. "Ana, wait!" I call.

"Hol-ee-shit, you really pissed her off!" the spiky-haired blond next to me exclaims. He's standing next to a guy I now recognize as Ana's brother, Trey.

I ignore them, limping after Ana, wincing from the pain shooting through my ankle. Trey and Blondie talk to each other behind me, but I'm too intent on catching up to Ana to hear what they're saying. Even with my handicap, I catch up with Ana before she gets halfway to her cabin.

Ever near, Rex pads to my side and watches.

"Ana," I say, reaching out.

She spins out of reach, turning to glare at me, her nostrils flaring. Her doe eyes flicker to Rex and soften, but then they flash back to me and the anger comes back as she shoots eyeball daggers. If looks could kill, I'd be a huge-ass dead man right now.

"What do you want, Aubrey? Didn't I tell you to stay over there?" she half yells, nodding toward my cabin. Her voice has so much anger, it's hard to believe it's Anabelle Tucker talking. She was always so sweet and endearing in high school. I never saw her get mad at anyone. I can't say that I don't deserve her ire or that she isn't sexy as fuck when she's pissed off. It makes her skin glow pink, and I wonder . . . does she still blush like she did when I stroked her nipples through her shirt for the first time? Ana, though, doesn't seem to remember. "Get to fucking stepping."

I scowl. I might be a bastard for what I did, but I'm not going to let her boss me around. "You're on *my* property. I'll do whatever the hell I please."

Ana scowls back and holds her palm out, turning her head away.

"Fine. Give me a refund then, and I'll be gone before you can even blink."

"Not happening," I say firmly, shaking my head. Sure, I'm being stubborn and a pain in the ass, but I'm an expert at both. And in this case, oh, hell no. I let her get away once. I'm not letting her get away again. "You're not going anywhere."

"Then stay away from me. I don't want to talk to you." She starts to turn, but I stop her with a firm hand on the shoulder.

"Ana—"

She recoils from my touch as if I'm a snake, throwing my hand off and sending me dangerously off-balance. I correct and find stable standing again to see her schooling her concern into a deadly look. "Don't touch me."

"I'm just—"

"I said stay away . . . and off your damn ankle!" she growls. "And if you touch me again, you're going to find yourself icing your balls along with your ankle!"

Message sent, she spins on her heels and marches all the way to her cabin, slamming the door.

God damn. You know you're an asshole when you can make someone who's as sweet as apple pie turn into a fiery siren ready to claw your face off. But she must care about me somewhat. Otherwise, she wouldn't be so worried about me staying off my foot. Maybe I should just give her a little space, then try to talk to her?

Fuck that. I'm not letting her just walk away without getting a word in.

I'm about to follow her inside when I hear the crunch of gravel behind me.

"I wouldn't do that if I were you."

I turn to see Trey and his friend, who seems to be gawking at me like I'm some giant Klondike bar.

"Trey," I say cordially, nodding my head in greeting. He and I got along pretty well way back when.

"Aubrey," Trey replies politely with a hint of steel, ever the protective older brother. I'm sure he knows what happened between Ana and me. They're close. He probably hates me too. But he doesn't know what I had on my plate. What I've gone through.

Trey looks like he's about to elbow his friend, who's still staring. But instead, he just gestures and introduces us. "This is my boyfriend, Brad . . . although I'm beginning to rethink that label. Brad, this is Aubrey."

"Nice to meet you," I say to Brad. I offer my hand, and we shake.

"I have to ask, when did they start raising giants around here?"

"This is Rex," I say, ignoring him and motioning toward the husky, who's been remarkably calm considering the situation. I normally introduce him whenever I meet new people. He might be a dog, but he's a person to me, loyal and always by my side. "My buddy."

"Hey, Rexy!" Brad chirps but is silenced by Rex's throaty rumble.

"What brings you guys up here?" I ask Trey, glancing at the cabin. Hopefully, Ana hasn't figured out how to detach the decorative axes from the wall or she might use me for target practice. "I wasn't expecting tenants so fast. I just put this rental on the market."

"Ana's been working hard at the hospital," Trey explains, "so she needed a vacation—"

"And something else," Brad chirps in under his breath, eyeing me up and down, "some big, fat—"

Trey gives Brad a frosty glare and he shuts up. "As for why she chose here," he continues, then shrugs. "Seemed like it had a special meaning."

She still remembers our place. Our special place. That means she has to still think about me.

The thought makes me feel hopeful about my prospects of getting Ana to listen to me.

"Hospital?" I ask. When I left, Ana was thinking about becoming a social worker.

Trey nods. "She's a nurse. She just moved back about a year ago and got a job at the hospital."

It doesn't surprise me she ended up in the medical field. Ana always loved helping people. Being a nurse definitely fits her personality.

"I thought she'd be married with a kid or two by now," I say after a moment, watching the cabin. It's an obvious dig for information, but I can't help myself. I *have* to know.

Trey shakes his head and I'm filled with relief. "Nope. No man, no kids. No time for a relationship, really. She practically lives and breathes her job. Coming up here for a little *me time* was the best thing she could do."

"Or maybe the worst," Brad adds. "I've never seen Ana get this mad before. She's always so sweet and nice to everybody. So honey, you must've done some pretty fucked-up shit to make her rage like that." He looks pointedly at me as if waiting for a response.

"It's complicated," is all I say. I don't know Brad. I'm not giving him my life story, no matter how curious he might be.

"Indeed, it is," adds Trey. I'm shocked he's not chewing me out or pressing me for more info on what happened. Seeing how angry Ana is, he has to feel some kind of way. "But hey, we're going to go inside and try to calm her down. I think it's best that you two stay away from each other. This is supposed to be a relaxing getaway. She doesn't need any added stress." He grabs Brad by the arm and drags him toward the cabin. "And listen to Ana. Stay off that ankle."

I stand there with Rex, wondering what I should do until I see Trey and Brad go inside and the two siblings start arguing. Sighing, I begin limping back to my cabin.

Stay away? Like hell. I'm not letting her go again.

"SO, THEY ARRIVED?"

I'm sitting on my bed, my ankle propped up on my extra blankets, and trying to keep my head straight. The pain's set in, and yeah, it hurts like fuck. Probably not the best time to take a phone call from Carlotta, but I don't want her to get worried.

"Yeah, arrived this morning," I reply, wincing as I adjust my body on the bed. This is really gonna suck, being laid up.

"How are you liking your new tenant?" she asks. "I heard she works at the hospital. I'm glad I dropped a brochure there."

"We have . . . history," I reply before I realize I probably should've kept that to myself.

"What kind of history?" Carlotta jumps in immediately. "Is there going to be a problem?"

"No . . . I don't think so. It's complicated."

On her end of the line, Carlotta sighs, and I can hear her

earrings clinking against the handset. "Aubrey, talking to you is like pulling teeth. So . . . how hot is this chick?"

Hot? Hot enough to bring the heat of full spring to this mountain valley about two months early. The entire time she was ranting at me, I wanted nothing more than to pull her down on top of me and taste those sweet lips of hers.

Not that I'm going to tell my cousin. "What kind of question is that?"

"And that answers my question. So, you want me to come play matchmaker or not?"

Damn. Busted. "Hell, no. What am I, eighteen? I'm a grown ass man, Car."

"Oh, come on. You might be a *grown ass man*." She makes sure to highlight the last part to mock me. "But you're way outta practice. And this is like some sign! I was just telling you that you needed a woman around there, and now this? You need all the help you can get! You've got two weeks to—"

I interrupt her, saying with force and hoping she'll listen, "Stop. no, just no. It's like riding a bike. I don't need help."

I'm playing it down. I don't want her to know my real feelings . . . how deep this goes. I look out my window, and in the distance, I can see Ana arguing with Trey through their window. She looks pissed. "Listen, Car, I'm gonna head out. We'll talk later."

"Aubrey—" Car says, but her voice is cut off as I hang up. I look over at the cabin, wondering what I'm going to do.

I'm not going to fuck this up like I did last time. Carlotta's right about one thing. I have two weeks . . . to make her mine. And I have every intention of making that happen.

CHAPTER 5

ANA

"We're gonna get a little sleep," Trey says, looking guilty that he and Brad need a little bit of couple time. It's late, and after a long day where Trey showed off his culinary skills and Brad's done his best to entertain me and get me out of my funk, they're just about femaled out. "You okay?"

"I'm fine," I reassure them, raising my glass of red wine. "See you in the morning."

They head toward the back bedroom and go inside. I wasn't so sure about their tagging along, even if it was only for a few days, but now that I know who's next door, I'm glad they're here.

I sit back, sipping my wine and finally taking a moment to enjoy the cabin. It's stunning. One large main room holds the living, dining, and kitchen areas, and there are two bedrooms, one off each side. Thank goodness the bedrooms are split because I have a feeling I will want to be far away from Trey and Brad's activities this weekend. I love them, but Trey is still my brother. The cabin is decorated in a true alpine style, with snowshoes on one wall, a pair of crossed axes over a stone fireplace, and a rustic charm that makes it feel like a mountain paradise. When paired with the views from the porch outside, I truly feel like I've found God's country.

If only it weren't for my neighbor to my back. I shake my head, looking out the back window toward his cabin.

His cabin is rougher, squatter, more . . . untamed than what I'm in. That was Aubrey today. Even though he was injured, he was wild, untamed, towering as he stood in the field on a leg and a half. His chest was huge, stretching the flannel shirt he was wearing and . . .

Fuck. I can feel the warm, instinctual tremble in my belly that I used to feel for him and it has me worried. He hurt me. He broke my heart. He's a bastard who should be left out here in the woods. Hell, if I'd known it was him, I would've left his ass lying there.

But it's a lie. I wouldn't do that to anyone, especially Aubrey.

Goddammit. I can't even be mad at him. I take a deep breath and pour myself another glass of wine, knowing I'm going to have a headache tomorrow but not really giving a fuck. If ever there's a time for a drunken trip down memory lane, it's when you see the high school sweetheart who was your first everything . . . including your first, and only, broken heart. Besides, I'm a nurse. I've got a half-dozen hangover cures. Some of them even work.

Taking a fortifying drink of wine, I decide to take the bull by the horns and dive into my thoughts about Aubrey from today. The fact is, ten years have made him even more handsome than he was. He always dwarfed me, but he's even bigger now, both taller and wider than the boy in my memories. And the soft sweetness he once had is gone. He's more rugged now, his hair a little longer, but the gruff look only makes him more delicious.

Fuck. I hate that last thought, but it's the truth. Even if we didn't have history, I want to feel what his body promises. I want to feel rough, calloused hands on my skin, squeezing my ass as his

44

lips nip at my neck. I want to climb him like a tree and trace every inch of his muscles. I want him to hold me up and pound into me so hard I bounce on his cock. But with the sweet agony of what we used to share mixed in with image of him fucking me hard . . . it's even more enticing.

Ugh . . . no, Ana. Stop right there. That's got *bad idea* written all over it. But it's the truth, as ugly as it is. I was angry today, still am, but there's obviously still something about him that calls to me, especially when he drops back into my life looking like a mountain man who could wrangle my body like a romance novel god. And I'm on such a dry run, my weak body might just overwhelm my responsible mind. I haven't had a lover since I moved back to town, and quite frankly, I feel like a freshly-dewed virgin again. Sounds like a bad porn movie, *The Twenty-Eight-Year-Old Virgin Nurse.*

Sighing, I drain half my wine glass and look into the drink's depths for answers. Maybe I should just say fuck it and leave? That's probably the smart thing to do. I've still got the time off from work. I can crash at home and just chill out, avoid the whole Aubrey issue, and just pretend today never happened.

An owl hoots outside, and I look out to see a beautiful landscape of the moon over the mountains. I walk out onto the porch and around, looking up at the perfect moon and the diamond pinpricks of the stars on the black velvet sky. It's amazing, and so peaceful I can feel the stress of the day almost dropping away as the moonlight bathes me in softness. I need this, a getaway from work, and if I go home, I know I'll end up covering some-one's shift again. But here? Here, I can just . . . be. No timeline, no demands on my attention, no life or death decisions.

Nah, no way in hell am I going to let Aubrey with his sexy brown eyes, chiseled arms, and rumbly voice chase me away from this. He broke my heart once, but we're adults now. He can stay on his side, I'll stay on mine, and it'll be fine. I realize that maybe doesn't sound like the most adult way to behave, but it's what I've got. I need this vacation, need some time in the woods, need to finally let the past go and move on for a better, fuller future.

"WHAT IN THE WORLD WERE YOU DOING OUTSIDE LAST NIGHT?" Trey asks as he slides my omelet from the skillet to my plate. "It was cold in here. It must've been freezing out there!"

"And I had clothes on. I'm still here. I didn't die," I reply sarcastically, pulling my fluffy robe tighter around me for warmth. "Felt warmer last night than it does now. Damn, Brad, how long's it going to take to get that fire going? Thought you were all domestic now."

Brad, who's kneeling over by the fireplace and fiddling with some log setup design more Lincoln log than fire-worthy, looks back and sticks out his tongue. "Bitch, I'm a domestic fucking goddess. But I'm a twenty-first-century domestic goddess, not this caveman shit."

Leaving Brad to whatever he's doing lest I get roped into helping, I look back to Trey, who's busy stirring the vegetable hash on the stovetop. "Figured you would've been too busy to notice me going outside anyway," I tease.

Trey blushes but winks at me, then he leans over to get a peek at Brad's ass before locking his eyes back on mine. "Just watching out for my little sister. Wouldn't want you to get eaten by a bear or . . . anything else." His words are more warning than an expression of concern, and I know he's telling me to watch out for Aubrey. I give him a little nod of understanding, knowing he's right and having already come to that conclusion myself.

Suddenly, Brad lets out a little cheering sound. "Yes! I have made fire!"

I look over to see a tiny little flame that's barely the size of my thumb, but it's there, and it's spreading quickly. "Woohoo . . . great job, Brad! From now on, let's just keep the fire going. Thankfully, we've got plenty of wood."

"Speaking of plenty of wood," Brad says, rolling his eyes when Trey snorts, "Not that, you pervert." He gestures to the pile of logs stacked next to him. "You know where all this came from, right? Big Stud next door."

"Don't even start," I declare, giving him a scowl before taking a sip of coffee.

Brad grows serious. "Okay, okay. But really, are you going to be okay with our neighbor on your own?"

"We're exes, Brad," I reply simply, not knowing just how much Trey told him last night. "But I'm not going to let him ruin a perfectly good vacation. He just needs to respect the boundaries and stay clear."

"You see, that's got me worried," Trey says softly. "Ana, I was there before. I saw how devastated you were back then, but you can't have this much animosity against him ten years later."

I half growl, cutting into my omelet. "He broke my heart, Trey. It's not like I still walk around pining for him, but I don't have to forgive him just because it's been a long time and he popped up in front of me."

"That might be true," Trey says, placating me. "But Ana . . . babe, this is a chance for you to heal that issue. I'm not saying to get back with him, far from it. Just a chance to get closure."

"Thanks, Dr. Phil," I grumble, though I don't mean to sound bitchy. He's probably right, but I don't know if I could have a serious conversation with Aubrey. I'd either start yelling, or crying, or jump his bones, and I don't want to do any of that. "I don't need to go back to that time. It's done and over with. I've

47

moved on, he's moved on . . . we'll just avoid each other and it'll be fine."

Trey doesn't say anything, just looks at me with those big puppy dog eyes of his as he eats his breakfast, a much healthier version of what he's giving me. Brad takes his seat and gives me a look, letting me know he's not done speaking by a long shot.

"Honey, from my point of view, you've got options. Talk to him or don't, fuck him or don't, ignore him completely or don't." Trey nearly chokes when Brad says, 'fuck him', and my jaw drops open in protest. Brad ignores both of us and barrels ahead. "There's not a wrong choice here. You need a vacation and you're here already. Just go with the flow, and whatever you decide to do, we'll back you."

He gives Trey a hard look, unusual for them since Trey is usually the sane one to balance Brad's craziness. But I appreciate their advice and especially Brad's promise that they'll support me. "Look, guys, I don't know what you want me to say here. I haven't thought about Aubrey in years, not really. And admittedly, running into him has me spinning. So my first instinct is just to avoid the whole thing. I wasn't looking for closure, don't need it or to reminisce about the good old days. I definitely don't need to fuck him, no matter how sexy he grew up to be. I just need a vacation. Some peace and quiet." Shit, probably shouldn't have admitted I noticed how hot Aubrey has gotten, but it's not like they didn't see for themselves.

Brad's eyebrows shoot together as he smiles. "I didn't see him before, but I will say that man is fine as fuck. No judgment if you do decide to go the sex route, but I will expect details."

"Enough," Trey says as he smacks Brad on the arm. "Ana, do whatever you need to do . . . avoid him or talk to him. Let us know if you need backup."

I notice he left out Brad's third suggestion because Brad is mouthing 'fuck him' at me with a smirk and nodding his head yes. I laugh out loud, and Trey sighs, the long–suffering sound more playful than truly annoyed.

"We're heading out for a hike today, if you're okay?" Trey asks, still looking a bit uncertain whether I'm going to dissolve into teenage broken-hearted tears once I'm alone.

"You two go have some fun. It's your vacation too. I'll be fine. I'm planning on doing nothing today but lying on the couch, drinking cocoa, and reading some romance novel involving a Mafia hitman who finds the woman of his dreams and hangs it up."

"Oh, I read that one," Brad says, getting up. "She dies and he goes all John Wick vengeance mode, ends up worse than he started. Sorry to tell you." He laughs, and I point a finger at him and narrow my eyes, wishing I were more threatening, even in a joking manner.

I wave him off and clean up the dishes while the guys get ready. After they leave, I grab my Kindle and try to do exactly what I told them, letting the heat from the fire warm me. I bury myself in the story, but every time I try and imagine the tall, dark hero, all I see is Aubrey in my head.

Sighing, I set my tablet aside, flopping back on the couch to look at the ceiling. Shit, I can't put up with this for weeks. I want to go talk to him, I want to take the axe on the wall to his balls, I want to hold those balls in my hand as I get ready to suck him deep and long, and I want to know what the hell happened back then.

Unable to just sit on my ass any longer, I get up, intending to go to the kitchen for a drink of water. As I reach for the kitchen cabinet, my hand freezes.

"Aubrey . . . what the fuck are you doing?" I whisper as I watch his front door open and he emerges. He's walking stiffly, but the main thing is, he's on his damn ankle. Crossing his front yard slowly, his dog at his side, he goes over to a chopping block before reaching down and grabbing the thermal undershirt he's wearing to peel it off.

His chiseled upper body emerges into the sunlight. He's massive, thick ridges of muscles on his abs leading up to a rock-hard chest, all of it covered in a fine coating of hair that has my mouth watering.

Damn it, he's doing this on purpose. It's cold as hell outside.

Reaching down, he picks up a log about the size of my waist before placing it on the chopping block, and then he turns to grab his axe. I'm treated to the sight of a back that looks capable of carrying the whole mountain.

I marvel at the perfection in front of me as he whips his axe over his head and it comes crashing down into the huge log, splitting it from top to bottom and sending the pieces tumbling. Damn it, the fool is completely ignoring my advice.

He limps over and picks up one of the halves, almost an insult to my nurse training as he leans on his axe for support again as he bends over to get the half.

Turning back to the chopping block, he stumbles, and that's enough. I run to my room, ditching my bathrobe and pulling on some jeans and the hoodie that I'd packed. Yanking my boots on, I walk outside, quickly making my way across the space between us as Aubrey brings his axe down again.

As I walk, I'm again struck by how beautiful the day is. The sun's rising high, the sky is so blue that it makes my eyes want to water, and the air smells so clean it's like filling my body with pure energy.

Aubrey is just as breathtaking as he picks up another chunk of wood, a light sheen of sweat already glistening on his body. His dog, Rex, I think, is lying nearby, just out of range of the flying shards.

"What the hell do you think you're doing?" I ask as Aubrey pauses, seeing me for the first time before setting his axe down.

"Chopping wood," he says, and this close, I can still see the pain etched in his face. "Same as everyday."

I glance over my shoulder, lifting an eyebrow. "Aubrey, there's a pile that runs the whole length of the cabin over there," I point out. "There's more than enough. Didn't I tell you to stay off your ankle?"

"Out here, you always need more wood," Aubrey replies, ignoring the part about the ankle. I look back at him, a naughty voice in my mind saying that yes, I do need some wood . . . but not the kind he can cut with an axe. "Besides, you're not a doctor." And the dismissal shuts that naughty voice right up.

"No, I'm the one who bandages stubborn asses like you up," I shoot back. "If you keep that up, you're going to make it worse."

I'm pissed at myself as I hear my voice, which sounds not stern or upset but worried about Aubrey. Dammit, I'm supposed to be stronger than this, but as he faces me fully, resting his hands on his hips and drawing my eyes to the V of muscle disappearing into his waistband, I know I'm weak. So fucking weak. I'm five feet away and practically drooling as I watch the sweat cool on his skin, making his nipples tighten. My own nipples stiffen, and I'm glad my hoodie is thick and I can't poke through.

"I'm a big boy. I can handle it," Aubrey replies, and the potential dirty twist on his words coupled with my own naughty thoughts makes me bark out a weird laughing sound. I slap my hand over my mouth, embarrassed at the noise.

He looks at me, a question in his eyes before pointedly letting his eyes slide down my body. I can read his look. He's thinking of a few other things his big boy can take care of. Honestly, I am too as I feel the caress of his gaze almost as a physical touch. There's a long moment of tension, the air thickening between us as I wonder what he thinks about what he sees. He's not the boy he once was, but I'm not the girl I used to be either.

He licks his lips like I'm a snack he'd happily devour, and I blush, which finally pushes me out of my desire enough to put a little bit of steel in my voice. "Fine. Have it your way. Make it worse for all I care."

I need to get away from him. My body's need for Aubrey's touch is driving me nuts, and I hate it. I hate that even as my mind says no, my body is definitely saying *yes, please*. And it pisses me off that he can get me hot and bothered with no more than a heated glance.

I turn on a boot heel and start to walk away. "Don't say I didn't warn you when you can't walk at all and you're in the hospital to get surgery. I'll say I told you so." I know it's bratty and bitchy, but they're the only defenses I can call up right now. And I need a defense, a big wall of space and time and distance between me and Aubrey before I do something epically stupid.

I stomp off, feeling like I'm about to catch fire in this hoodie, heat rising in my body from embarrassment, arousal, and anger. I pray he doesn't tell me to stop because I might. I might stop, turn around, and run to him. Fuck the past and let him just fuck me now.

CHAPTER 6

AUBREY

I watch Ana's ass as she walks away, my cock hardening in my pants. The way each cheek clenches as she takes a step, trying to look angry as she stomps on the cold ground, is both cute and arousing, and next to me, Rex whimpers.

She left me high and dry yesterday. Not this time. I'm not going to stand here, my cock aching in my jeans and words on the tip of my tongue as she leaves me. Not this time.

"Rex . . . get her," I say with a snap of my fingers, and Rex is off like a shot. To him, this is all a game. I've spent a lot of time training him.

Ana doesn't know that though, and as Rex barks, she lets out a yell that echoes off the mountains before taking off, trying to get to her cabin before Rex closes in on her. She never has a chance. It's too far, but that doesn't stop her from trying.

Rex plays the game, though, bounding around in front of her and steering her away, sending her curving this way and that like he's herding her. Suddenly, she trips over the mess of her feet and Rex's and tumbles to the ground. Rex is on her in an instant, standing over her and probably ready to lick her face off. He might look dangerous, but he's the furthest thing from it.

"Fuck! Help!" she screams as he stands over her, waiting for my command.

"Rex . . . kiss," I say as I walk up. Rex leans down and licks Ana's face, the screams continuing but changing into peals of laughter as Rex gets her face good. "Okay, off!"

Rex gets off, trotting happily as he comes back to my side. Ana wipes at her face, anger, laughter, and more burning in her eyes. "What the fuck was that for?"

"What'd you expect me to do, run you down?" I ask. "Let's talk."

Ana goes to get up, but when I look at Rex, she stops, staying on her butt. She looks up at me, sass filling her tone. "Fine, talk. What about? The weather? Sports? Politics?"

I shake my head, holding out my hand to help her to her feet. She looks at it like it's a snake, so I'm surprised when she actually takes it. Pulling her up is easy. She's as light as a feather, and as she gets up, her chest brushes against my body briefly. My cock jumps in my jeans as I feel the soft smoosh of her breasts against me, and she freezes, feeling it too.

Slowly, so as not to scare her or more likely piss her off any more, I move to brush off some dirt that got on her sweatshirt. As I do, a desire, powerful and deep, pulls inside me, and Ana's face darkens as she pulls away. "There . . . cleaner now."

"Don't sic your dog on me and I'll stay clean," she replies, but I can see it in her eyes . . . she wants to be dirty but she's fighting it. Her face is flaming that pink shade I always adored, and her eyes are big and dilated. She wants me as badly as I want her. "That was a dick move, sending your dog after me."

I shrug, wanting to touch her skin again but knowing this isn't the right time yet. "What can I say? You told me not to strain my ankle, and Rex likes to play."

"But I don't," Ana replies, stepping back another step and dusting off her butt. "And I would appreciate if you left me out of the games."

I step closer. "And I would appreciate if you'd stop trying to shut me out. We need to talk."

Ana snorts, looking at me out of the side of her eyes. "About what? The brochure said no refunds." She's fighting valiantly to stay off-topic, ignore the elephant in the room, but I can't let her.

I shake my head, taking another half-step forward and looking into those eyes it broke my heart to leave. "Us."

Ana swallows, trying to hang onto the remnants of her anger as she looks up at me, but her voice is soft, vulnerable. "Aubrey, there is no *us*. Hasn't been for a long time."

I reach out for her hand, but she pulls back slightly so I lower my hand. "I want to explain."

It's Ana's turn to shake her head, her eyes glistening with bad memories. "There's nothing to explain. It was years ago, and it's over and done with. You left me high and dry and it hurt. It broke my heart, but I'm over it now."

She tries to say it with conviction, and it almost sounds like something she's said before, maybe more than once. There's no anger in her voice, just sadness and the raw vulnerability that I'm seeing now, and I know she isn't over it. Her actions have all but said otherwise.

I scratch my cheek, wishing I'd trimmed my beard a bit, and search for the words to get her to listen, just for a moment. "I know I fucked up, but I really need for you to know why. I'm just not good at this and don't know how to tell it."

Ana stops, crossing her arms and nodding. "Okay, sure. Go ahead and get it off your chest so *you* feel better. Why the hell not?" Her voice is dripping in sarcasm, which tells me how much pain she's in because Ana is sweet . . . always. She couldn't have changed that much. But she's on a roll now, even as her voice loses the harsh tilt in favor of a sadder tone. "Why'd you shatter me in front of everyone and leave me looking like a damn fool, my heart in a million pieces? Why'd you haunt my dreams for years afterward? Why'd you have to poison every other relation-ship I've ever had since then? Trust me, there's not a thing you can say that'll explain *that*."

Holy fuck. Talk about a bomb dropping on my head. She's been underneath this crushing burden that I laid on her shoulders, and I'm just now seeing it.

I open my mouth, but my tongue's tied. How can I tell her what happened so that it will make sense to her? If I tell her the truth, it might sound like bullshit. I realize now that it's going to take some time to help her understand. Time she may not give me.

But I'm still going to try. "It's complicated. I can't just say it in a few sentences."

Ana snorts derisively. "Complicated?" she parrots disbelievingly.

I nod, keeping my face calm. "We should have a seat and I'll try to explain."

Ana studies my face for a minute, searching for something, then sighs. "Fine. Where?"

I turn, gesturing with my hand. "My cabin."

Ana glances over, her face blushing. I can tell what she's think-ing. She'd be in my space, alone . . . in close quarters. "I don't think that's a good idea."

I step closer until our bodies are just a few inches apart, pulled toward her like a magnet. This close, I can see that she's barefaced and so beautiful, her natural color making her glow in the morning light. "I think it's a great idea. You and I can finally come to an . . . understanding."

Ana says nothing, but her breathing quickens. Taking a risk, I reach out, pulling her close and letting her feel the hard thickness of my cock against her warm body. She whimpers softly, and I take that as a good sign. I lower my head, bringing my lips close to hers. "Come with me, Sweet Ana."

I'm on the verge of kissing her when she pulls away, her eyes flashing with genuine anger. "*Sweet Ana*. That's what you used to call me. In fact, those were the last words you ever said to me before you disappeared. So don't ever think you're going to just give me some *Sweet Ana* this and *Sweet Ana* that and suddenly, I'll forgive and forget. Just leave me alone."

She takes a step back, raising a hand warningly when I go to reach for her before turning and running away. Next to me, Rex jumps to his feet, wondering if the game's ready to start again, but I shake my head. "Down, boy."

If only my cock would behave as well as he does.

It's okay. I saw her eyes and heard what she said. Forgive and forget? No, my Sweet Ana. I know that's impossible. But forgive and move on? Maybe there's a chance. I'm making progress, even if it's two baby steps forward and a big leap backward.

CHAPTER 7

ANA

The trail is beautiful. Too wide to call it a hiking trail but too narrow to be a road, I guess it was originally made for dirt bikes and ATVs.

Either way, it's just another amazing sight after a whole day and a half of amazing sights.

Like Aubrey sweating in the sun and the feel of his cock pressed against me.

I stumble a little, frustrated at my lack of control over my thoughts. The fact is, though, that since yesterday morning's little 'conversation' with Aubrey, I've been having a hard time concentrating on anything.

I take that back. I have been concentrating . . . but all I've been able to focus on is Aubrey. The way he looked in the sun, the smirk on his face, even the low, gravelly growl of his voice. All of it is the stuff of distraction.

That doesn't even begin to address what his words did to me. I want to be angry. I want to tell him to take whatever excuse he has for running off and shove it straight up his ass. I want to know why—of course I do—but I'm scared to hear it too.

There's nothing he can say that will make what he did to me okay, and at least if I don't know, I can fool myself into thinking he didn't have a choice. Like maybe his family got swept into witness protection or something huge like that. Because I'm pretty sure it's nothing that noteworthy. More likely, he was just done with me, and I don't think I can handle hearing that the boy who held my entire heart in his hand just decided he didn't want it anymore. It took me a long time to get over us, and seeing him brings up old anger, old pain, old insecurities.

But it brings up old heat too, embers I didn't know were still smoldering and have quickly and easily been fanned into flames. I want him, even if it's just physical. Actually, if I did give in, it'd have to be purely physical. I don't think my heart could take being broken again, but God help me, his touch on my body and the feeling of his lips being so close to my skin yesterday have left me needy and wanting, unable to do anything about it.

Okay, I *could* do something about it. I could go over to Aubrey's cabin and get fucked three ways from Sunday. I heard it in his voice, saw it in his eyes. It's what he really wanted. Sure, maybe he'd try to explain things, smooth it over with me in an attempt to assuage his conscience and get in my pants, but his real goal would be to bend me over and pound me into submission. And it would be fucking *glorious* . . . as long as no old feelings rose up with the heat surrounding us. But something tells me a deep dose of Aubrey's huge cock and massive body isn't going to help on that side of things. That could get . . . addicting.

"Hey, Ana, you getting winded?" Trey asks, pulling me out of my thoughts. "You're slowing down."

"I'm fine. I'm just enjoying the scenery," I quickly lie, because even though the scenery is fucking amazing, I've barely noticed a thing. "Remember, I'm here to relax, not train for a triathlon."

Trey chuckles, slowing down. Brad follows suit, although he can't help but put a little dig in by pumping his arms exaggeratedly and swinging his hips like he's speed walking. "Let's see those elbows, ladies!"

"Okay, I hear ya," Trey says, dropping back next to me. "Listen, I don't want to sound like a broken record here, but you're going to be fine on your own, right?"

"Why not?" I ask, wiping my forehead. "You guys damn-near filled the house with food. I'm not going to starve." I'm hoping against hope that he'll take the bait and let it go. The last thing I need to do is talk about my love life with my brother. I've done more than I care to already.

"You're already starving," Brad quips. "And there's a whole sausage buffet right next door."

Trey growls at Brad, who giggles and sprints ahead, leaving us alone. "Seriously, I'd at least like to know you and Aubrey have your boundaries set before we leave. There's a lot of . . . tension between you two."

I snort, glad that I didn't tell Trey and Brad the details of my encounter with Aubrey while they were out hiking yesterday. They only saw my frustration when they got back, and I'd mumbled something about Aubrey being a stubborn pain in the ass. "Tension?"

Brad, who has some of the sharpest ears I've ever encountered, turns around up ahead and calls back, "Damn right, tension! You two are so ready to fuck each other's brains out I can practically smell the pheromones."

"That's disgusting!" I laugh as we catch up to Brad. "But trust me, there's no sexual tension between us. No way. Just anger and an ugly past."

"Please, honey. Keep telling yourself that," Brad jokes. "But I saw him, and I know you. More importantly, I know *just* how long it's been since you've gotten any." He nods his head like my fucking Aubrey is a foregone conclusion, and I'm instantly pissy.

"Give it a rest already. I said there's nothing between us." My voice is snappish, way harsher than I'd intended, but his words reminded me of the exceedingly long dry spell that I'm suddenly feeling oh, so ready to break.

Brad stops, looking at me with more curiosity than hurt on his face. But I feel bad for speaking sharply. "Sorry. I just don't want to talk or think about Aubrey anymore. I just want to leave the past in the past and have a decent vacation."

I start walking again, hoping they'll let the matter lie. But I see the look that passes between them. I'm not fooling myself, and I'm definitely not fooling them.

I STOP, FROZEN AS I OPEN THE DOOR TO THE CABIN. AUBREY'S standing at the table, dressed in a fresh pair of jeans and a clean black denim shirt. He's laid out a lunch for us on the table, and from the looks of it, he's been going at it for a while.

"What the hell are you doing in here?"

Before Aubrey can say anything, Brad speaks up, sounding more than a little guilty. "Uhm, I kind of invited him to lunch."

I turn to Brad, lifting an eyebrow. "Why?"

"Just wanted to get to know the big beast before we leave. To ease Trey's mind that Bigfoot here isn't going to drag you off in the woods and we'll never see you again."

He's joking, but both Aubrey and I narrow our eyes at him, and I grit my teeth.

Trey clears his throat, and I realize this wasn't all Brad's idea. I sigh, and I glance at Aubrey, who hasn't said a word but his eyes still burn with intensity. I can feel the trickle of sweat going down my neck, and I know his eyes are following it, wanting to trace my skin with the tip of his tongue. Or that's just what I want him to be thinking . . . what I want him to do.

"Fine. Let's have lunch," I declare. "Give me two minutes to change shirts."

I go into my room and pull my top and sports bra off, ignoring the tight tingling in my nipples as I pull on a comfy bra and a casual T-shirt. Emerging, I find the boys sitting politely at the table, each of them with a glass of water in front of them. Aubrey rises, slightly old-fashioned, and I notice the only open seat is next to him.

Fuck it. Taking a steadying breath, I come over and sit down, looking at the spread. "This is impressive."

"One of the things I *can* cook," Aubrey grunts, opening the big pot of stew. The smell's rich and heady, and while I've never been much for stew, this smells like it's better than anything I've ever eaten.

"What's in this?" Trey asks as he takes a big bowl from Aubrey and sniffs. "It smells great."

"Deer, mostly," Aubrey says, spooning up another bowl for Brad. "Some potatoes, they're easy to grow, and a few other vegetables."

"Yeah, well, smells delicious," Brad exclaims, taking a bite. "And tastes good too. So . . . what has you living out here? And where'd you get deer?"

"I hunt, try to be as self-sufficient as I can," Aubrey says, his voice polite but still short on his words. Next to him, I feel dwarfed, and I'm constantly distracted as Aubrey and the guys talk. Instead of the stew or the conversation, I'm tuned into Aubrey's every move . . . the bounce of his knee when he gets a bit nervous, the way his eyes keep cutting to me as if making sure I'm really there, and the nuance of every expression that crosses his face. Aubrey's presence is like a burning stove next to me, making me feel feverish.

"You like it up here?" Trey asks. I can sense what he's doing. He wants to ask the same question Brad did again since Aubrey avoided it, but he's coming at it from a different angle. "I remember you liked the outdoors, but I didn't think it was enough to live out here by yourself."

"I like the peace and quiet," Aubrey replies. "The land was a good bargain, and I have an agreement with a few local stores."

"What's that?" I ask, curious.

"I clear trees on the property and sell the firewood. It's just me, so it's not a lot, but I don't need much cash . . . enough for the taxes on this place. Which is what the cabin rental profits are for now."

I can see Aubrey's on to Trey's game, but Trey pushes on, not quite satisfied. "You don't need money for anything else?"

"I hunt for food and grow the rest," Aubrey replies. "I use a bow, so supplies are cheap." He turns to me, changing the topic off himself. His leg presses against mine and makes my body rev into overdrive almost instantly. "What about you, Ana? How are you enjoying being a nurse?"

"I love it," I reply, trying to keep my mind on anything other than the feeling of Aubrey pressed against my thigh. It's narcotic, my head swimming as I find myself unable to think of anything other than the intense desire building inside of me and the hunger to feel the hard 'third leg' of his with my hand. If Brad and Trey weren't here, I'd just be able to slide my hand . . . "I like helping people."

"She's the best damn nurse in the hospital," Trey brags, and

Aubrey smiles a little, making my stomach flutter. His leg presses harder, and I glance down to see the swelling bulge in his jeans. He's not hiding it, knowing the thick plank table isn't going to let the guys on the other side of the table see, but I see, and my mouth goes dry.

God, could I even fit that in my mouth? Aubrey would love that, and his eyes twinkle as he sees my dilemma. "I bet. You're a natural for it, I'm sure. And by the way, my ankle does feel a bit better. The boot helps some too."

"What did you do?" I ask, and Aubrey slides away just enough to show me the boot he's wearing, a high all-leather boot that's tightly laced. It also gives me a view of his cock pressed against the denim of his jeans, but I'm able to restrain myself enough not to slide under the table and start nuzzling him. "That'll help . . . but you still need rest."

"Maybe," Aubrey admits. "But stuff's got to get done."

I see Trey trying to catch my eye, but it's okay. I'll be fine. I'm not going to have a nervous meltdown up here alone with Aubrey. "Well, if you can behave better than a caveman, I might give it a look and make sure your foot isn't going to rot off."

We wrap up lunch, and Aubrey stays more or less silent as he cleans up the dishes while Trey and Brad get their bags together. "You sure you'll be okay?" Trey whispers quietly after they've packed the rental SUV. "You know I—"

"Will be back to pick me up," I reply with a smile. "I've still got my phone, and Aubrey's got an ATV if I need it. Now chill out. This was *my* vacation, remember? I didn't ask you to tag along, but I know you mean well."

I give Trey and Brad hugs, watching with amusement as my brother and Aubrey square off with each other. I've always thought Trey was a pretty muscled-up guy—he's a personal trainer, after all—but seeing him next to Aubrey puts things in perspective. Like just how *big* Aubrey is.

Trey offers his hand, and Aubrey takes it, shaking. Both of them are squeezing hard enough that their forearm muscles look like a bundle of cords for a moment before they both relent. Trey nods. "Thanks for the good stew. Have a good couple of weeks."

Aubrey nods and steps off the porch, pausing to watch Trey and Brad get into the SUV and drive off. When they're gone, he turns and looks at me, his eyes still glowing with that heat I felt all during lunch. I'm already expecting him to attack me, knowing I'm weak and want his kiss, his body. What I'm not expecting are his words. "I'll see you around."

Any other time, I might think it sounds distant. Like, maybe I'll see you next year. But this is a promise, and as I watch him slowly walk away, I find myself looking forward to it.

CHAPTER 8

ANA

*A*ll alone. Just me and Aubrey here in this place. Everything is telling me this is bad idea. I wanted him so badly sitting at that table. Even now, sitting out on the porch, I can't help but want to go around back and see what he's doing, to get closer . . . to see if that offer to go into his cabin still stands.

But it's the lust talking, it has to be. I don't know him anymore. He's practically a stranger. So am I. I'm not the 'Sweet Ana' who used to be aflutter in his letterman jacket and who wore nothing but good girl white cotton panties and dreamed of the two of us having a fairytale wedding before going off on a honeymoon to Disneyland.

No, we're different now. He seems to have become Rambo Bunyan or something, bow hunting and chopping wood, a survivalist. And I'm . . . me. Maybe more jaded than I used to be, definitely more careful, and less trusting. I'm not broken, not anymore, but there are some cracks in my shell. And he's the one who put them there.

Am I even capable of acting on the lust and not letting old feelings resurface? There's no chance of rekindling a relationship with Aubrey, but the idea of casual sex, something that normally would be an automatic no, is beginning to seem more reasonable. An evil corner of my mind even thinks about fucking Aubrey, getting him hooked on me, and then ditching him the way he ditched me. Turnabout is fair play, after all. The thought is maniacally devious, far beyond anything I'm actually capable of doing. But the sex part of the plan does seem doable. It could possibly even be a good thing. Let the steam out, take the edge off.

I'm justifying it, and I know it. I'd be a fool to even entertain it. But my body wants what my body wants, and I definitely want Aubrey. But just for the sex. Let the past stay in the past and give in to the lust he's awoken in me. That's perfectly reasonable, right? Even I know it's a bad idea, but I'm not sure I care.

Sighing, I head to the shower room, which is delightfully separate from the toilet. I close the door, letting the natural light fill the space from the big picture window that extends into the shower itself. The view outside is breathtaking, the trees and forest rising up behind the cabin so that it feels like I'm a forest fairy bathing in the rain. The idea is whimsical, even silly, but it appeals to me somehow. I take a careful look outside, making sure I'm as hidden as I think I am. Realizing that it really is a private view, I decide to be a bit decadent and indulge my forest fairy fantasy. Maybe even a bit of a mountain man fantasy too.

Turning on the rain head shower, I strip quickly and hop under the warm spray. Even the drops of water along my skin reignite the fire of sexual heat Aubrey has been stoking inside me for the last two days.

Slowly, I trace my hands along my skin, imagining they're his hands. I caress and cup my breasts, teasing the caramel nipples with my thumbs as I push the mounds together. I remember how hard and big Aubrey looked in his jeans just from our legs pressing together and wonder what seeing my breasts would do to him. Would he get even harder? Would he lick and suck the tips until they were achy and pearled with want?

A moan escapes my lips and I let my fingertips trace down my belly to cup my pussy. I buck my hips into my own hand, imagining Aubrey whispering in my ear to *'Fuck my hand like you want to fuck my cock.'*

I'm tempted to speed this up, knowing from experience what will set me off, but I take it slow, teasing myself and letting it build into something bigger. I slide a finger down to my entrance, coating it in my juices, and spread the slickness along my clit, slow and easy. Back and forth I rub, spreading my legs as wide as I can. Needing more, I lean back against the cool tile wall, propping a foot up on the shower edge, picturing Aubrey settling between my thighs.

I dip a finger into my pussy, pumping slowly and deeply a few times before adding a second finger. My palm bumps against my clit with every thrust of my fingers, and it builds faster than I'd planned. I'm so on edge from all of Aubrey's teasing, and just his presence, that the slightest touch is gonna set me off.

I press my free hand to the glass, needing to be grounded because I can already feel that this is going to be a big one. My fingers pound into me, my hips bucking for more as I cry out, the orgasm hitting with a fierceness I rarely feel.

The waves wash over me, and I pry my eyes open, wanting to finish my forest fairy fantasy. I see the trees, a blanket of green surrounding me, and the sky, an umbrella of blue and white above. And I feel small, rocked by the rain, by the crashing of my body, a tiny bit of sweetness in a wild world. And I love every moment of it, touching myself lazily long after the shudders have subsided and my breathing begins to return to normal.

I'm smiling to myself as I begin to wash my body, luxuriating in the sudsy bubbles that roll down my skin. I look out the window, noticing that it hasn't fogged up. Maybe Aubrey uses something on the glass? It feels naughty to be so exposed, even if I'm really not. I'm alone in the cabin, the view is of the empty woods, and Aubrey's cabin is around on the other side, far from the serene view I'm currently enjoying.

That was just what I needed. A little something to take the edge off. Hopefully, next time I see Aubrey, I won't be so easy to rile up. Maybe we can have that conversation like adults. Or maybe not and I stick with my plan to avoid the past and skip that confrontation. All I know is that I feel boneless and satisfied, and that's enough for now.

Aubrey

I wasn't sure I could believe my eyes when Ana opened the curtain to the master bath shower in her cabin. I'm not that far away, and I saw her scan the woods outside the big window. I figured she'd see me out here among the trees, especially since I'm not hiding, just slowly gathering kindling, but maybe not? My moment of confusion ends abruptly when she starts taking her clothes off. I should move, give her the privacy she likely thinks she has, but I'm frozen in place, mesmerized as Ana gets into the shower.

I'm expecting her to just wash the day's sweat away, but when she dips her head back to get her honey hair wet, she arches her back and her tits rise deliciously. I feel the blood rush to my cock, instantly hardening against the visual onslaught of Ana's naked form. She's not the skinny girl I remember, all angles and edges. No, Ana's soft and curvy now, her body a winding seduction.

My breath quickens as I watch her hands trace along her skin the way I want to, wondering if she's as silky as I remember, as smooth as she seems now. She touches her breasts, teasing herself, and my jaw drops. Is she ... oh, fuck, she is.

I groan at the sight of her pleasuring herself, dropping the armful of wood I'd gathered. I palm my cock, thick and hard in my jeans, knowing I'm fighting a losing battle. As Ana's hand snakes its way down her body to her bare pussy, I follow her movements, running my hand down my abs, feeling them clench as my cock jumps.

As she cups herself, I give in and desperately unbutton my jeans, shoving them and my boxer briefs down to release my cock and balls, which are already heavy with need. Precum drips down my shaft, easing my way as I take myself in hand.

Her movements are hypnotic, her fingers dipping in and out of the pussy I want to claim so desperately, gliding across the clit I want to lick and nibble and taste. I start to pump my cock, using my thumb to smear my precum all over my tender flared head, making it glisten in the afternoon light.

"That's it, rub that sweet pussy for me. Get it nice and wet for me. I'll bend you over and bury my tongue in deep before lining this cock up and . . ."

My words are constant, a continuous stream of telling Ana what I want to see even if she can't hear me. Ironically, as I whisper out loud to the trees, "Spread yourself wide, let me see all of you," Ana actually does what I said. I slow my hand's up and down motion, watching raptly as Ana widens her stance, putting a foot up for leverage as she presses her fingers in deeper, fucking herself with her hand.

I match her pace, stroke for stroke, imagining it's my thick cock filling her tight little pussy, making her mouth drop open in a gasp I can't hear. I pump my cock in my fist, my balls churning and the tension rolling down the back of my legs to make my toes curl as I imagine her taking me in deep, calling out my name.

I'm nearly there, ready to blow my load when she presses a hand to the glass. Logically, I know she's just balancing, but it feels like she's reaching out to me. And that's enough.

I'm pushed over the edge, and I grunt, a choked cry tearing from my lips as I come hard, spurts splattering on my hand, on my jeans, and even on the tree beside me. My hips buck as I wring every drop of pleasure out of the orgasm, my muffled sounds stirring a flock of birds into fleeing the suppressed roar of a nearby predator.

My eyes stay locked on Ana the whole time, and though I just came violently, when I see her lost in her orgasm, my cock hardens a little again. I watch her head thrash back and forth for a moment before she lifts her face to the window, looking into the depths of the trees.

I swear she's looking right at me, but surely not. Ana, my Sweet Ana, wouldn't tease me like that . . . would she? Hell, I don't actually know anymore. Who is she now? Who am I? Because I'm damn sure not some perv who watches the woman he wants without her knowing, and I've lived in these woods for years and have never once jacked off in the trees. But she's doing something to me . . . making me crazy, making me think, making me feel.

And though I should run like hellfire from that, I know I should. The fact that it's Ana triggering these thoughts makes me wish for things that could've been . . . if only I'd stayed.

CHAPTER 9

AUBREY

*T*his has got to stop.

It's been two days since Brad and Trey left, and other than little waves as she's left on her daily nature walks or from her window, she's totally avoided me since our lunch.

It's gotten so bad, I've spent nearly as much time fantasizing and jacking off as I have eating.

Even if Ana didn't know I was watching her shower show, she has to know what the flirting at lunch did to me, her heated gaze on my cock turning me on so hard and making me want her so badly. I wonder if she knows that she licked her lips, leaving no doubt what she was thinking about.

Ever since, my fantasies have been about that tongue on my cock, my hands replacing hers as I trace her curves the way she did in the shower. My mouth waters to taste her pussy, and I mentally see a looped image of my cock sliding in and out of her, covered in her sweet-girl cum.

I'm going crazy, but I saw her face. She's just as heated up as I am.

I thought she might come to me, or that maybe a little time would do us both some good. But I can see that I was wrong. We've had time, too much of it . . . ten years' worth. I'm going to have to hunt her, chase her.

I grunt at the thought. Big, bad wild man chasing after the skittish, sweet good girl. There's a twisted part of me that likes the idea of dirtying up my Sweet Ana. But a thorn twists in my gut that she didn't used to be so gun-shy. I did that to her, made her afraid to trust. I hate myself for it, but I was just a kid myself and didn't know what to do, how to handle things. I thought she'd be okay, I really did, even if knew I would never find someone like her again.

I don't know that she'll talk to me, hear me out. But I do know that she wants me, maybe as much as I want her. And I'm not too good to use her desire against her, use my body to draw her closer, take what we both want. And maybe, just maybe, she'll listen to me if I make her boneless with satisfaction, her legs too jellied to run away. Maybe then, she'll listen. Maybe then, she'll forgive me.

But it's been rough getting around with my bruised ankle. I've made do, getting chores done slower than usual but done nonetheless. But it's time to tempt her, tease her, get her to come to me. The best hunters know you have to attract the prey, get it on your turf, on your terms. Yeah, I'm giving chase, but I'm not gonna run after her. In fact, she's gonna run right into my arms, but I'll be there to catch her this time.

Adjusting the tank top I'm wearing today, I head outside. I've still got plenty of work to do. I've got nearly three whole trees' worth of logs that need to be turned into firewood, and the work will help with my plan.

Walking outside slowly, limping a bit more than I really need to, I get my axe and start picking out logs to split. Rex is with me, lazing in the sun once he realizes what I'm doing. With each step, I play up my ankle a little, ready for Ana to come storming out of the cabin to tell me how much of a fool I am. I can see the curtains flutter. She's probably watching, and I know it irritates her so much as I work.

With every chop of my axe, I expect her to come out, and with each split log that falls to the ground to be tossed across the yard to join my slowly growing pile, I find my irritation growing instead. My ankle starts to throb, and soon enough, my limp is real and it hurts to do my work.

I don't stop and just keep setting up logs, swinging my axe, and making the pieces fly. Sweat starts to trickle down my chest, and I keep going, not letting Ana win this one. She's got to come out, dammit.

But why like this? You damn fool, my inner voice says. *Maybe you should just make this easier and go knock on her door.*

Maybe . . . but this is *my* way. Besides, getting work done at the same time. Two birds, one stone. I lift my axe and bring it whistling down again, another two chunks going flying. My ankle is in agony as I lurch over to the pieces and pick them up. My left side has a severe stitch, the muscles threatening to cramp as I bend over, and I know why. I've been trying to balance on my left side almost this entire time, and my muscles are doing double-duty.

I grunt as I gingerly toss the lengths into the pile, feeling like an idiot. It was stupid to think that using the same trick twice would work. Maybe I've underestimated her. Maybe she can hold out longer than I can. Maybe she's not as crazy for me as I am for her.

I'm so distracted by the pain that I don't see the log in front of me until it's too late, and I fall, gasping in pain as my ribs hit the ground. I plant my hand on the ground and try to get to my knees, but my right foot digs into the ground and I collapse back down. Even over Rex's concerned barks, I hear her mumbled, "Dumbass."

Hissing with pain, I turn over, somewhat surprised when I see a shadow over me. A petite, sexy shadow that looks pissed off. "I said to stay off your damn ankle. Why the hell won't you listen?"

"What can I say? I'm hard-headed," I say, grinning. I'll never admit it, but having Ana here makes relief wash over me. I really thought she wasn't going to come out. I don't let it show as I give her my best boyish grin. "I'm doing just fine. Was just taking a little break."

Ana snorts. "Sure, you are. You look like you're getting ready for a dirt nap. Now lie back."

Ana kneels down, examining my ankle. She moves it in my boot slowly back and forth, each movement making me groan in agony. "Goddamn. You getting a kick out of torturing me?"

"Shut up, you big baby," Ana says, amusement and frustration in her voice. "See what you did? Now you *really* can't walk on it."

"Hey, I had to get you out here somehow," I admit, letting her help me up. "It worked, and now I get to go put my feet up. Want to be my Naughty Nurse?" I say it lightly, teasingly, wiggling the carrot to get my prey closer, where I want her.

She blushes but ignores the invitation. "Yeah, you can put your feet up, and if you even think of getting up again, I'm going to handcuff you to your bed," Ana says, moving next to me and putting my right arm over her shoulder.

"Mmm, definitely a Naughty Nurse thing to say. Is that supposed to be a threat? Because if you're into that, I could be too." I give her my boyish grin again and wiggle my eyebrows at her. It's over the top silly, something I haven't done in years. It feels good, reminds me of who I used to be before I was the asshole on the mountain who growled at everyone.

Ana rolls her eyes, huffing out a laugh unwillingly. I'm counting that in the point column for me. She wraps an arm around my waist, holding mine to her shoulders. "Now, lean on me when you use this foot."

Together, we limp inside, my body totally aware of hers pressed against my side. The pain's enough that I don't pop wood as we walk, and that increases as she helps me into my chair and I hiss when my ribs have to flex. "What did you do?"

"Just sore."

Ana runs a hand over my side, tutting softly even as her hand strokes my shirt slowly, tenderly. "These will need to be looked at too. You're stubborn as a mule."

It's hard to hold in my grin. It took a little pain, but this is working out even better than I expected. "It's a fault, but also a strength. Thanks."

Ana helps me get my feet up before standing and looking around. "Where are your First-Aid supplies?"

"I have a kit under the sink, but it's just Band-Aids and stuff like that. What do you need?"

"We're going to need to wrap and maybe even splint this for a few days," she replies, sighing.

I try to bend forward and untie my bootlace, but no dice. Instead, I lean back and let Ana get the supplies she needs. I hear her rummaging around in the kitchen for a minute and wonder what she's up to since she said the Band-Aids in the First-Aid kit definitely wouldn't be useful for this.

"Well, you're going to have a funky splint then," Ana says, undoing my boots. She doesn't make a peep as she helps me out and takes off my socks, only wincing a little when she sees the deep purple bruising on my skin. "Fuck me."

77

That was the plan, I think, smiling to myself as she goes about her business. It takes her about five minutes, but soon enough, my right foot is fully wrapped, and I've learned a new use for wooden spoons.

"Now," she says, dusting her hands and looking at me, "I suppose you're going to need someone to take care of you too. Just one rule . . . no bedpans."

I grin, nodding. "Deal. So . . . hungry? We could do a late lunch."

Ana thinks, then nods, smiling a little. "I suppose. You wait here. I'll be right back."

Oh, I'm not going anywhere. Not this time. Not when I have her exactly where I want her.

CHAPTER 10

ANA

*A*fter a light lunch of soup and some bread from my cabin, I help Aubrey over to his couch, where he can lie down while I look at his injuries more closely. "Okay, off with the shirt." My voice is all business, professional as always when I'm in nurse mode, but underneath, I know I need to prepare myself for what I'm about to see. Aubrey is like a walking, talking dream in clothes. Shirtless, he's the stuff fantasies are made of, judging by how many times I've pictured him the last few days.

Aubrey grunts, lifting just his right arm. He gets his left up only a few inches before his face tightens and I put a hand on his wrist.

"I'll help you with it," I say calmly while wanting to slap him right across his handsome face. The dumb, stubborn idiot. He intentionally hurt himself just to try and get me out of the house to talk to him. I mean, showing off a little, not giving up? That's one thing, but this . . .

I ease his tank top up and off his body, my breath catching a little.

I know I should be detached, keep a clinical mind to assess his injury. But a baser, more needy side of me notices how close he his, the way his chest is heaving a bit from the work of taking his shirt off, and how the dusting of hair runs down in a line into the waistband of his jeans, making me want to follow it. His abs clench, and he hisses as he tries to explore his injured side himself. Clearing my throat, I try to focus on the more immediate problem as I run my hand carefully over the area, looking for any tender spots. My fingertips burn where they touch his skin and I wonder if he feels it too. "You did this on purpose."

Even though he all but admitted it earlier, Aubrey plays innocent, grunting at me. "Had work to do."

Shaking my head, I press gently, not feeling anything broken there at least. "Sure. Now you're worse off than you were."

Aubrey looks at me through hooded eyes, watching my hand trace along his skin. His voice is gravelly, deeper than usual, although it doesn't seem to be from the pain. "I'd say I'm better. Got a pretty girl taking care of me. You know, you're a hard one to crack. Almost as stubborn as me."

The compliment and the admission that he knows he's a stubborn ass make me blush, and I keep rubbing his skin, moving over his chest and biting my lip as I feel the rock-hard muscle underneath. I pretend I'm still searching for injuries, but we both know that's not true. I appreciate that he lets me keep up the façade, though, because if he called me on it, I'd stop and we both know it. "I should've let you lie out there until your dog dragged you back inside." My voice is a whisper, more seductive than admonishment.

"But you didn't," Aubrey says, covering my hand with his. "Because you care." There's a moment, both of us frozen, and I can feel his heart beating fast and hard under my hand. His eyes are locked on mine, daring me, begging me. It would be so easy to slip into his lap, carefully to keep from hurting his ribs, straddle his cock, and take his mouth. Let him fill me, shatter all this tension coiling through my core. So easy, and yet . . . so hard on my heart. He's dangerous.

I don't respond, letting the moment stretch until it snaps as Rex grumbles in his sleep by the fire. Thankful for the reprieve, I decide to change the subject. Getting the rubbing alcohol, I wash his ribs and a few scratches I find, not sure if they're new or old, looking for another subject to focus on. Anything. "You sure have a lot of wood lying around. You must get a lot of splinters."

Aubrey shrugs, looking at his calloused palms. "You get used to it. And I like to keep plenty handy for when I'm in the mood for woodworking." He gestures to a large chair. "Made that." He says it casually, like making a freaking chair is no big deal.

"Really?" I ask, glancing back. The chair is massive, definitely Aubrey-sized, with smooth runners to let it rock back and forth, a high back, and wide armrests. I have a flash of Aubrey working night after night by firelight to shape the posts just so. Then I picture him sitting in it, my legs spread wide over the armrests as he pumps up into me, rocking with the motion of our bodies joining. Fuck, I've got to stop. I gulp. "You do good work."

"I'm good with my hands," Aubrey says, his voice thick with meaning.

I breathe in sharply, wondering just *how* good and knowing that I've got to redirect the conversation to something safer or I'm going to fall into his trap, willing and begging. "I can't imagine living out here like this. No Starbucks? No takeout Chinese? I'd go insane."

Aubrey looks out the window, seemingly lost . . . in the woods? In the past? In something, for sure. "At first, it was a big change for me. I traveled around, just sort of drifted for a while, trying to find peace. To find what I really wanted. But when I came here, it was like finally, everything was calm. I started to feel right at home."

Trying to find what you really wanted? I thought I was what you wanted, I want to scream. It takes effort to shove down the anger and to not burst out and tell him the heartache he'd caused me. But what good would it do now? It's been ten years. And until this trip, I was all but over Aubrey O'Day.

Aubrey, though, seems to notice my expression. "You're mad at me."

"Annoyed," I partially lie, "for your being a damn fool about your foot."

"No," Aubrey says quietly, his voice a low rumble that has my belly filled with butterflies and my pulse starting to race, "No . . . you're mad at more than that."

I scoff, but it's weak, unconvincing. "How would you know? You don't know me. Not anymore."

"Oh, I know you well," Aubrey says. "But even if I didn't, you're practically thinking out loud. It's written all over your face."

I pale, wondering what's slipped between my lips as I've been trying to find something to distract myself. I get up, gathering the mess of cotton balls and supplies from my earlier doctoring, but Aubrey reaches out and grabs my wrist. "Hey . . ."

Without thinking, I yank my hand away, needing the distance. But Aubrey hisses in pain, his eyes tightening, and I immediately feel sorry even though he grabbed me.

Shit, he jerked and tweaked his ribs when I pulled my hand away. "Aubrey, are you okay?"

"Fine," he growls. "Probably deserved it."

I sit and place my hand on his ribs again, not pressing hard but just feeling his warm skin. "How does that feel? Any pain?"

Aubrey winces slightly, but not much. I move my fingers gingerly, watching his face for signs of pain. "Not really. I think it's lower," he says, heat rising in my chest as I move my hand lower, just to the edge of his ribs, almost to his abdomen. I glance at my hand, noting with a hitch of breath that he has not a six-pack but an eight-pack. So unfair when I'm trying so hard to be good. God, why does he have to be so tempting?

"Here?"

The corners of his lips tilt up, so slight I wouldn't have noticed if I wasn't watching so closely, and his voice lowers to a commanding rasp. "Lower."

In almost a trance, my heart racing and my pussy starting to ache, I move lower. "Here?"

"Not quite."

I slide my hand lower, almost to his waistband, where I can see his happy trail begin. I watch, seeing the bulge in his jeans thicken, my cheeks red-hot as Aubrey growls. "Ana . . ."

I jerk my hand away, blushing fiercely. "Keep dreaming, asshole." I stand once again, needing even more to get away before I do something stupid. His cock was right there, barely an inch from my hand, and my fingers tingled to touch him, stroke him.

Aubrey sighs, trying to sit up. He gets about halfway up before he flops back, groaning in pain. His fist punches into the couch cushion on his good side as he mutters, "Fuck, fuck, fuck."

"What happened?" I ask, my nurse instincts immediately taking over. "You may have a fracture . . ."

Aubrey grunts, shaking his head. "It's not the ribs, just put too much weight on the ankle. Help me over to my bed?" The tension is gone, replaced with frustration on his part. I get the feeling he's mad at being hurt, hates needing help. I think maybe he's accustomed to being alone, not needing anything or anybody.

I nod, helping him up. I'm fully aware of how close his stripped and ripped upper body is as he leans on me, hopping on his left foot as we make our way to the bed. It's awkward and time-consuming because he's so much bigger than I am. "Three . . . two . . . one," Aubrey says as we get closer.

"Okay, nice and easy," I whisper, my hands holding him tighter as I move in front. I can't help it. I feel the swell of his cock press against my belly as I look up at him, my hands on his back to steady him. "Now down in one . . . two . . ."

Aubrey sits down suddenly, pulling me with him so that I land on top of him in the middle of the bed, my legs splaying to feel him pressed against me. I look down at his prone form beneath me, pissed but also so turned on I just want to stay here for a while. He hisses in pain, and I try to shift off him.

He grabs my waist, holding me still. "Worth it," he grunts.

"Don't tell me you faked that. You bastard."

Aubrey's hands stay on my waist, just above my waistband as he smirks up at me. "Not quite. Hurts like a bitch. But you love it. You want me too."

"Ugh," I growl, pushing up, but that just presses me harder against his bulge, and I whimper. "You don't know *what* I want—"

Aubrey interrupts me. "I saw you. In the shower."

I freeze. *No . . .God, no.* I look in his eyes and see that he's telling me the truth. I blush furiously, embarrassed that he saw me . . . like that, doing that. I'm well on my way to covering my embarrassment with righteous anger when he continues. "It was the sexiest fucking thing I'd ever seen."

I bite my lip, the heat from the anger turning into lust as I imagine him watching me, what he thought, what he did. Needing that visual, I whisper, hoping that if I'm quiet enough, I won't have to admit that I asked. "What did you do?"

Aubrey's hands drift lower to rest on the top of my ass. I want to pull away. I know I should . . . but I can't. Too much of me doesn't want to.

"I jacked off for you too. Right there in the woods, leaning against a tree with my hard cock in my hand, watching you fuck your fingers, wishing you were taking my cock in that sweet little pussy." His words are dirty, letting me picture him that way too. It's something I'd like to see for real, if I'm honest, this wild, untamed beast pumping furiously as he watches me with an intense predatory gaze, knowing that it's all because of me.

I feel like prey, even now as he stares up at me, but there's a hint of control in knowing that he's following me, wanting me.

"I think I'd have liked to see that too," I reply, my voice catching as another tingle runs up from my pussy. God, I'm so wet. Why am I even fighting this at all?

"My balls are *still* aching from it. I haven't come that hard in . . . forever."

I look down, my voice a needy rasp. "Good."

"*Good?*" Aubrey snarls, his hands dropping to cup my ass fully. He squeezes, and I can't help it, I whimper. "Oh, Ana, that's far from good. You know why?"

"Why?" I almost whisper, trying with all my might to not just start riding him right now.

"Because I promised myself I was going to give you just as big a load as you got out of my cock when I came all over myself watching you. All over your tits, your ass, in your pussy. Wherever you'll let me."

His words are like a punch to the gut, my breath taken away. It takes a moment for me to gather myself. "In your dreams," I reply, but it's a futile argument, and I know it as I look into his smoldering eyes. *And in mine, too.*

Aubrey seems to read my mind and pulls my hips down until I'm pressed against him, another helpless whimper rising in my throat. "In my dreams, I fuck you hard until you're screaming my name," he growls. "Deep, hard, and raw until you can't take any more."

Oh, God, Aubrey never used to talk to me like this. *No one* has ever talked to me like that. I love it. I don't even want to protest. I'm so turned on my pussy is aching, desperate for him to make good on his promise, at least this time. His big cock filling me until he empties every last drop he's got inside me? Yes, please. But I'm breathing so fast and my heart is pounding so hard I can't even speak.

His hands squeeze my ass, hard enough to leave fingerprints, and then he moves deeper, between my legs. I cry out softly as he cups my pussy, his arm so long he can reach all the way around. "I want to fuck you, Ana. Right here, right now. I want you to come all over my cock 'till you beg for mercy. What's it gonna be?"

Even with how turned on I am, I'm unsure. My body is screaming *yes*, but a tiny niggle in my brain gives me pause. Can this just be physical? Can I do this without having closure on why he left? Am I setting myself up for a broken heart again?

He grinds his cock against me and my body wins the argument. Fuck it. Fuck him. And please . . . fuck me.

I lean down, and our lips meet in a fiery kiss.

CHAPTER 11

AUBREY

*A*na's eyes burn into my very soul. For years, I dreamed of this, the way Ana gave herself to me fully, the shock that crossed her face the first time our bodies joined. God, that image is burned into my brain as the most beautiful thing I've ever seen. But slowly, over the years, the dreams faded, almost as though it never happened. Now that I have her in my arms again, the memories of the past and the desire currently racing through me are building up to a firestorm. I'm not going to pass up this opportunity, even if there's so much left to talk about.

Pulling her down, I crush her lips with mine, claiming her in a deep kiss that's hard and rough, my need overtaking my control. Ana responds, her tongue meeting mine as she fights me with her lips and tongue, but her hands pull me tighter, her body grinding against mine.

"I think you've wanted this as much as me," I growl into her ear, holding her hips against my cock as I thrust against her through our clothes.

Ana groans, her head thrown back and her hands clenching against my chest. "You might be right, but you're hurt."

"It's fine. You said stay off my feet. I'm staying off my feet," I tease as I reach for the hem of her T-shirt. It comes off easily with a single jerk, revealing a simple bra that strains against the swell of her breasts, her nipples already hard and poking through the thin cotton. "Mmm . . ."

"You—" Ana says, her words cut off as I pull her down to suck and nip at her neck. I let myself be guided by the way she moans and my own hunger, nibbling down her neck as I reach up, squeezing her right breast and sliding her bra down. Ana cries out softly, pushing her chest to meet my hungry mouth.

I find her nipple, just as perky and tightly brown as it was in the window, like a caramel sitting on top of her breast. I capture it, sucking hard as she moans, my hands sliding around her back to hold her to me as I feast on her. My cock is rock-hard and throbbing as I grind against her, her hips bucking against me as she seeks her climax.

"Oh, no, you don't," I growl, pulling back and grabbing the waistband of her pants. "You're not coming until I let you."

Ana whines in need as I tease her with the bulge in my jeans, keeping her trembling on the edge. "Goddammit, Aubrey—"

"Shut up and grab the headboard," I command her, reaching up and unbuttoning her waistband. I pull, and she wiggles, helping both her soaked panties and pants slip down her legs and off, the pile of her clothes growing on the floor.

I pause, looking down at her sweet, glistening pussy hovering right over my hips. In my jeans, my cock jumps, trying to get closer to her. I growl, licking my lips. "Looks like you want to come."

"Yes . . . fuck, please, Aubrey." Her hips are bucking in the air above me, searching desperately for relief, tempting me to just plow into her and unleash every bit of my control.

But I hold the reins back for a little longer, wanting to tease both of us, needing this to last as long as possible because I know there's going to be hell to pay. It's up to me to make it worth it for her because I'd gladly pay whatever the price to own her body once again.

"Did you come in the shower too?" I ask softly, guiding her up my body to straddle my face. She settles above me, her hands on the headboard and her pussy hovering inches from my mouth. I inhale her sweetness, her scent so familiar but almost forgotten. "What did you think of when you touched yourself?"

"You . . . fucking me," she admits, her blush deepening. "Fucking me relentlessly 'till I came."

"Good," I rasp, my breath hot along her lips. "Now come for me."

I lick her clit hard and fast, my hands keeping her thighs clamped tight to my face as I suck and nibble. Her juices are sweet and tangy, and I gulp her down thirstily, devouring every drop. I look up her body and see that her chest is quivering, and a split-second later, I can feel the first tremors of her climax sweep through her.

"Aubrey . . . fuck . . . yes!" she cries out, her honey coating my mouth as Ana comes. I suck harder, drawing it out and swallowing a mouthful of her wetness, loving the way she gives in and fucks my face wildly, searching for every bit of pleasure.

As the last shudders rack her body, I toss her off me, pinning her to the bed beneath me. A sharp pain shoots through my ankle at the sudden movement, but I'm far too gone in Ana's eyes to care, and the pain subsides quickly as my lust takes over. I fumble with my jeans, shoving them down and pulling my cock out. I'm aching, and I've waited long enough. I thrust hard into her with one stroke, pausing halfway in as Ana gasps, her fingernails digging into my arms and her pussy clamping down at the intrusion. "Holy fuck!"

"Take it . . . all of me," I growl in her ear before nibbling her earlobe. I'm not brutal, but I need to make her mine, own her body the way she's always owned my heart. I pump in and out insistently, letting her adjust. She's so tight, I'm amazed I even got half my thick cock into her with the first thrust, and as Ana whimpers, the soft sounds of pain turn to sounds of pleasure as I start to bottom out inside her. "That's it, let me in, sweetheart. You're so fucking tight . . . need you to cover me in your cream so I don't hurt you."

"Mmm. Fuck, this is better than I dreamed," Ana says breathlessly. "Tell me I'm not dreaming."

"You're not dreaming, Sweet Ana," I promise her as I pull back.

I keep my eyes locked on Ana's face as I pound her, watching every expression that crosses through her features—the surprise, the desire, the pleasure. The steel frame of my bed creaks with every stroke, a musical accompaniment to our grunts and cries.

Ana squeezes me, her pussy clenching around me tighter than a fist. I reach up, grabbing the headboard, getting leverage over her body to give even more to the intense thrusts. She does the same, her hands flat against the headboard so that she can push away. The combination of her pushing and my pulling against the headboard lets our bodies meet in a punishing power, every slap of our hips vibrating through us in a forceful build toward climax.

We're not tender. We haven't earned that yet, and my control is far too shredded to be gentle right now. But still, Ana gives me all she has, her eyes wide as her body totally submits to my savage will.

"Aubrey . . . oh, fuck, I'm . . . oh, oh, oh!" Ana cries out, her pussy walls fluttering around me. Her moans and the "O" framed on her lips pushes me over the edge. I'm so overwhelmed that I don't even think to pull out but instead drive my cock deeper, my back arching as I fill her all the way. The feeling of my hot seed filling her makes Ana gasp, and she comes again, bucking against me as her pussy milks my cock for every drop.

I stay deep inside her as my orgasm peaks and finally subsides before pulling out, a single final spurt coming out just as I emerge to ooze down her body. The visual of marking her, inside and out, releases a knot in my gut that I didn't know was there. Seeing my cock glisten with her juices helps too, knowing that she's marked me, on the outside just now, and on the inside, many years ago.

As my eyes trace back to Ana's face, I'm not sure what I'll find, which makes me nervous. Is she mad? Satisfied? Confused? Because I sure as fuck am. All those emotions, and a million more. We've been through so much, and so much time has passed, but that was epic. The best fuck I've ever had, by far. And I want more of it, more of her. I want all of her.

Ana looks to be in shock though, still shaken to the core as she tries to speak, "Holy shit, I feel like I just exploded and got put back together with a bam . . ." She mimics the words with her hands, letting them burst outward before slamming her palms back together. The smile on her face is beautiful and makes me feel like a god. I did that, helped put that happiness on her face.

That puffed-up feeling lasts but a split second as her face contorts. I feel the cum leaking out of her pussy, dripping down my balls where they rest against her. I grind against her, keeping it there, smearing it along her skin like an animal marking its territory, and she gasps slightly. In this moment, I'm probably more a wild beast than a man, but she didn't seem to mind a minute ago when I was riding her, slapping against her in earth-shattering waves.

"What are you doing?" she squeals, wiggling beneath me but only succeeding in rubbing against me even more.

I want to admit that I'm marking her, but it's too soon and I know it'll send her running for the hills. I have no doubt she still thinks this is a quick fuck, one and done to get it out of her system. She hasn't realized that this was just the first of many times I'm going to take her and that before long, she'll be begging for it. For now, I have to keep it dirty, just light enough that she doesn't spook. "Just enjoying the feel of your pussy so full of my cum you can't hold it all."

She tsks but subtly shifts against me so I know she liked that answer even if she won't admit it. "Not that you asked, but I'm on birth control and I'm clean."

I growl, knowing that I honestly didn't even think about whether she was protected. I would've come in her even if she hadn't been. I just wanted her and couldn't stop. Although her needing to be on birth control for whatever fuckers she sees back home does make my gut tighten in jealousy. "I'm clean too."

As the adrenaline of the moment passes, the pains start to set in, my ribs and ankle complaining at their overuse. I flop ungracefully to the bed beside Ana, reaching my arm up behind my head to stretch out the muscles in my torso and adjusting my jeans back in place but leaving them unbuttoned. Just in case she's interested in round two.

Ana hisses, sitting up to loom over me. For such a tiny thing, she's surprisingly intimidating when she gets that Mean Nurse look on her face. "Damn it, I'm supposed to be treating your injuries, which you made worse in some juvenile attempt to lure me over here." Her eyes flick down to my ankle, still laced into my boot, to my bare chest as she checks out my ribs. Her eyes repeatedly jump down to my crotch, though, and my cock responds, hardening more every time she glances its way.

"I gave you what you wanted, what I wanted too," I murmur, the admission easy for me. "Admit it, Ana."

I know I'm right. And in that moment, neither of us cared about anything else, the past, the future all giving way to the present moment. But she's in denial, the fog of desire clearing from her mind and leaving her in doubt about what we just did. I can feel the retreat as she moves away to sit up on the edge of the bed, her back to me.

"We shouldn't have. I shouldn't have," she says, shaking her head.

I can't see her face, but I can hear the tinge of regret and it cuts me to the core. I don't want to be her regret, a mistake. I regret enough for the both of us, and it's an ugly emotion that eats away the core of your spirit. I don't want that for Ana . . . especially not about me. She needs the light casualness still, even though there's so much more going on. I'll continue to give her the out for now. "Let me fuck the shit outta you?" I rumble. She doesn't respond, so I continue, adding a hint of something deeper to test the waters. "You know there's always been something combustible between us. That hasn't changed, Ana. I don't think it ever will."

She looks back at me over her shoulder, her eyes tracing my body, and I fight to stay still, to not sit up and pull her to me, for another go or just to hold her, I'm not sure. But with a sigh, she stands and moves away from the bed, and the spell we've been under is broken, snapping as she gains distance from me.

She bends to grab her T-shirt and then yelps as she jumps. "Ahh." Her wide eyes look around her feet and then she laughs. "Holy shit, Rex! You scared me!"

Rex barks back, answering to his name, and then plops his head up on the edge of the bed for a loving pat. "Good boy, Rex."

"Did he just watch us have sex?" Ana asks, horror blushing across her face as she holds her shirt to her chest. Like Rex gives a shit about her bare breasts.

"I think he came in while you were busy riding my face and

93

coming in my mouth," I tease. Her mouth drops open in a pretty 'O' that I'd love to fill with my cock. I never saw Rex come in and wouldn't have given it a second thought even if I had. But I can't pass up the opportunity to tease her a bit.

She snaps her mouth closed as I grin at her, swiping my thumb along my lip as if there's still some of her cream there. There isn't. I've long since licked every drop of it from my lips.

Rex heads back into his favorite corner, the one where the sunbeam hits just right for him to sunbathe. His eyes are closed before he even settles on the floor.

Ana watches him, then turns back to me. "I need you to know this doesn't change anything. Just a momentary lapse of judgement, giving in to all that . . ." She gestures her hands, apparently meaning all of me.

I'm on the verge of protesting, of pushing the matter and forcing her to admit that there's more between us and always has been. But I'll use whatever temptation I have at my disposal to keep her close. If it's my body she wants, I'm not opposed to that . . . at least, for now. I stand from the bed, suppressing the wince from the movement to crowd right in front of her, our bodies inches apart. I casually reach down and adjust my cock with my palm, enjoying the way her eyes track my every movement and knowing that we both wish it were her hands on my cock. I can see the hitch in her breathing, the flush rising on her cheeks again. "Understood," I say.

She looks disappointed at my lack of argument, and for a moment, I almost give in, but I know it'd backfire and give her ammunition against me, sending her running off once again. No, holding tight on my tongue, I let the silence stand, hoping that soon, I'll be able to speak more freely and tell her the truth about what happened all those years ago and that she'll actually listen to me.

Letting the seed plant and hoping that it'll lead to her wanting more, I switch topics to throw her off-balance a bit. "You know what you need?" I let the question hang in the air and watch the dirty thoughts race across her face with a groan. "Mmm, yeah, that too, but I was gonna say that you came up here to get away, be with nature, and have an adventure. Right?"

Ana bites her lip. "Well, yeah. It's supposed to be a vacation, to relax and unwind. Not nursing a stubborn oaf who won't do as he's told. Speaking of, no more games to get me running over. You could've really hurt yourself. Also, you're on your feet . . . again." Her tone belies the suppressed eye roll.

I shrug. "It was a calculated risk. And it was damn worth it, if I say so myself. You know what you do to me, Ana." I let my need for her into my voice even though I honestly mean more than the physical effect of being near her, but her eyes track right back to my cock, thick and hard between us. I groan, the warning clear in my voice as I chastise her. "Ana, I'm trying to have a conversation with you here, but if you keep looking at my cock, I'm gonna push you to your knees and make you suck me into that mouth that keeps dropping open in invitation."

There's a beat of hesitation where we both think she might actually do that, especially when I see the way her bare thighs are pressing together, but it passes with a huff of indignation. "Ugh . . . such a caveman." She turns to stomp off, but I catch her arm in my hand.

"Ana, what I was trying to say before we both got so distracted . . ." I pause, giving her a hard look, daring her to disagree with me, but she stays silent so I continue. "is that you should let me take you hunting. I told you at lunch that I hunt most of what I eat. Cutting logs in the middle of nowhere doesn't exactly afford weekly trips to Trader Joe's. Let me show you. Let me take you on an adventure."

"I don't think so. You need to stay off your ankle, not go

traipsing through the woods," she argues. "I can't allow that. Nurse's orders."

"You act as though you have a choice. I'm going hunting, need to so that I can eat. You can stay here, holed up in your cabin and worrying about me. Or you can go with me, see some beautiful scenery, and make sure I'm being a good boy and don't do anything too stupid." It's a risk and I know it. She might rise to the challenge or ditch me in favor of couch surfing.

The 'no' is on the tip of her tongue, but I can see the 'yes' swirling in her eyes as she battles internally. Finally, she reaches a compromise . . . with herself and with me. "Fine, but only if we wait until tomorrow. You've already overdone it, so stay off your foot for the rest of today. Then tomorrow, we'll go hunting. As long as the trip is short, and heavy on the sightseeing more than the hunting. Deal?"

"Deal," I growl, more than satisfied with her terms.

CHAPTER 12

ANA

I should've fucking known better. I thought I'd sketched out a pretty fair deal where Aubrey would spend the remainder of the day resting his ankle and ribs. I'd pictured him propped up on the couch, dozing with his eyes closed as he followed my orders to stay off his foot. That picture also included me going back to my cabin for a nap and a night by the fire. Alone.

When Aubrey agreed to wait for our hunting trip, he'd pictured the two of us hanging out in his cabin for the rest of the day and evening. I'd done my best to argue, but deep down, I'd known I was going to stay. And that's how I find myself, once again, warming up soup and serving him dinner on the couch. At least there's a fire.

Wait. He started a damn fire while I was in the kitchen. I give him a side-eye of disapproval, but he just slurps his soup happily, ignoring my silent reprimand. That man. I don't know whether to wallop him upside the head to force him to stay down or marvel that he's able to be up and around at all. Most guys would take advantage and hold court on the couch, not bothering to lift a finger to help. But not Aubrey. He's fighting to still do things . . . work and take care of himself and me. The thought gives me a warm fuzzy for a moment before I remember that he wasn't always one to fight for me. He was the guy who just walked away.

I shake my head, letting the thought rattle loose. If this is going to work, these days next to each other, especially the time spent together, we're going to have to stay solidly in the present. No past, no future, no big conversations about what happened. I won't say that I'm not curious, of course. I've spent nights awake, tossing and turning, wondering what the hell happened. But it's been years, and nothing he can say would make it okay, so it's better to just live in a fantasy world for the next week where we are strangers who just met and have amazing chemistry. Nothing more, nothing less. A short-lived adventure.

Sounds easy enough, but it makes conversation a veritable minefield where every personal question could explode in my face. Thinking carefully, I venture, "It's beautiful up here. Do you get many guests at the other cabin?"

Shit. Way to go, Ana. That totally sounds like you're fishing to see if he's fucking a different woman every week. Well, actually, I would kinda like to know that. But surely, most guests to a remote cabin aren't single women, right? I bury my face in my soup bowl, hoping he doesn't see the embarrassment on my face.

He grunts. "This is my favorite place on Earth, I think. Just me and Mother Nature, peace and quiet. You're actually my first guest at the cabin. Carlotta just made the brochure and the online ad for it."

I feel the flinch before I can stop it, and know Aubrey saw it too by the grin on his face. "Carlotta is a marketing genius. And my second cousin, so no need to get jealous."

I sputter helplessly. "I'm not jealous. You just seem to like being alone up here on your mountain of solitude, so I was surprised you had someone to help you with the advertising." The argument sounds weak even to my ears, but thankfully, Aubrey lets it go unchallenged.

"I have spent the better part of a few years alone up here, so I was glad to have her help. Seems to have worked better than I'd ever hoped." The comment hangs heavily, but I don't give in to answering. After a moment, he continues, "So, tell me about you, Ms. Nurse Extraordinaire."

It's small talk, a capitulation to my stated desire to keep things light, casual. I both appreciate it and hate it. I feel like the most wishy-washy of women in the history of time, wanting him to force the topic to the elephant in the room while simultaneously wanting to run lest that elephant stomp my heart to smithereens once again.

Fear of the true story of our past makes the decision for me, and I launch into a superficial answer. "I went to nursing school and worked my ass off for top grades so that I could get the placements I wanted. After school, I was lucky enough to get on at St. Joseph's Memorial Hospital. I spent a year working whatever shifts, whatever department they needed me in, basically being low man on the totem pole and taking what I could get. I've paid my dues a bit now and have learned a lot, so I'm lucky to work in critical care more often than not. It's my favorite, helping people through crises, but getting to know them longer than just a quick run through the emergency department. It was actually a patient who first gave me the prompt to take a vacation."

I smile as I think of Mrs. Smith and hope she's okay. By the time I left for vacation, she had been discharged and was happily and healthily under the care of her children once again. I think she'd be proud that I actually followed through and went on vacation.

I wonder what she'd say about the whole situation with Aubrey, though.

Aubrey smiles as I talk, listening intently. He raises his glass of tea in salute. "To your patient's good suggestion." He takes a drink to finish the toast and then continues as I drink too. "Sounds like you work hard, but I can tell you love it by the way you talk about it."

I nod. "I do love it. I love helping people, caring for them when they need it, ensuring they get better and can return to their lives. It's fulfilling. What about you? What do you do up here everyday?" I purposefully word the question carefully, not asking how he ended up here, sensing that might take us down a dangerous road.

Aubrey swallows another sip of tea, looking out the window. "Mostly chop wood . . . for myself and for the businesses I contract with. I deliver into town once a week or so. I hike out to clear felled trees when possible. Sometimes, I hike for the hell of it or play fetch with Rex, hunt, and tend the garden as it needs it. It doesn't sound like much, but keeping everything going is a full-time job, sunup to sundown."

"It sounds very . . . outdoorsy." It truly does, but that wasn't my first thought. My first thought was that it sounds really lonely. I knew he was alone out here, had even joked about the solitude. But I guess I figured he saw people more than once a week. I try to reconcile that with my life, the constant conversation with patients, the chatter at the nurses' station with coworkers, the phone calls with family and friends. By the end of the day, I usually crave some quiet. But I think Aubrey would crave conversation. But maybe not? He's out here alone for a reason, after all, whatever that may be.

"Yeah, it definitely is that. But I like it. I did the rat race thing for a while, and it wasn't for me, the hustle and bustle, the competition for no good reason beyond bragging rights, and the constant need for more status, more money, more power." He shakes his head, obviously remembering those times, and I wonder when that was, how long after he left me, and what got him there. But I hold my tongue and don't ask. "Out here, I feel calmer, more connected with what's really important, just me and Rex hanging out, appreciating the beauty of the woods as they go through the seasons."

Deciding the question is worth the risk, I wade into the deeper waters. "Don't you get lonely up here? If you only see folks in town once a week, how do you keep from going stir-crazy?"

He hums, obviously thinking about his answer, which I appreciate. "I do sometimes, I guess. Carlotta comes for dinner a couple of times a month, and my days in town are usually long, so by the time I get home, I'm all peopled out. But mostly, Rex and I manage just fine. Unless it's weird that I talk to him and he talks back? That's not weird, right?" He's joking, his eyes sparkling even though his smirk is hidden in the tight line of his lips.

I adopt a wise doctor affect as I give my diagnosis. "Nope, talking to your dog is perfectly normal. As long as he only barks or eyeballs you back, I think you're fine. If he's talking in actual words, it might be cause for concern."

Aubrey laughs a full, hearty chuckle from deep in his throat and the rumbles vibrate the room. It's a melodic sound, baser than a tolling bell, and it makes my belly flip-flop. I smile back, confessing, "I don't have any pets—way too busy to take proper care of them. It wouldn't be fair, but I have been known to talk to my plants. Studies show it helps them grow and stay healthy. So I think we're both perfectly sane."

The smile on his face says clearly that he's certain neither of us is entirely sane, especially given the circumstances of where we're sitting and the danger we're playing with. "Come here," Aubrey murmurs, more demand than request. I should run back to my cabin, back home to the city, but I don't. Instead, I walk slowly toward the couch, following his commands and sitting down gingerly beside him so as not to hurt his ribs or ankle.

"I'm not broken, woman." Aubrey wraps his arms around me, manhandling me to move us both into the position he wants. I find myself lying on my side, half-on and half-off Aubrey as he lies on his back on the couch. It's warm and comfortable, which makes me tense. But slowly, his fingers running up and down my arm soothes me and I relax against him.

After a few minutes of quiet stillness, I realize that Aubrey's breathing has evened out and he's drifted off. He must've been more tired than either of us realized after his wood-chopping stunt and then the energetic fucking. His body is probably drained, without reserves to use to heal. I decide to let him rest and snuggle up against him, bound and determined to rest myself too.

But my mind roars with questions. What happened back then? Do I really want to know? What the hell happened today, and am I going to do it again? Do I want to? Does he?

I try to be still, not wanting to disturb him, but I eventually give in and get up carefully so as not to wake him. I stand over the couch, watching with bated breath to insure Aubrey continues dozing. Rex lifts his head from his paws, his protective gaze evaluating me, and I give him a pat to the head to reassure him that I mean no harm.

Quietly, I gather our soup bowls and tea glasses, moving into the kitchen to wash them. Once that's done, I feel an overwhelming urge to snoop, to find the answers to some of my questions without going to the source. But I won't do that. It's wrong, and if I'm going to give in to the urge to know, I want to hear it straight from Aubrey's lips and watch his eyes when he tells me why he did what he did.

In an attempt to busy myself without waking Aubrey, I wander outside to the back porch. There's a cushioned rocking chair and a small table with what looks to be a half-formed wood figurine on it. I smile, realizing that although he didn't mention it, Aubrey must do a little whittling too. The image of him rocking the evening away, deeply concentrating as he putzes with tiny slivers of wood, is adorable in my mind's eye.

I step off the porch, my eyes sweeping along the expanse of trees and sky, taking in the beautiful grandeur with an inhale of fresh air. Lifting my face to the sun, I say a vow of thanks for the day, this messy, dirty, emotional, lovely day, with Aubrey in this forest paradise.

My thoughts turn to tomorrow and the promise I'd made. I'm going hunting? There are so many things wrong with that idea it's not even funny. I'm gonna get lost, or starve to death, and definitely get attacked by a bear. Trey is going to blame himself for leaving me alone up here with an injured mountain man who couldn't protect me from the vicious grizzly attack, and Brad will bawl big, melodramatic tears at my funeral while looking spectacular in head-to-toe black, of course.

Okay, so maybe it's not that bad. But I do worry that Aubrey is overdoing it, as evidenced by his impromptu nap right now. Especially considering he said he's usually going sunup to sundown. Hiking and hunting may not be the best idea tomorrow, but I have no faith in my ability to talk him down from his plan.

Deciding that I should take a play from my nursing guidebook, I begin searching for a long, thick stick that would make a good walking stick. I know better than to call it a cane because a man like Aubrey would never use a cane or a crutch. But a walking stick is a tried and true hiking aide, one that I can hopefully get him to use.

The mission gives me focus as I search far and wide for the

perfect option, making sure to keep the cabin in sight the whole time just to be safe. Finally, I kick a thatch of fallen leaves and the perfect stick emerges from the pile. I pick it up, pulling a few thin sprouts of twigs off and smiling. I need to get the bark off because it's rather brittle, but I think it'll work.

I test it out as I walk to the back porch and decide that this is going to be a negotiating factor for tomorrow. Aubrey is using the stick to help him walk or we're not going. And I know he wants, maybe needs, to go hunting. I settle in the rocking chair, picking at the bark to get down to fresh wood as I watch the sun dip below the horizon line and listen to the forest come to life with the buzz of night creatures.

It takes me a long while, and eventually, I even use Aubrey's axe to get a few stubborn areas of bark off. But my work pays off, the surface of the tall stick smooth to the touch and just what Aubrey will need tomorrow.

I lean the stick near the back door, knowing that I'll have to surprise him with my gift in the morning if I have any hope of his actually using it. Sneaking quietly back inside, I see that Aubrey is still asleep but has rolled to his side, trying in vain to somehow fit his huge form onto the skinny couch.

With a small smile, I gently rub his shoulder. "Aubrey, wake up. Let's move you to the bed so you can get comfortable." It takes a couple of repeats, and some cringes from discomfort on his part, but I manage to help him shuffle to his bedroom and lie down.

As he plops onto the bed, he mutters, "You too, Sweet Ana. Stay with me, at least for tonight."

I don't answer, my voice stuck behind the lump in my throat. But I pat him, trying to get Aubrey to settle back to sleep without an agreement from me. But he's not having it, and he pulls me to the bed next to him. I let out a cry as I tumble down, trying desperately to not smoosh him, especially on his sore ribs. "Whoa! Aubrey, get some rest, okay?"

He opens his eyes, bleary but still focused on me. "Stay, Ana. Please." His voice is rough with sleep, sexy and rumbly, but it's the 'please' that does me in.

"Fine, I'll stay. But let me fix your ankle up." I sit up on the bed, carefully unlacing his boot and pulling it off. He winces at the pressure, his eyes popping open, clear and brown and staring daggers at me. "Sorry, need to check it out and prop your foot on some pillows."

He's already back to sleep before I finish my explanation, muttering something that sounds suspiciously like "Nurse Ratchet . . . nice, my ass."

I hold the giggle in, ever the consummate professional. Or not, considering present circumstances. I do a quick check of Aubrey's ankle, noting that the swelling does look significantly better and the bruising is already starting to change colors as it goes through the long healing process. I cradle his foot, slipping a stack of pillows underneath it, and then I stand back to assess.

I should sleep on the couch. I'd still be staying like he asked, but not so dangerously close to him. Even as I talk myself into it, I know Aubrey will give me shit about it in the morning if I do that.

Pausing in the doorway, I realize that I don't want to sleep on the couch. I want to sleep in this big bed with this big beast of a man, curled up against his body. It's stupid, clearly a rash decision made more on lust than logic, but how many opportunities like this come up in a lifetime? None? One? Maybe more if you're lucky enough to get some sort of fairytale miracle?

Decision made, I slip my jeans off, leaving my T-shirt and undies on for polite manners and slide into the bed next to Aubrey. He instantly wraps his arms around me, holding my cheek to his thick chest and cupping my thigh where it lies across his. I fall asleep without a single question on my mind, the simple feeling of settling in Aubrey's arms as comfortable and easy as coming home.

CHAPTER 13

AUBREY

*T*his is crazy. I was sure that Ana hated my guts. I'm still not convinced she doesn't, but after the past two days, I'm so fuck-drunk that I'm willing to admit there's a chance she doesn't.

We didn't go hunting the day after our first fuck as I'd made her agree to. Instead, she convinced me to stay home one more day, promising to spend the whole day and night with me. It was a price worth the delay, and we spent the next twenty-four hours in my cabin, eating food from the fridge between bouts of sex.

I'm not naive enough to think it was anything more than two people relieving a desperate need. Lord knows, I'd gone so long without sex I had enough stored inside my balls to fill a water tower, and poor Ana has just been the receptacle for all my raging lust.

But from her moans and enthusiasm, I know for a fact she's enjoyed every minute of it. I swear, I've woken up more than once where instead of nursing my ankle, she's nursing me back to another hard-on so she can get another dose of my cock.

What isn't important are the positions, the multitudes of times

I've left her full of cum, or whether she came on my fingers, my tongue, or my cock. What's important is that we haven't spoken about the past.

She's declared over and over that it doesn't mean anything and she wants to stay focused on the here and now, calling me a stubborn asshole every time I try to bring it up or talk about something more serious than 'where do you want it?'

But I have hope. Hope that she'll eventually listen. Hope that she might find it in her heart to forgive me.

It's just going to take time. And with her only being here for a short time before she returns home to care for folks who actually need her help, time might not be on my side.

Our issues aren't going to be resolved by me unburdening my heart. You can't just forgive and forget in an instant after all these years. And she needs to know that I didn't run because I'm a coward, even if I do feel like one right now because knowing that I'm going to have to come clean scares the shit out of me. All this time, I've dealt with it in my own way and without talking about it to anyone else. The burdens of the past have weighed heavily on my shoulders alone.

"You're all set," Ana says, bent over at my knee. The bandage and brace aren't pretty, but they'll fit inside my strongest boot, and that'll have to be enough. "You shouldn't put much weight on it, but it doesn't seem like you listen to a thing I say."

"I'll be fine," I reply, standing up and testing my ankle. It's a lot better than I expected. Who knew that taking a day off my feet would help so damn much? Guess I just needed the right motivation for staying in bed. "I'm gonna let you do most of the work anyway."

Ana stands up, gazing up at me and looking sexy as fuck. She's dressed like some hunting calendar dream, cute in her jeans, boots, and a borrowed camo shirt that's tied off. She's not wearing a bra, and the curves of her breasts pressed against her shirt look tempting as fuck. The sight of her nipples pressing against the shirt is just for me. The whole picture is topped off with her bare face and a messy knot of her honey hair underneath one of my old ballcaps. "You sure keep saying that. Sounds like you want us to starve."

I grin, knowing she's mostly teasing. "We both know you brought enough food for a month, so we aren't starving either way. Besides, even if we weren't going out, Rex has to get out for a walk sometimes. No way he'd let me sit in here all day, jacked-up ankle or not. Unless you want to take him for a stroll while I kick back?"

Ana glances at Rex, who's sitting by the door, ready and waiting, silently saying, *Let's go, let's go!* She shakes her head. "No, thanks. I'm still not convinced he likes me. I might just end up being the food."

I laugh, teasing back. "Well, I'd happily eat you morning, noon, and night every day."

She flushes and then says, "Close your eyes."

I wiggle my eyebrows at her meaningfully. "Okay by me, but we are getting out to hunt at some point today so it'll have to be a quickie this time."

I hear her quiet giggle then a put-upon sigh. "It's not always about sex, Aubrey. I have a surprise for you."

I grin, keeping my eyes closed. "That still sounds like you're talking about sex, best surprise I can think of." The banter feels good. It's been our go-to mode for the last day. Easy and light, nothing dark or heavy to test the blossoming connection we're rekindling. That'll come. It has to. But for now, this is working.

I hear the back door open and then close, then Ana says, "Okay, open." I open my eyes to see her standing directly in front of me, handing me . . . a stick? I take it from her, confusion written across my face.

"It's a walking stick, to help with your ankle while we're hiking today," she explains, as though that should be obvious. Actually, now that she says it, that's completely apparent. I just didn't think of it because I'm a stubborn asshole, as we've well established.

"No way. Where'd you even get this?" I ask, trying to hand it back to Ana, but she shoves it back toward me with open palms.

"I made it for you. And you're using it today on our hunting hike or we're not going." Her voice is serious, inviting no discussion or argument. I realize this is her professional, I-mean-business tone.

I look at the stick again, turning it in my hands. It's crude, nothing fancy or polished, just a long length of smooth wood. But she made this for me, spent time searching for the right one, debarking it, and prepping it. All the while, thinking of me. My heart fills with warmth. Progress. I'm making progress with her, slowly but surely.

I nod and plant the end on the floor. It's perfect, just long enough to give me good support, and strong too. It's slightly against my dignity . . . but it's only temporary, and besides, Ana made it. "Fine, fine. I'll use it. Ana . . ."

I wait for her eyes to meet mine, the smile already plastered on her face at my agreement to use the stick, and I realize she expected much more of an argument. "Thank you."

Her smile spreads wider and her eyes shine, and I think she might actually be tearing up a bit. Shit, is that good? Bad? I don't know for sure, so I redirect as quickly as possible. "Come on, I've got the place picked out already."

We go out to my ATV, quickly loading up with what we'll need for the day as Rex runs back and forth from the shed to the house on a loop, following in our footsteps. Apparently, the day indoors yesterday made him a bit antsy too. I give him a pat on the head and instruct him to 'watch the house', and he lopes off, setting a path around the perimeter of the cabin. Ana laughs, but I assure her, "Don't worry, he won't walk paces the whole time we're gone. Just for a bit until he's confident there's nothing looming, then he'll take turns on the front porch and then the back, laying out and dozing off and on."

She shakes her head in disbelief but climbs on the ATV behind me and we drive out. It feels good to have her arms wrapped around my waist even over the jackets we're wearing, and I'm a little regretful when it's over. "We walk from here. Don't worry, it's not far, just about two hundred yards."

The day's beautiful as we slowly make our way through the woods with clear blue skies above us. A cool wind is coming down from up-mountain, and the hint of moisture in the air's even better. It's exactly what we need to stay fresh as we hike the short distance. Of course, I use the walking stick Ana made me, willing to ding my own ego if it puts a smile on her face.

"Here we are," I note as we reach the spot, a deer stand that I use a lot. "Up and at 'em."

I unsling my light pack and climb the handful of steps using just my left leg in an awkward hopping motion, leaving Ana down on the ground, scowling at me. "What the heck are you doing?"

I reach the top, and it's hard not to laugh as I look down at her. She's so cute when she's indignant. "You told me I need to stay off my ankle. That's what I'm doing."

"And what am I supposed to do?"

I grin, pointing back at the cases on the ATV's cargo rack. "All the work. While I watch."

"You're out of your mind!" Ana says, huffing. "I have no idea what I'm doing."

"You'll learn, Miss Nurse," I joke.

Ana throws her hands up, picking up the smaller of the two hard cases. "I can't with you! You know this is blackmail, right?"

I smirk at her cockily, wagging a finger. "It's just about patience. How are you supposed to nurse my ankle if you don't have any patience?"

"Trust me, I have a lot of it," Ana says as she hands up the first case. "Just not much for an overgrown asshole."

I grin, looking into her beautiful eyes and lowering my voice until it's husky the way she likes. "Don't forget, this overgrown asshole knows how to dick you until you're screaming at the top of your lungs. So I'm useful for *something*, at least."

Ana drops the few feet down, growling as she stomps over to get the next item to hand up.

I have to grin as she stomps off, nearly foaming at the mouth. I enjoy seeing this side of her. Sweet Ana, all flustered and sassy with pink cheeks, turns me on. She stays gone for a good five minutes before coming back to hand me the second case. Then she stands there with her hands on her hips, looking up at me.

"Alright, what am I supposed to be doing?"

I look down from my seat and nod, grinning. "I knew you'd see it my way. Climb on up here, and don't forget the knapsack."

Ana obeys, and when she reaches the stand, she looks around. It's a little tight, but not too bad. I didn't build this thing to have more than one person in it, but she's so small, we can squeeze in. "No funny business. You might not believe me, but I *do* know my way out of here. I'll leave you high and dry."

"Then you'd be guilt-ridden forever," I tease, opening up the smaller of the two cases and taking out the pieces. "Now, here's what you'll be using."

"A . . . crossbow?" Ana asks before stopping.

"Yep. You can't learn to use a bow in one sitting, but a crossbow's a lot like a rifle," I explain, locking the pieces into place. "Aim and shoot. Ever shot a rifle?"

"Only shooting I've done is laser tag with Trey," Ana admits. "Does that count?"

"It could," I hedge. I finish assembling the crossbow and then set it aside to put together my bow. "This is just in case you need backup. Now, let's see how you handle the crossbow."

I demonstrate, putting a bolt in an old target I have set up on a tree before handing it to Ana. "Your turn."

She looks at the bright green bolt sticking out of the tree, then looks at me. "You want me to do *that*?"

I nod. "Bring the stock up to your shoulder . . . just a little higher. Get this on your cheek."

I guide Ana through how to shoot, moving behind her and adjusting her as needed. Holding her still, I'm aware of her body and how warm she feels in the cool stand, but I keep myself professional even as my cock hardens and presses against her ass. "Now, when you want to fire, you stroke the trigger. Don't yank it."

Ana lowers the crossbow, looking back at me. "Stroke it, don't yank it? *Really?*"

"I didn't mean it as a pun, but it does sound like fun, doesn't it?" I grin, leaning in and kissing her quickly and deeply. When our lips break, I'm smirking hard. "Now, you ready to try and fire something?"

"I still don't get why you don't use a gun," Ana says as I recock the bow and seat a bolt. "Isn't it easier?"

"It is, but this always feels like a more balanced battle to me. Now, just like we practiced."

Amazingly, Ana's a natural, hitting the black circle I've painted on the target wood with her first three shots without even needing a single hint. "Wow, I'm a deadeye."

"Don't get too cocky. Now we wait. The boar come through here, usually around sunset."

"Sunset?" Ana asks, surprised. "But it's barely after lunch!"

"And we needed time to make sure you could shoot right and not scare off the boar," I explain. "Now . . . quiet."

Silence drops between us, the crossbow set aside as we settle in to wait. I let her sit up front, my body close to her so I can talk quietly with her. "How'd it feel to hit the target?"

"Good," she whispers back.

"You're a natural. Ana, look, I feel like I should . . ." I start, my voice barely a whisper in her ear as I tempt fate, and her anger, by trying to explain about our past, about what happened.

She knows where my mind is heading, though, and puts the brakes on that train of thought with a sad sigh. "Don't, Aubrey. Really . . . don't. This is nice, we're having fun, and I don't want to turn the rest of my time here into a trip down memory lane, especially when it's a sad and angry trip."

I nod and feel her tense up, feel the gap widening between us, yawning wide and dark and dangerous. It takes every bit of strength I have, but I push the words deep down, trying to respect her wishes even though I desperately want to force her to listen.

It's quiet for a long few minutes, the tension slowly melting as we wander through the past in our minds, in our hearts. We stay close, our bodies pressed against each other, even if the distance of our souls stays static, much to my frustration.

We wait as the afternoon stretches on, not saying much as we wait. When my watch says it's getting close to four, I recock her crossbow and set a hunting broadhead into the groove.

I get my gear ready too, my bow poised in case Ana needs it. About thirty minutes later, I hear the first rustles in the woods, and coming down the game trail is a doe, still skinny after a long winter. But that's not what we're here for, so we let her pass.

Ten minutes later, there's another rustle, and a boar emerges. The Bear Mountains actually have more boar than bears nowadays, too many hunters looking for a trophy and too many developers taking the bears' territory. Boars, though, are officially vermin by the state because they're so prevalent, and they're fair game.

But this boar is small, likely still young, and not suitable to hunt yet. I whisper to Ana, "Not this one."

We wait for over an hour, watching the sun dip toward the horizon and the forest come to life with nocturnal creatures. But though we see a few more deer, no more boars come near our hunting post. I do need to hunt to restock my freezer supplies, but I'm just enjoying being wrapped around Ana, her back to my front as the orange light casts a glow over us.

Finally, we give up and head carefully back to the ATV for the ride back to the cabin. We might not have had a successful hunt, but I feel like Ana is slowly warming to me, even if she did shut me down on having a serious discussion again. But I'm wearing her down, and if nothing else, she's getting more comfortable around me, letting her guard down more and more, letting me in. Eventually, she has to listen, or maybe we can just pretend the past never happened and move forward from here.

WE DON'T HAVE FRESH MEAT FOR DINNER, BUT LUCKILY, I'M always well-prepared and Ana really did stock up for her vacation. Rex is practically drooling on the ground as the low flames lick at the chicken breasts we've skewered and placed on a makeshift grill that lays on the open firepit.

"So this is what your life is like," Ana says as I turn the skewers. "You do this often?"

"More often than not. Usually not chicken, though I'll admit I go into town to get some things."

Ana shakes her head, looking at me sideways. "I've imagined what you'd be like, where you'd be, many times over the years. Never expected this. You were so . . . different." She chuckles. "You were about as far from a loner as it gets. And look at you now!"

I swallow, looking down. It's the first time we've mentioned our pasts, and suddenly, it's my time to feel nervous. "It's what I had to do to survive."

She can see the darkness in my eyes and turns, tilting her head as she looks at me carefully. "What do you mean, to survive?"

I stare at her long and hard, trying to think up a way to start because this is the opening I've been waiting for, my chance to explain how my life went sideways and I left her behind, even if I didn't want to.

Before I can answer, a growling sound with a familiar stench wafts our direction.

"What the hell is that smell?" she cries, backing away. "God, that's fucking rank!"

"Skunk," I growl. "The fire scares it so it's scenting, I guess. Probably just wants food."

Rex barks in the skunk's direction, the scruff of his neck rising.

"No, Rex!" I command, hoping Rex remembers. The last time he tangled with a skunk, he got sprayed. It took a day for him to see right and a week of tomato juice baths to get the smell out of his fur.

"Let's get back," I growl, pointing toward the cabin. "You don't want that smell getting into your clothes and your skin, trust me."

Ana doesn't need any more convincing, running while Rex stays with me as I follow, limping along. I think about how funny it is. The conversation I've worried about having for years . . . and it's stopped in its tracks by a skunk.

CHAPTER 14

AUBREY

"Oh my gawd, that smell!" Ana gags, out of breath. My ankle's not too bad, but I'm glad that we're stopping. Ana shakes her head, waving her hand in front of her nose. "I've never smelled something *that* bad . . . and I work in a hospital!"

I chuckle. "Good thing you're a city girl then. It's happened to me a few times out here. Never pleasant."

A shudder rushes through her, so I move closer. "You're shivering. From the cold or the smell?"

The stars twinkle above us like diamonds glittering on blue-black velvet, and Ana takes a half-step back, turning so that I'm hugging her from behind as she looks around. "Both maybe. Maybe something else though." She looks around, scanning the darkening tree line, and I catch a hint of a smile as she notices the sparking lightning bugs who have come out for the evening. "This reminds me of our special place. I wouldn't even remember how to get there from here though."

I nuzzle at her neck and kiss her just below her ear. "I know where it is. Too far of a walk right now, but this can be our special place for tonight."

Ana moans softly, pressing back against me as I bring my hand around and cup her breast, the perfect handful for my touch. Her breath catches, and she looks back, her eyes two more diamonds in the moonlight. "Uh, should we go in the cabin?"

I look over my shoulder at the cabin then back to Ana. "I don't think I can make it. Might have to stay right here." I grin as her face goes from an expression of 'oh, no', thinking my ankle hurts too much to let me walk the handful of yards to the cabin, to one of sexy sassiness as she gets my meaning.

Ana nods, reaching up to cup my neck as I lower my lips, tasting the curve of her neck as I pull her tighter, my hands roaming her body.

We sink down to the grassy earth, our hands exploring each other as we shrug off our jackets. I pull Ana on top of me, stroking her thighs and ass. "Ana . . . my Sweet Ana."

"I think part of me has always been your Sweet Ana," she whispers, nipping at my neck. The confession feels big, an acknowledgement of what we once were to each other. "But I'm more now."

I slip my hand inside her jeans, humming happily as I cup her pussy. "I've noticed." I slip a finger along the edge of her panties, dipping in to tease at her slit. "You've grown, inside and out," I say, placing my other hand on her heart.

"So have you. *Everything* about you is bigger." She gasps as I tease her pussy. "Or maybe I'm just imagining things."

"It's in the food up here," I joke, rolling her over to kiss down her neck. It's pretty chilly, so I suck on her nipples through her shirt, saying, "I don't want you to freeze, so we'll have to do this half-dressed, okay?" She moans, which I take as agreement considering her back is arching as I tug on her stiff nubs, so I push her pants lower, leaving her trapped with them around her knees. "God, you're fucking beautiful."

"Aubrey?" Ana says, twisting her hips. I get up, and she turns over, getting to her knees to present herself to me. "Please?"

I can't resist the sight of Ana, her eyes gleaming in the starlight and her ass swaying hypnotically back and forth in front of me. Reaching forward, I grab her ass, spreading her cheeks wide to let me see her wet pussy, relishing the heady punch of her arousal that hits my nostrils. "I need a taste."

"Oh, fuck, Aubrey, yes," Ana cries out as I bury my face in her ass, my tongue lapping at her pussy from behind as I feast on her. She's so delicious, and I squeeze the handfuls of her ass again and again, kneading her flesh and knowing I'm likely leaving fingerprint marks on her skin. "Oh, fuck . . ."

I jab my stiff tongue deep in Ana's pussy, tongue-fucking her forcefully before pulling out to stroke her clit, covering my mouth and lips in the sweet wine. I give her all I have, trying to show her that I'm not the boy who left her . . . that I'm more, that I've grown like she has.

Ana trembles, her fingers digging at the soft grass until she cries out, her back arching as she comes, calling out my name softly. "Aubrey . . . oh, God, you make me feel so good." It's a breathy confession that pulls at my heart.

Give me a chance, and I always will, I want to promise her, but instead I pull back, shoving my jeans down my thighs and freeing my cock. I'm ready, and I can feel my pulse through my skin, precum already oozing from my tip.

I tease my head along her folds, coating myself in her slickness and taking a moment to lock down my control. "Are you ready?" I ask. "Ana, I feel like . . ." My voice is soft, a whisper in the open air, but the strain is evident.

"No," Ana says, looking back at me. "Aubrey, I understand what you're doing. You want to be tender and sweet, show me that I'm

121

special, that this space is special. Want to know what'll make this special?"

"What?" I ask, curious.

"You . . . just be you. Don't hold back. I want you to pound the fuck out of me like the big beast that you are. Blow my fucking mind like only you can."

It's a dare, and part of me knows she's trying to avoid the emotions that are thick in the air, using the darkness inside of me as the smoke screen instead of her usual light banter. It almost angers me, the way she keeps minimizing what we were, what we are. But it intrigues me too, the thought that I don't have to hold back with her, that she wants me wild, rough, untamed.

The animal, the beast, as she calls it, roars in response, and I grab her hips, pulling her back against my stiff cock. "Is that what you want?" I snarl, biting her neck. "To get fucked on your knees on the ground like an animal?" My filthy words excite her, judging by how she's pushing back, searching for my cock. "Then take it all."

I thrust all the way in with one stroke, deep into Ana's tight pussy until my hips smack against hers. She cries out, screaming my name in pleasure and pain as I pull back and pound into her, bottoming out with every long, deep stroke, my balls swinging up to slap against her clit.

Ana tries to push back, but I'm too strong, and I take over, pulling her pussy onto my cock as I thrust, controlling the tempo, the depth, and not giving her any space to limit anything. I growl in her ear, "This is what you want? To be taken, fucked, overpowered?"

"God, yes," Ana moans, her body flattening out. I let her stretch out, straddling her thighs and hammering her tight pussy as I pin her to the ground, pressed into my jacket and the ground as my cock swells. "Fuck, Aubrey, I—"

She never completes her statement as I roar, my climax jolting me like a bolt of lightning as I fill her pussy with everything I have, gasping as she clenches around me, another orgasm sweeping through her. A strangled cry that sounds like my name reaches my ears, but I'm still riding high, her name inarticulate on my lips behind a locked throat.

We collapse, and I immediately roll to the side so I don't crush her, cradling Ana's tiny figure in my arms. She stays there, the two of us looking up at the stars together until my cock softens and slips out of her. She twists to lie on my chest. "Well, I asked for it." There's a smile in her voice, but I need to be sure.

"Are you okay?" I ask, stroking her hair softly. "I didn't want to hurt you."

"You didn't," Ana says, laying a hand over my heart and feeling the racing thunder in my chest. "It was amazing."

It's quiet for several minutes, both of us lost in our thoughts . . . of the spectacular fucking we just had, of the stars blanketing us above, of the past.

"You know, it's been so long, I can only remember some parts of our days together. I feel like bits and pieces are so vivid, but others are hazy, lost to time," I whisper, holding her close and praying she doesn't shut down on me. "The good parts, mostly. We had a lot of good times."

"I can remember all of it," Ana whispers back, but while there's a little sadness in her voice, there's a mix of other things too. Things that make me feel encouraged.

"Can you?"

"Yes," she says before chuckling. "Like when we first . . ."

CHAPTER 15

ANA - HIGH SCHOOL – JUNIOR YEAR

"That should stop the bleeding," I say, putting on a Band-Aid for my friend who cut her hand while doing a cartwheel during gym class. Of course, how someone cuts their hand doing a cartwheel is pretty damn fantastical, but for some reason, Coach Smoak insisted on our having class outside on the soccer field today . . . and nobody checks those fields for sticks and rocks in the off-season.

"Damn, girl, you should be a doctor," my best friend, Marissa Palmer, says. She and I have been friends since elementary school, but she won the puberty lottery and the skinny, kinda geeky girl I used to do sleepovers with turned into Great Falls's teenage dream. Blonde, blue-eyed, and a body that leaves boys drooling behind her, but she's still sweet and we have lots of fun, even if most guys just see me as a stepping stone to get them closer to her. And that's if they see me at all.

"It's just a Band-Aid," I point out, closing the kit. "Coach didn't want to send you to the school nurse."

"That's because ol' Sourpuss didn't want to get in trouble. Thankfully, I've got the best doctor this side of Meredith Grey on my side!"

I laugh. Marissa's more into the sexy drama of the new show than the actual medical side of things. Meanwhile, I geek out and look up the medical jargon to check for accuracy. "Trey always tells me that, but I don't know. Med school is a lot of work and takes forever. But I love helping people so I'm thinking along the lines of a social worker or vet. Probably social worker. I love animals, but some of them scare me."

"Ha, good point," Marissa says before biting her lower lip, looking as if she'd rather not say what she's about to say but is forcing herself to do it anyway. "Hey, girl, I've been meaning to ask you something."

"What's up?"

Marissa looks down, blushing a little. "Well . . . does Trey ever ask you about me?"

Uh-oh. Marissa gazes at my brother with stars in her eyes every time she comes over, sometimes even resorting to obvious flirting. He's older and cooler, and even I can see that he's cute. I can see where this is going, and while Trey's never told me . . . I mean, he is my brother. I sort of know these things or at least suspect. But it's not my place to share his business. Time to play it dumb. "What do you mean?"

Marissa shrugs, looking like she'd rather be anywhere else right this instant. "Like . . . you know, don't make me spell it out! Every time I try to talk to him, he's just . . . uninterested."

I pause. I don't know what to tell her. "Look, he's kinda in a different world than we are. He's graduated and has all this pressure to be an adult. I think he just sees me as a kid still, and by extension, you too." It's the truth. Well, one of them at least. I'm pretty sure Trey doesn't swing this way, but even if he did, I'm not sure a high school kid would be on his radar considering the throngs of people at the university, even if we are only a couple of years apart and have always been close and part of the same bigger group of friends.

The bell rings, and for once, I'm glad I have math on the far side of the school. I'll have to haul buns to get over there in time. "Gotta go. I'll meet you at lunch!"

Marissa looks chagrined but doesn't argue. "Okay, girl, catch you later."

I rush all the way across campus, hurrying up the stairs and getting into class just as the bell rings. I sit down, pulling out my pre-calc book, but just as I do, I feel the hair on the back of my neck prick up. *Oh, God, he's looking at me.*

I can't help but glance back to see Aubrey O'Day, the cutest boy in school, looking at me. Tall, lean, and with a body that's made him star of both the football and the basketball teams, Aubrey's been the biggest jock to come out of Great Falls in years. There are already rumors that come next year, it's not going to be a matter of *if* he's going to get a full-ride scholarship to some big college, but which ones.

Just about every girl in school's got a crush on him . . . well, except for maybe Marissa, and rumors abound about whom he's going to ask to homecoming.

Aubrey winks at me, and I feel like someone just turned a blowtorch on my face. I blink rapidly, gasping in shock. My heart pounds as I turn back, trying to focus on what a derivation is for and failing miserably. It's like a scene from some old teen movie . . . the nerd that can't handle even the slightest bit of attention from the object of her crush. Is he laughing at me and my awkward response? I would be. If only I had a scriptwriter setting the scene for the big turnaround moment where he realizes he loves the quiet nerd. *As if,* I snort to myself.

Can't blame me for freaking out though. He's just so hot. He's been the most popular guy in school since last year, when he ran for the touchdown that made us district champs.

All the hot girls are always crowded around him like a pack of groupies whenever he's in the lunch room or even just hanging out with the guys before class. Seriously, for Aubrey O'Day, school is nothing more than easy pussy on parade . . . if he wanted. Which I don't know anything about, because I try desperately to not hear any gossip about that.

I've caught him looking at me from time to time in class, but he never talks to me, and that just reinforces my thoughts that he's secretly and silently making fun of me, even if he's never given a single indication that it's true. Teenage insecurity? Definitely. I'm probably right though. I think he likes just looking at me to mess with my head because I'm not popular in the least.

I'm the good girl, the one who studies and doesn't go out to parties, and I've got the stats to prove it. Been kissed three times, had my admittedly small boobs felt once, and I've seen a guy's dick exactly zero times if I don't count on the internet. Even that wasn't on purpose . . . some asshole sent me a dick pic. It wasn't anything to be proud of, that's for sure.

I spend the next half hour trying to concentrate and listen to the teacher, but I can't focus. Every time I look back, I see Aubrey looking at me, his eyes proudly not skittering away when I catch him. His gaze is just this side of staring, except that he cuts his eyes back to the board every once in a while. When the bell rings, I'm putting stuff in my backpack when I hear big feet approach.

"I creep you out yet?" a deep voice asks. It's a man's voice, not a boy's, although there's a hint of humor to it.

I turn, my neck craning as I look up into Aubrey's handsome face. He's grinning, and the amused twinkle in his eye flusters me so much I need to take a moment to respond. I have to try and put on a casual front and not show that I'm nervous as hell, recognizing that as a death sentence in high school, especially when someone like Aubrey is talking to you. "I was wondering why you were looking at me," I finally tease back. "Is there something on my face?" I scrub at my cheeks, letting the coolness of my hand ease the pink flush.

Aubrey shakes his head, smirking. "Nope. But math's so boring, looking at your pretty face is the only way I can get through it without falling asleep."

His bald-faced compliment brings me up short, a furious blush returning to my cheeks with a vengeance. "I, uh, gee, thanks. I'm glad I'm more interesting than calculus, I guess," I say with a laugh. It's not the best compliment I've ever gotten, but I'll take it, considering the source.

"You're welcome, and trust me, you're more interesting than a lot of things. Maybe even football." He says it conspiratorially, looking around to be sure no one hears him say that. It's silly and cute and makes me smile, like I'm in on some big secret with him, even if it's all in jest.

Aubrey suddenly looks a little unsure of himself, and he scratches at his short hair, almost as if he's nervous. But why would someone like him be nervous talking to me? "So, uh, listen. The big game is tonight versus Elgin, and those fuckers have been talking shit about us for so long I can't wait to beat them."

Elgin. Great Falls's biggest rivals and constant shit-talkers. I nod, adjusting my backpack. "I hope you do, too."

"The team's ready, but I think I need a cheerleader to help me out and give me motivation," Aubrey says, nodding. "So I was thinking . . . if we win, you go out with me tomorrow night?"

I gawk at him for a moment, taking a second to realize what he's saying. "Me?" I ask incredulously. And I swear to God, I actually turn and look behind me to make sure he's not talking over my head to some cheerleader behind me, but there's no one there. He can't be talking about me. He can have any girl he wants and *I'm* supposed to be his motivation? "Are you messing with me? Is the punch line coming?"

Aubrey's eyebrows furrow, but then he smiles. "Why wouldn't I be serious? Be there tonight, on the edge of the bleachers near the locker room. I'll be looking for you."

I nod, not even thinking, unable to say anything as he walks away giving me a little wave. As he turns the corner, I can only think of one thing. *Marissa's gonna freak when she hears this.*

***

THIS HAS TO BE THE MOST MISERABLE I'VE EVER BEEN IN MY LIFE.

Seriously . . . why is football like the only sport that they don't stop the game due to rain? Or maybe that's not true? I wouldn't know because I don't do sports. Yet, here I sit in the drizzling rain that hasn't let up for the past few hours. If this is a trick, Mother Nature is fucking in on it too.

"I can't feel my toes," Trey says next to me as we huddle together. "And my butt's frozen."

"I know, but we gotta stick it out," I reply, yelling over the frantic blasting of the band. Elgin's got the ball, and the drum section's determined that the more noise they make, the bigger the chances Elgin's going to screw up.

"Why, because Stud Boy asked you?" Trey asks, smirking. "Didn't think you even cared about football."

I glare at him, trying to look angry and failing. He's right. I don't know much about what's going on, but I can see the score, and I see Aubrey. But damn, this rain's making things miserable.

Elgin punts, and Great Falls gets the ball back with just under two minutes left. We're down by five, and it's going to be tough to avoid the tenth straight loss to our rivals.

"Come on, Aubrey, you can do it!" I yell as he straps up his helmet to return to the field after a conference with the Coach. I can barely read his number right now—there's so much mud and he's been banging for tough yards all night.

I know Aubrey can't hear me, there's too much noise, but I watch in shock as he stops, looking in my direction. I swear I see him smile and nod before he jogs out to the huddle, and I sit down, wondering if I'm going nuts. "Did he . . .?"

"Look at you?" Trey completes next to me. "Either that, or he was giving me the look. Doubt that though."

The first two plays are quick duds, handoffs that get stuffed at the line, and on third down, Aubrey's pass is dropped. It's down to the last few seconds, and across the field, the Elgin fans are raising hell, trying to distract us as they line up for the last play of the game.

My heart's in my throat as Aubrey looks left, then right, his eyes freezing on me for a moment. He calls the rest of his signals, and the ball snaps, Aubrey tossing the ball to one of the running backs. Blayden starts running right, and my gaze follows him, but out of the corner of my eye, I see Aubrey taking off the other direction, running downfield and making quick headway on the left side of the field. Next to me, Trey's getting to his feet, excited.

I gawk as Blayden stops, turning and throwing the ball just as a defender smashes into him. It's an ugly throw, but Aubrey adjusts, catching it on the run. I'm on my feet, cheering madly as he jukes a defender before bulldozing over another, and Aubrey's off to the races, streaking down the sideline like a gazelle for the touchdown.

"Oh, my God, we did it!" I'm screaming, jumping up and down while hugging Trey. The clock buzzes. We won! For the first time in ten years, we beat Elgin.

I run onto the field with a bunch of other people congratulating the players. It's a chaotic celebration, people hugging each other and randomly shouting out their excitement. I lose Trey in the masses, but the crowd's too big and I can't see him. I don't know where Aubrey is either. Even in the crowd, I start to feel a little lost, lonely as I admit to myself that I'd hoped I'd see Aubrey after the game.

Saddened, I finally give up just as the rain stops and the stars start to peek out. I'm still looking at the scoreboard, a small smile on my face, when Trey walks up. He's blushing a little, and I wonder who he was talking to. "There you are! You okay?" he asks. "You look . . . sad."

"I guess. I don't know, I was hoping . . ." I reply, shrugging. I hear squelching behind me, and I turn to see Aubrey grinning as he runs up in his muddy uniform. "Aubrey?"

"Sorry, celebrating with the team for a minute and then Coach wanted me to say something to the radio people," he says, shrugging. "Hey, Trey."

"Hey," Trey replies, glancing at the two of us. "Uh, I think I'll go get the car warmed up. Maybe I'll be able to feel my ass in a few minutes."

Trey disappears, and I look at Aubrey, whose hair is plastered to his skull and his skin's flushed. Still, he looks so hot that I'm barely able to speak. Finally, I bite my lip and search for words. *Ana, for the love of God, say something, anything.* "Nice game."

"Thanks. We did it," Aubrey says, grinning. "By the way, I got something for you."

He takes a ball out from behind his back, beaming. I look at the wet ball, tilting my head, my confusion obvious on my face.

"It's the game ball," Aubrey explains. "Coach gave it to me, and I'm giving it to you."

He tosses the ball to me, and I catch it on pure reflex, blushing hard. "Stop it! You're the reason we won. It's yours!" I say, trying to give it back.

"Seriously," Aubrey says, stepping closer. "Without you, we wouldn't have won. When I was getting ready for that last play, I looked up and saw your pretty face, sitting in the rain and cheering me on. I said to myself, by God, you gotta make this play or you'll never get another chance. Ana will probably never go to another football game for you, and she definitely won't go on that date." He's teasing, but there's an undercurrent of truth to the words, an honest admission that my being here meant something to him.

I swear if someone took a picture of me right now, I'd be bright red. "You're teasing me." Even I can hear the hopeful note to the words, basically pleading with him to mean what he's saying.

"I'd never do that," Aubrey swears, and in his voice, I can hear it. He's being honest. Aubrey O'Day thinks I'm pretty! He brushes a lock of wet hair from my forehead, and I nervously look down. I notice a date and time on the ball. "Hey, this is wrong. Shouldn't it be today's date and time for the game? This is tomorrow's date."

Aubrey smirks, confidence oozing from his every pore as he bends down to whisper in my ear, "That's tomorrow's date and time because that'll be our first date. The first of many. Pick you up at seven?" he says, tapping the time on the ball.

I nod, looking up at him and grinning. "Seven sounds great."

CHAPTER 16

ANA

"*J* remember that game. It was probably my best ever, considering the conditions," Aubrey says, chuckling. "I was so worried you'd hold me to that promise, that you'd not go out with me if we lost."

I chuckle, nuzzling against him. My body's sore, my ass bruised from the pounding he gave me, but this feels good, a tiny bit of tender with the rough. "I honestly thought you were just playing a game with me. I didn't think someone like you would ever go for someone like me. I was waiting for the punch line for a while."

Aubrey nods, stroking my shoulder in the darkness. "I know what you're talking about. And I'll be honest. I felt a lot of pressure back then to fill the role people thought I was *supposed* to fill. But I've always liked the idea of a sweet, wholesome girl. One you have to be a better man to deserve, who makes you think of porches and kids in the yard on a tire swing. The kind you can take home to Mom and not worry a bit. You were just . . . everything. You were—you are—perfect."

I sit up, staring at him. Is he serious? I mean, if I was so perfect, why did he just up and leave without so much as a word? That just makes no sense.

He seems to read my mind. "I didn't want to leave. I really didn't. But after what happened, I was just lost. Completely lost," he says mysteriously. "I thought I'd just bring you down and ruin your life. It was why I never came back."

I frown, feeling like we've been dancing around this subject for too long already. It's time to stop hiding from it and address it head on. There's something in our past, and I need to know what that is, even if it's going to hurt like a son of a bitch. I have a feeling Aubrey needs to tell this story too. I never considered that he was as deeply affected by the whole thing as I was, that whatever pulled him away might be just as painful for him as it was for me. In my head, he was the villain, the bad guy who lured me in, made me love him fully, and then disappeared with my heart. That there might be nuances beyond what my young self could fathom never entered my mind back then, and honestly, I just avoided all thoughts of Aubrey for years after that, forcing them away with a scoff of ugly regret and a wash of righteous anger. I give in to the curiosity, the need to know, recognizing that I'm rewriting my stated purpose for spending time with him this week but realizing it was inevitable and we both knew it. "Aubrey, what happened? To you, to us?"

He scratches at his jaw, and I see pain flash in his eyes. For a big brute like him, I know whatever it is has to really hurt him. He takes a deep breath and sits up, adjusting his clothes a little before letting out a long, trembling sigh.

"Well—"

Before he can say anything more, the heavens erupt with a crack of lightning that arcs down, the veins of electricity bright and white across the dark sky. Rain immediately follows in a quick deluge, and I'm struck by the overwhelming sense of irony that

I'd just shared a memory of being soaked to the bone and here we are again, getting wet. "Ah, shit!"

"In the cabin!" Aubrey says as the rain gets heavier second by second. "These storms can get nasty quick!"

Aubrey gets up, using his walking stick but leaning on me too as we make our way back to the cabin as quickly as possible. As we get closer, Rex runs out to greet us, barking and circling around us, urging us to move faster. "I know, Rex. We're doing the best we can!" I tell the dog, realizing that I'm talking to the dog like Aubrey does and not feeling the least bit crazy for doing so because what he's saying is so obvious.

The walk is hell. Aubrey's prediction of the storm getting bad quickly proves true as lightning stabs the sky in strobe light flashes that dazzle my eyes, and rain quickly turns the grass into a wet, slippery mat dotted with tripwires of bushes and rocks. Aubrey stumbles more than once, and I grab him around the waist as his leg gives out. "Oh, no, you don't! I'm not treating a broken arm too!"

Aubrey gasps and laughs as we keep moving. "I'm sure if I fall, you'll catch me."

Nice to know he can still joke with the pain I know he's feeling as we haul ass back to the cabin. "More like I'll pad your fall and you'll squish me," I manage.

He grunts on each of the four steps to the cabin, and thankfully, the rain and lightning have chased away our skunk 'friend'.

Opening the door, Aubrey's limping badly, and we freeze once we're inside, safe and a little warmer once the cool rain isn't pelting us. I'm soaked, my nipples stiff and easily showing as my shirt's clinging to my body. "Shit," I mutter as I close the door and look down, "I forgot my jacket."

"That's okay," Aubrey says, wincing as he turns around. "We'll get it later, and you look even more beautiful all soaked." He lets the double-entendre float in the air between us, rumbling his approval as he looks me up and down.

Heat warms my belly, and I smile, running my fingers through the mess of my hair. "You've been up in the mountains too long, Aubrey. I look like a wet mop and you know it. Let's get these wet clothes off and get a fire going so we can warm up." The busy work of getting undressed takes our attention, letting the moment we almost had outside pass with barely a notice.

I peel Aubrey's shirt up and off him, laying it on the back of a chair to dry. My heart flutters at the sight of his chiseled upper body. The chill has turned his skin almost marble-like, and though I'm tempted to trace the lines of muscles and scars that pepper his body, I get on my knees, undoing his pants and tugging them down his tree trunk legs. "You were a lot leaner back then," I huff as I untie his boots. "How'd you put on this much muscle? Chopping wood?"

"Pretty much," Aubrey says, looking down at me. I can feel the desire bubbling up inside me as I glance up and see his cock outlined against the soaked fabric of his boxer briefs. It'd be so easy to slide them down and take him into my mouth, but my caretaker instincts are stronger at the moment. I get up, guiding Aubrey back into a chair as I help him off with his boot. "Ouch."

"I bet," I reply as I unwind his bandage. It's pink, and nobody's example of a strong ankle, but amazingly, it doesn't look any worse for wear. I guess those two days in bed helped more than we realized. "See? This is why you should have stayed inside today. It's just going to take longer to heal every time you push it."

I step back, stripping to my bra and panties and laying my wet clothes out to dry too. Then I fiddle with the wood in the fireplace, determined to start the fire myself and knowing Aubrey is watching my every move. Once it's roaring, I stand, holding my hands to the flames before turning around to let it warm my backside.

"I thought it was worth it myself," Aubrey rumbles, looking at me. "We got to spend time together, and you have to admit . . . today was fun."

I want to argue with him, to tell him how, as a medical professional, I should never have let him do the things he did today, but instead, I simply sigh, knowing it's a battle in futility, so I nod along, agreeing with him. "Okay, okay. I learned some new things, and yeah, we had fun. But I can't encourage this behavior. You're lucky it's just swollen."

"Yeah, you had fun," Aubrey says, his voice dropping as I suddenly become aware that his eyes are tracing along my body, leaving goosebumps in their wake. My nipples are still hard and press against the thin fabric of my bra, begging for his eyes, his hands, his mouth. "But I know what would make this even better."

"What?" I almost whisper, agonizingly aware of how close his cock is in those wet undies of his.

"Fucking that sweet pussy again, right here, right now," he growls. "That'll warm us up, too."

I shake my head, though my body is begging for what he offers. "Out of the question. Too much of a risk you'll get injured doing that," I purr, ignoring the fact that I welcomed him just a short time ago without argument about his ankle or anything else. I reach for his shorts and lay my hand on top of his cock. "But . . . there's no risk in sucking you off though."

Aubrey smiles, leaning back in his chair as I step closer. Getting back on my knees between his thighs, I see he's already rock hard and my mouth waters at the sight of his big dick straining against the boxers. I trace my fingers along his length through the cotton, up and down till he groans.

"Fuck, Ana. You're killing me," he rasps.

I hook the waistband of his boxer briefs and pull them down, working them under his hips and down his legs with his help, leaving him bare before me. His cock is long and thick, proudly jutting up to his belly button and bobbing toward me with every heartbeat. He's glorious, the stunning example of manhood I've held every other man to and that no one has ever lived up to.

I lick my lips in preparation, and Aubrey's hand jerks to the base of his shaft, squeezing tightly as his breath hitches. "Woman, you keep looking at me like that and licking your lips, and I'm gonna come before you even touch me with that naughty tongue."

I smirk at him, letting the velvet-over-iron skin glance along my cheek, rubbing him softly. "Well, if I can't look at how gorgeous you are and I can't lick my lips at how delicious I know you're going to taste, what can I do?" I tease, knowing my words will rile him up even further.

"Suck me off, Ana. Like you said. Suck my cock in that pretty little mouth, past your pouty lips and down your tight throat." His thumb swipes at my bottom lip as he tells me exactly what he wants, spelling out exactly what I want too.

No longer willing to tease either of us, I follow his request—okay, his demand, but I happily oblige. He groans as I take him in, deeper and deeper with every bob up and down his length. His precum tastes good on my tongue, salty and sweet like the man, and I work to get more and more of the treat, wanting every drop until I get his full release.

His hands grip the armrests of the chair tightly, the wood squeaking under his grip. I rise to the head of his cock, swirling my tongue lazily around the crown and hollowing my cheeks as I lift his hands, guiding them to the sides of my head. He looks down, the question in his eyes. "You sure, Sweet Ana?"

I nod, never letting go of my suction along his cock and

humming my agreement. I feel him jump in my mouth in response as his fingers curl, grabbing handfuls of my hair. I let him guide me, not surprised when he goes deep, holding himself in my throat for a second before retreating to do it again. I fight to swallow with him in my throat, the difficulty worth it when he cries out in pleasure from the tightness around his cock.

And that's enough to release his control. He begins bucking wildly, gripping my hair tightly and moving me with him as he fucks my mouth, shallow but fast. His breathing is choppy above me, and I have spit oozing from my lips to run down my chin, coating his balls. I run a finger along the midline of his balls, feeling the mess we're making and loving the raw filthiness of it. I grip them, urging him to release, and get a split-second of warning as his balls pull up tight before he explodes in my mouth.

I gulp him down, rope after rope filling my mouth as he roars above me. I suck him clean, getting every drop and wringing every bit of pleasure from his body until he collapses bonelessly back in the chair.

I listen as his breathing recovers, my cheek pressed to his thigh and his fingers tracing lazy circles through my hair, soothing where he'd gripped me. We're quiet, the crackles of the fire and Rex snoring in the corner the only sounds in the cabin as the storm rages on outside.

My voice is quiet, not wanting to break the spell but needing to return to where we were before, when I decided I was ready to know. That was a big step for me, and while I'm still terrified that whatever he says won't be enough to justify his actions, I recognize that we've both come a long way and have been through a lot since then. "I wasn't ready to listen before, but I am now. What happened back in high school?"

Aubrey swallows, the audible gulp a reminder of how hard this is for him too. "Oh, yeah. The storm interrupted us."

Outside, there's a rumble of thunder, and I stroke along his thigh, encouraging him as I look up at him. "Don't rush. I'm not going anywhere. I promise."

Aubrey lets out a sigh and nods slowly. "I can't start the night I left . . . there's too much background. I have to start earlier, when I got the Oregon offer."

"I remember that. Things were going so well."

Aubrey nods. "I thought I had everything. School was kicking ass, football was going well, but most of all, I had the world's best girlfriend. I thought my life was on the highway to heaven . . ."

CHAPTER 17

AUBREY - HIGH SCHOOL - SENIOR YEAR

*T*he stands look nearly empty, but it's still the biggest crowd I've ever played in front of. I mean, Great Falls High plays in a stadium that seats eight thousand . . . and State U's stadium seats over fifty thousand. Tough for our little town to fill that many seats, even if everyone and their long-lost cousins attended.

I'm not worried about most of the fifteen thousand people in attendance. I'm worried about the Barton defense, which has been giving me hell this second half with their whip-fast adjustments. Their head coach was a pro in his younger days, and his defense plays like he's drilled their playbooks into their heads.

We line up, and I take the snap, dropping back five steps just like I'm supposed to. I've grown another inch over the past year, and I can see over the defensive line, easily seeing Brett already with two steps on his guy. I let it go and watch as Brett takes it in stride, running as fast as he can . . . Touchdown!

I do a little dance as I run up the field to congratulate Brett, banging helmets with him. "Fuck, yeah!" Brett screams as the crowd cheers. "Title's ours!"

His prediction proves right as the final seconds tick off the clock and we win the 2A State Championship for the first time in our school's history. Dozens of fans crowd around me, pounding me on the back as they yell their congratulations.

"Good game, O'Day!" says one while I bro-hug with Roger Illium, the linebacker who's led the defense all year. He's got the MVP ball, and he earned it with two sacks and an interception that was a key turning point in our favor.

"Yeah," Roger adds. "Glad you finally pulled up and I could stop carrying you. My back was starting to hurt."

"Fuck you," I laugh back, but Coach Orton runs up as we laugh, maybe more excited than any of his players. Then again, he's been coaching high school ball for twenty-five years and this is his first state title. "Boys, you both worked your asses off today and earned this win." He smiles wide, a little lost in the moment, just soaking it all in, but then he seems to remember he had a mission. "Oh, Roger . . . there's a man from the paper wanting an interview with you. And Aubrey, I need to talk to you for a moment alone."

I scan the crowd, wishing I could find Ana, but it's a madhouse around us on the field. *Where is she?* The disadvantage of falling in love with a short girl, I guess. That's okay. If I don't see her, I know she'll be waiting with my folks right outside the locker room like we arranged.

I've been with Coach a long time, and this is the cherry on the top of our years of work, so I take the moment he asks for. "Sure, Coach."

Coach leads me toward the goalposts, where the crowd's thin. "You played a hell of a game, Aubrey. Best I've seen since my son was going here."

That's a compliment. Tim Orton tore it up in his college days right here on the State U field until he had a career-ending knee injury. "Thanks, Coach, but it was everyone. I mean, Brett played amazing."

Coach smiles at my textbook answer, focusing on the team, highlighting teammates. He's taught me well. It's never a one-man show on the field. "I've got some good news for you, Son. There were some recruiters here. You're going to have some offers coming your way."

"Really?" I ask, grinning. "Where? Please say Oregon."

I've let it sort of become known that I want to go to Oregon, not because I particularly like ducks or green and yellow . . . but because Ana and I figured out it had the best mix of football opportunities for me and social work programs for her. She says she likes the trees, and that's good enough for me.

Coach nods, holding up a letter with a big 'O' in the corner, and I gawk. "Are you fucking serious?"

Coach chuckles. "I think I'll let that slip . . . this time, boy. Go on, get changed. And Aubrey, that won't be the only one. Mark my words, you're going to get to choose where you go to school."

That's cool, but I already know where I want to go. I can't fucking believe it, and I feel like I'm floating as I get changed. Leaving the locker room, my family and Ana are waiting for me.

Ana runs into my arms, throwing hers around my neck. "Con-gratulations, champ!"

Everything else fades away as I exchange kisses with Ana, holding her tightly. We're totally in love, and it's like I have everything I could want in life.

"It's all because of you, babe" I reply, setting her down. "My Sweet Ana, my strength."

"Nah, it's not me, it's those wide shoulders you've suddenly sprouted," Ana teases, smiling up at me. "You'd better slow down, by the way. I thought you were supposed to stop growing at seventeen?"

I chuckle, leaning over to plant my chin on top of her head. It's true. I know I tower over her and often have to bend down to kiss her . . . but we don't mind.

My dad clears his throat, and I wince a bit, so excited at celebrating with Ana that I almost forgot to include my mom and dad. I offer my dad a handshake and he takes it, pumping my arm hard before pulling me to him in a hug with a fierce pat on my back. "Great job, Son! I'm so proud of you!"

My mom's reaction is more hysterical as she reaches up, forcing me to bend down to hug her. She's blubbering, repeating, "My baby . . ." over and over. I cringe, even though I'm secretly pleased to have made them so proud.

"Ah, well . . . hey, I got some more good news too," I tease them all.

"What?" Ana asks, hopping up and down as I drive her nuts with my hemming and hawing, letting the pause lengthen dramatically. "I swear, Aubrey, if you don't tell me . . ."

"Okay, well . . . here."

All I have to do is flash the envelope's logo, and Ana squeals, jumping up and down in excitement as she snatches it out of my hand to read the details. My parents move in for another hug, congratulating me. I know it's a weight off their shoulders, a relief that they're not going to have to finance four years of college for me, but more importantly, they're genuinely happy to see my dreams come true.

"I'm so happy for you, babe," Ana says as I lift her up again, kissing her as the happiness of the moment washes over us.

My parents beam at us, and I love that they approve of my relationship with Ana. It'd be hard not to. She's the epitome of what every parent wants their child to end up with . . . sweet, caring, kind, strong, and with just enough sass to keep me in line. They've gotten to know her bit by bit over the last year, and I think she's finally comfortable around them too, forgetting her nerves and just being her adorable self more and more.

"We're gonna go, let you celebrate with your friends for a bit," my dad says, pulling my mom away gently.

"But don't be too late getting home. You're still my baby!" she reminds me, and I laugh, far too excited to care that she's calling me a baby when I tower over her and am off to college next year.

Ana and I join the crowd of folks in the parking lot, meeting up with what basically constitutes our entire senior class. Single-file, we caravan away from the stadium and head back to Great Falls, ready to celebrate our win. I feel like I'm celebrating even more though . . . my future with Ana.

***

THE NEXT MORNING IS ROUGH, THE ADRENALINE AND EXCITEMENT taking it out of me almost as much as the game itself. Not to mention the late-night celebration.

But Mom perseveres, opening the curtains and letting the midday sunshine into my room. "Aubrey . . . rise and shine, porcupine. Get up. We're calling Gabe in a few minutes."

That's enough to get me going again. I miss my brother. He's been overseas in the military for a few years now, just coming home for short leaves, and getting to talk to him face-to-face is rare, even if it is digital. Usually, we resort to emails and phone calls, even letters.

Assured that I'm awake, my mom flits out to answer the ringing doorbell, and I hop up, pulling on sweatpants and running my fingers through my hair. Not that Gabe cares one iota if I look like shit, but he'll definitely comment and tease me about it.

Heading out to the living room, I see Angie, Gabe's long-time girlfriend. They've been through some rough times but seem steady now, and she's standing by him through these long deployments, so she's good in my book, even if we don't see her much since she lives a few towns over. I give her a hug, teasing, "You ready for this?" She looks nervous and I'm not sure why.

It takes us about twenty minutes to get Gabe on the screen. Running the system where he's deployed takes time. When he comes on, we all crowd around the screen, Mom and Angie sitting at the table with Dad and me standing behind them, everyone waving and greeting him at the same time.

"Man, you better have good news for me." Seeing Gabe and hearing his voice tightens the knot in my gut. I know I'm just the brother, not the parent or spouse, but man, I miss my partner in crime. Having this connection with him, even for a moment shared with others, is special.

I grin at Gabe. He used to be taller than me, and wider in the shoulders, but since my last growth spurt, I bet we're pretty spot-on. I've looked up to him since I was little and can honestly say my big brother is my role model. "Well, nice to see your scraggly ass too, Gabe. Haven't they taught you to shave in the Army?"

Gabe rubs his chin, laughing. "What can I say? This ain't Stateside. So how was the game?"

"Oh, that . . ." I reply before grinning and launching into the details. I have to keep it short. Gabe's only got twenty minutes, and I don't want to hog the time for myself when my parents and Angie have stuff they want to tell him too. "And also, I got this," I say, holding up the offer envelope. "Your little brother might be throwing balls around Oregon next year!"

Gabe whistles, grinning. "Fuck yeah, Aubrey! Way to go, man!"

"Thanks, bro! How're things for you?"

The light in Gabe's eyes dims a little, and it pains me. We haven't talked much over the past few months, but he's sent me emails telling me how hard it is. I wonder how much he shares with me versus what he shares with Mom and Dad, or Angie.

But Gabe's always one to do his duty. "I'd be lying to you if I said things were great," he says, scratching at his cheek. "The stuff I've seen lately . . . you don't wanna know. I just can't wait till I get out of this shithole."

None of us quite know what to say, and Gabe shrugs. "I'll get over it. Just need to through for a bit longer and then I'm done. My enlistment will be up and I'll be home for good."

The words seem directed to Angie more than the rest of us, and she takes over the conversation.

"Hey, honey. I miss you!" We all try to give them the semblance of privacy even though we're sitting right here, listening to every word. I notice Angie is fidgeting with her fingers a bit, and again, I'm struck by the thought that she seems nervous for some reason.

"Hey, Gabe, remember your last visit Stateside?"

Gabe grins wolfishly, enough that my mom clears her throat in warning. "Yeah, of course. Thanks again for coming up to Virginia to see me." Gabe had been on US soil for less than forty-eight hours and was granted a four-hour leave pass. With school, I wasn't able to go, and my parents were hesitant to leave me alone, so Angie had gone out by herself. I think it was a good thing for them, solidified them a bit.

"Well, it was a rather, uhm, productive visit. You're going to be a father."

There's silence on the other end of the line, then Gabe jumps up, punching the air and cheering. We follow his lead, cheering right along with them as my mom hugs Angie tight, promising to help with whatever she needs.

The next few minutes are crazy, and by the end of Gabe's time, everyone's pretty emotional. Even Gabe looks like he's crying. "Congrats, man," I tell him when I can get a word in. "I'm honored to be an uncle . . . and don't you worry, I'll make sure Angie's taken care of while you're over there. I'll drive her to doctor's appointments if I have to or do midnight runs for ice cream. I'll do you right, take care of your girl the way you would."

"Thanks, man," Gabe replies. "I love you guys!" We all tell him the same, begging him to be careful, as if that's his choice, and say our goodbyes.

After we hang up, we all hug Angie and Mom agrees to drive her home while I go grab a shower.

CHAPTER 18

ANA

"I remember that . . . you talking about how excited everyone was that Gabe was gonna be a dad," I say as we lay in bed, still spent after three massive orgasms in one night. Another rumble of thunder rolls, but they're fading. I guess the storm's over for now.

I'm already anxious to know what happened next. The state championship game was in December, and everything was fine after that for a while. Hell, it was better than fine. We'd made plans for months, talking about college, getting married, having kids.

But then, he just disappeared that spring. He didn't even show up to graduation, and his whole family just sort of vanished off the face of the earth at the same time. It was the talk of the town, kids at school looking at me with pity and everyone gossiping about why the whole family would disappear overnight. Admittedly, those theories fed my imagination for a long time, sometimes helping lessen the sting by thinking that he had to stay away for his own safety or for mine. Other times, I'd be sure that he'd just ditched me and was off living some different, happier life without me, and I was so angry.

Aubrey nods, and I can see he's still deep in his own head. "Yeah. It was a big moment for him. It was a ray of light in all that darkness he was in."

"That's awesome. I'm sure there's a reason . . . but what does this have to do with what happened with us?"

Aubrey is slow in responding, and I can tell whatever he's going to say next isn't something he likes to talk about. He looks tired, drained from telling just that much of the story.

I place my hand over his heart, patting his chest softly. "Please? I want to understand, Aubrey. I want . . . this is hard, but I want to understand you. Us. This. And to do that, I have to know what you were going through, what happened."

I'm shocked at my words. Us? Do I mean the 'us' of the past or now? I'm honestly not sure. Can there an 'us' again? Aubrey notices my words too and smiles softly.

"Do you remember that winter? The formal? God, you were so gorgeous. That was the happiest night of my life, baby."

He might be stalling a little bit, but a chill goes down my spine at the word. *Baby*. I was Sweet Ana from the beginning, but Baby only after we said our *I Love Yous*. We share a smile, both in on the secret code of the nickname, the memories flooding back in a wash of warm fuzzies.

"Well, I remember thinking you looked so handsome in your tux. And that your jaw dropped open when you saw that my dress was strapless because I'd kept that a surprise. I loved the way your arm felt wrapped around my bare shoulders all night. The school gym actually looked nice, all sparkly twinkle lights and tulle draped from the rafters."

I ramble on about that night as if it happened yesterday, the past fresh once again. "Oh, and hey, remember . . ."

I hear a soft snore above me.

"Aubrey?" I ask, looking up to see his eyes closed and his head cocked back.

He looks so pale and exhausted, and I realize I'm not going to get the rest of the story out of him. At least not tonight. That's okay. I've waited this long. I can wait a bit longer, and we have time . . . but I know it's not *too* much time before I have to leave.

The thought of going home, back to work and the city, hits me awkwardly. I would usually be excited about that prospect, but something about leaving Aubrey up here in the woods alone feels wrong.

BRIGHT LIGHT PIERCES THE VEIL OF SLEEP I'M HAPPILY HIDING behind, rousing me from a rather erotic dream. I grin, stretching long with a groan before peeking through hooded eyes at the still-snoring behemoth beneath me. His chest rumbles with every breath, rattling my cheek where it's pressed to his muscles. I sigh happily, snuggling in for a moment before realizing that nature is calling. Urgently.

Trying to be quiet, I gently get out of bed and tiptoe to the bathroom to take care of business before sneaking back into the tempting warmth of the big bed with Aubrey. The movement rouses him and one brown eye pops open to glare at me. "What are you doing, woman? Get over here," he says, grabbing at me.

I squawk, feigning to get away, but let him pull me back to his side. "Mmm, that's better," he says, tracing his fingertips along my arm and leaving a smattering of goosebumps in his wake. I return the favor, running my hand along his chest, down to his abs, exposed as the sheet has worked its way down and is barely covering his hips. Beneath the fine dusting of hair, I can feel the ridges of muscles, but also the occasional scar, just a few little lines here and there. But rather than mar the perfect sculpture of his abdomen, they add interest, and I want to hear the story that accompanies each one.

"I like this, waking up with you," Aubrey says, his voice soft and sleepy. "You should just move your gear over here, stay with me every night, fall asleep after I fuck you senseless, cuddle all night, and wake up in my arms."

I'll admit I like the sound of that, but I goad him anyway. "Did you know you snore?" I ask quietly, a smile in my voice.

His chuckle vibrates as he confesses, "Yeah, not too bad though, hopefully. You sleep okay? Have sweet dreams about me, Sweet Ana?"

"Maybe I did, maybe I didn't," I tease back.

"Well, I definitely had some sweet dreams about you." He shifts, and I can feel the hard line of his cock against my thigh.

The soft pillow talk feels good, comfortable. I think I'll always be up for sex with Aubrey, but we should get back to where we were last night before sleep overtook us.

"Wanna hear about my dreams? I think you'll like them." Aubrey is already moving against me, warming me up and letting me think that maybe we can delay the conversation for a few minutes, considering we've got all day.

I open my mouth to answer, but a loud slam on the window causes us both to jump with surprise, and my heart pounds in my chest as I look out the window and see Brad's face, smirking in an obvious 'gotcha' expression.

"Whoo! I *knew* I'd come up here and find you two up to some kinky shit. Well done, Ana. Well. Done," he says loudly. "Hey, Trey! Come check this out!"

"Oh, my God!" I yell, blushing furiously with embarrassment. I hop up, grabbing the blanket and tossing it to cover Aubrey up, not wanting my brother or Brad to get a view of what Aubrey's packing. I'm struck with a shot of possession . . . he's mine, and I'm not sharing, not even a peek! The blanket lands somewhere over his head, turning the bed into a fuzzy mountain of knit cotton.

As I grab his shirt from the floor, pulling it over my head quickly, I look back at him, watching as he pulls the blanket from his head. He's grinning like a loon. "Are you hiding me, Ana? Pretty sure that ship has sailed," he laughs.

I cringe, but it's with a smile. This is kind of ridiculous. Yeah, I'm totally busted, but I'm a grown woman. Trey has no right to give me shit about having a sex life. Of course, he will anyway. That's what big brothers do. "Get some clothes on. I'll be right back."

"Where are you going?"

"To find that crossbow you showed me how to use. I'm not gonna kill him . . . just put an arrow in his ass. Maybe teach him a lesson about sneaking up on people and spying like a pervert."

"Your voice may be full of vinegar, but I know you love Brad and won't hurt him too badly . . . probably. Maybe. Hell, should I get dressed fast to save him?" He tries to get up, but it's a slow process of staggered movements, pushing up from the bed and swinging his feet to the floor. Normally, I'd rush over to help him, but right now, I have bigger fish to fry.

I smirk evilly, telling Aubrey, "Just thank your lucky stars you're not on the receiving end of my plotting right now. Maybe you should just stay there. You don't want to see this."

I stomp to the door, standing to my full height and my face hard. Using my no-nonsense tone, I demand, "What the hell are you guys doing here?"

Brad is standing with his hands on his hips, his delight at being correct surrounding him in an air of cockiness. "Bitch, you are sooooo busted."

I look to Trey, who is eyeing me with raised brows. "Really, Ana?"

I sigh. "Well, guess you should come on in then." I invite them into Aubrey's cabin like it's mine, like I have any right to do so. "Guess I'd better make some coffee."

Brad laughs. "I think you already got your morning shot of wake-me-up, didn't ya?"

Trey gives Brad a sharp look, but we can both see the tilt of Trey's lips as he fights the grin. That's one thing I can say for Brad. He makes my brother happy, makes him more chill and smiley. Right now, as much as I might smack Brad, I'm probably lucky he's here to keep Trey from going too far into protective big brother mode.

"We came to check on you because you haven't answered your phone. I was afraid you were dead in the woods somewhere, hoping for a rescue. Oh, I brought you another six-pack of that nasty soda you like, too," Trey says.

"If you thought I was dead, why'd you bring me soda?" I say with a smile before telling him, "Thank you. For the soda." I stick my tongue out at him like the brat he used to tease me about being when we were little, and he rolls his eyes.

From behind me, I hear the *clunk-clunk-clunk* of Aubrey coming into the room, dressed on his own, down to his boot. The nurse in me can't help but feel a little guilty that I didn't help him bandage his ankle, and I bite my lip, wondering if he did it properly. Or at all. Stubborn man.

He sits down at the table across from Trey, both of them eyeing each other up. "G'morning, guys. Good to see you."

There's a breath of anticipation in the air as Brad and I wonder what our guys are gonna do, but then Trey breaks the silence with a smile. "Just wanted to check in, make sure my baby sister was doing alright." Okay, so maybe a bit of a veiled threat there, but Aubrey takes it mostly in stride.

Aubrey looks to me, his eyes working their way from my mess of hair, across my bare face, and down my chest before meeting mine with a big wink. "She's looks just fine to me." It's bold and maybe even a bit confrontational, considering the compromising position we were just found in.

Trey looks at me with narrowed eyes, and between the two of them, I've had it. "That's enough. I am fine, not that either of you actually seems to care while you're busy puffing up at each other. Why don't you both just whip 'em out and see who's bigger?" I say exasperatedly. I hear Brad's intake of breath and stop him with a finger before he can say a word. "Nope, rewind. I take that back. Everyone with a penis, keep it in your pants."

"Spoilsport!" Brad pouts.

CHAPTER 19

AUBREY

*O*nce the verbal well is tapped, Ana and Trey start chattering back and forth, somewhere between bickering and catching up. It's oddly sweet, the way they give each other shit, but you can tell that if either of them were threatened, they'd team up against the world.

I'm watching their verbal sparring when my phone rings. Ana looks surprised when I grab it from the nearby counter. It virtually never rings. That's how I know without even looking that it's Carlotta. She's the only one who ever calls me nowadays.

I give a nod to Ana while she, Trey, and Brad catch up over an edited version of our last several days, heaving myself up. "Gotta take this call." I limp outside to the back porch, dropping into the chair as I slide my thumb across the phone screen.

"Well finally," Carlotta growls when I answer. "I was about ready come up there to check in since you weren't answering. Wasn't sure if you'd scared the poor girl off and were pouting or if she'd killed you for being a grumpy asshole. At least give me a few grunts and let me know what's going on."

I can't help but smile . . . Carlotta's reaction. If she'd walked in on Ana and me over the past few days, it would have left her shocked. "Well, hello to you too. I'm fine. I'm alive, and so is my guest." I intentionally don't give her the details she's sniffing around for, knowing it'll drive her nuts.

I can almost hear Car roll her eyes, and I definitely hear her sigh. "Great, so you're alive and she's still there. What's the status?"

"What do you mean *what's the status?*"

"With the girl, Aubrey!" Carlotta growls in exasperation. "Please tell me you've figured out your *complicated* shit with her. I don't care if it's with words or actions. Please say you've actually connected with a human being other than me."

"Aww, I thought you liked being my *person*. My feelings are hurt," I tease her, thinking that I've definitely connected with Ana through actions . . . several times over.

"Holy shit. Was that a joke? Mountain man recluse Aubrey just made a joke . . . about feelings. What is she, a fucking miracle worker?" Carlotta sounds incredulous as she teases me back.

I laugh a little. The banter with Car feels easy, unlike the usual way she begs me to lighten up and I shut her down with grunts. She's right, Ana is changing me, quickly and for the better. But I can already feel that the rebound back from this time with her is gonna be a bitch when she goes home and I'm alone again. It never bothered me before, but now, it does sound lonely. "You've got an unhealthy interest in my private life. Worry about your own." The dark thoughts have crept back into my voice a little and Car notices.

"Argh, you're so infuriating!" Carlotta yells. "Get my hopes up that you might be an actual human being, just to shut that back down. But I'm guessing you're making progress because you at least sound a *little* happier."

"Just fine weather and good livin'. Does wonders for the spirit," I say dismissively, hoping she'll drop it. She has no idea just how right she is . . . but shit, I thought I was still in full-on asshole mode. Am I really sounding less grumpy?

"Whatever, asshole. It's fine if you don't want to share. But just listen." I'm quiet for a moment, so she takes that as agreement and continues, "You said the two of you have history. The fact that you told me shows you care, that she was important to you back whenever that that was. So don't let this opportunity pass you up. You owe it to yourself to reach out to her, see if she can bring you back to life a bit."

Owe it to myself? I don't know about that, and Ana might breathe new life into me, but at what cost to herself? I can't self-ishly use her to soothe my damage, and she's such a kind person, she'd do whatever she could to help me, even if it's a useless endeavor. And if she won't forgive me, it'll be another mark in the 'Aubrey's Fuck-Ups' column, and that tally is pretty damn high already. It doesn't need another boost.

But she's right about not letting this opportunity go. The last few days have definitely proven that there's still something between Ana and me. If only she can forgive me after hearing the whole story.

"We'll see," I tell her noncommittally before wrapping up the conversation. "Great talking to you, Car. I'll talk to you again soon."

Carlotta, of course, isn't pleased. "That's it? Maybe I was wrong, you stubborn sack of—"

Her words are cut off as I hang up and make my way back inside. At least everyone's still alive and sitting down, so the fallout can't have been too bad. But I'm not sure if I trust Brad's look. He totally looks like the kid who got into the cookie jar.

Ana gets up, helping me over to the sofa. It's a fairly obvious ploy to delay whatever conversation I interrupted when I came back in because we both know that I can amble around the house pretty well now. We both ignore the pointed looks from Trey and Brad, and I'll admit, I lean against her more than I need to, giving her shoulder a squeeze of support. I'm solidly in Ana's corner, no matter what . . . us against them, if need be.

"Sorry about that. Had to take a call. My cousin, just business stuff. Everyone cool here?"

Ana nods and sits next to me almost automatically. "Yeah, everything's fine." The words seem directed to Trey more than to me. He dips his chin in acquiescence, and Ana takes the win of whatever their argument had been. I'll admit to being curious, but since it's obviously centered around me, I'm not sure I need to hear the details just yet, so I keep my mouth shut and follow Ana's lead. "Would you believe these two have come up with an idea?" she says laughingly.

"We want to go kayaking and think it would be cool if you guys came with us," Brad says. "I packed my favorite Speedo!"

Ana shakes her head, crossing her arms. "Absolutely not. His ankle is still on the mend and—"

Maybe they didn't just come up here to check on her. That, or they just came prepared with an excuse. Either way, we're going. The other option is to sit here while Trey stares me down. "I think it'd be a ton of fun," I counter. "I know some good spots where the feed rivers are a decent whitewater, not too rough this time of year. Although, I'd definitely skip the Speedo in favor of some warmer gear," I say, my mouth tilted up as I joke with Brad. Huh, maybe Carlotta's right. I am less . . . grumpy.

Ana scowls murder at me. "What? Let's not even talk about the cold, but what about the, I don't know, *raging river currents and rocks?*"

"We don't have to raft with them. We can just watch from the shore and have a picnic," I reply, the compromise taking shape in my mind. "We'll make a day of it. Me, you, and Rex."

Ana goes quiet. "A picnic?"

Brad claps his hands together, sensing he's going to get his way and obviously pleased. "Perfect! Trey and I can raft while Ana gets herself a nice relaxing picnic buffet! Bring the hot dogs . . . oh, guess that's you," he sasses, pointing at me.

A bark of laughter erupts, surprising us all, me most of all. But it seems to be the seal of approval on the whole plan.

It takes us about twenty minutes to drive to the drop-off point up the mountain. As we unload the rented kayaks, I quiz Trey. "You've done whitewater before?"

"Yeah, a dozen or so times," Trey confirms. "Don't worry about us. We'll be fine."

"Alright then, you two be careful. There will probably be other rafters along the river too, so you won't be alone out there. And remember, when you come out onto the main lake, turn right to get to the shore near the parking area."

Ana helps the boys launch, both of us waving. Trey looks back, giving me a warning glare, but when Brad peeks over his shoulder, he flashes a huge wink at us before turning around quickly before Trey can catch him. Ana laughs, and we jump into the guys' SUV to drive down to the lake.

It's close, only ten minutes down the winding road, much faster than the hour-plus it'll take the guys to navigate along the offshoots of the river to get to the main body of the lake. Ana looks over at me as I drive. "You know, Trey approved of you . . . before."

"Hope he will again," I reply simply as we reach the shore.

"He's just protective of me because he saw the aftermath when you left. He doesn't want me to get hurt again," she says softly. She's framing it as what Trey is worried about, but I can recognize that she's the one pleading for me to be careful with her heart.

"I don't want either of us to get hurt, so I understand his protectiveness."

It's quiet as we approach the parking area. There's no one around as we unload, walking down along the shore to set up a picnic area. I spread out the cloth before seeing Ana trying to lug the big cooler down, and I rush up as best I can, putting my hand on her shoulder. "Uh-uh. Let's just grab our lunch and drinks and leave that heavy beast in the truck. Neither of us should be hauling that thing."

"Oh, so you *can* give in to reason," Ana jabs, but she grabs the food and helps me set everything up while Rex dances around, excited to be running in a new area. "Should we watch him?"

"He knows the lake, and he won't venture far off," I reassure her. "Come on, let's have some food."

It's so different, watching the quiet lake lap at the shore as I sit down with Ana. Part of it, I think, is that while there's attraction between us, the scenario's sort of tamped down our perpetual desire to rip each other's clothes off, considering Brad and Trey will be back shortly. I should probably use the time to tell her more of the backstory, but I'm leery of sharing too much with potential witnesses to the fallout. I think I'll take her lead for now, considering it's her brother who's invaded. Looking across the water, I feel her out. "Never would've predicted this. Chicken?"

"Sure," Ana says, taking a piece of cold fried chicken from me. "Predicted what?"

"That I'd be having lunch with an incredibly beautiful woman who's nursing me back to health . . . and who was my high school sweetheart."

Ana blushes furiously, giving me a small smile. "It's funny how things work out, isn't it?"

"Never thought it'd happen," I admit, the rest of my story trembling behind my lips. "I actually avoided you for the longest time, scared that you were still mad at me. Probably more scared that you'd moved on and had this whole happy life without me, even if a part of me wanted that for you. The one we'd dreamed of . . . with some other asshole who brought you flowers, made you smile, and got to hold you in his arms all night. I've been lonely . . . I just didn't know it. After a while, it all felt routine, and years passed without my even being aware of it."

Ana nods. "There hasn't been anyone, Aubrey. Not really, just casual boyfriends, nothing serious. I couldn't trust anyone anymore, and guys could sense that, I guess, could tell I wasn't whole, that I'd given my heart to a boy as a kid and never gotten it back, never had closure." Her voice is sad, a dark shadow on the bright day, cutting me to the core. "I saw that brochure, the pictures so beautiful and reminding me of before, and I just came here because . . ."

"The memories," I finish quietly. "Same reason I bought my place. Because believe it or not, it reminded me of the best times in my life . . . of my time with you. That was the last time I felt right, happy. Ever since then, things just went so wrong."

I'm on the verge of continuing my story, taking the painful trip through my past, *our* past. But Ana stops me with a kiss, her lips pressing to mine, soft and sweet. A surprise. It takes me a heartbeat to catch up and kiss her back, cupping her head and enjoying the taste of sunshine on her lips.

After one more smack, she pulls back and smiles at me. "What was that for?" I ask. "Not that I'm complaining."

"Not right now," Ana says with a shake of her head. "I want this to be an afternoon of good memories for us, and for those two to have fun on the river, and I don't want to ruin it. I promise I'll let you tell me. Hell, I'm going to *make* you tell me. But I have a feeling it's going to be heavy and take more than the time we have right now. It's waited for years, and we've avoided it for the last week. What's a few more hours? So, how about trying this apple with a taste of honey?"

I want to press her. I need to get this off my chest. It's been buried for so long, festering deep inside, and somehow, I think she's the only one who might understand. But this has got to be on her terms. I'm the one who fucked up, and I'll do whatever it takes to make that right, even if it's pushing the painful words back deep into my gut. I take a breath, attempting to let the past go and reset my mind to this moment.

Ana dips an apple wedge into some local honey and tries it. "I was thinking you were going to try and seduce me with fruit," I say, falling in line with her orders for fun and uncomplicated.

"I thought about it," she admits, licking her lips. The sight of her pink tongue sticking out draws my focus. I grab another apple slice and dip it, letting her eat it from my hand, groaning as she starts sucking my finger, making me hard in my pants. "But I see you already had that idea."

"Guilty as charged," I admit. "We were interrupted this morning, remember? And I don't like being interrupted."

"Oh, really? What did you have planned for us before we were so rudely interrupted by my well-meaning and pussy-blocking brother?" Her voice is full of bedevilment.

"This," I growl, moving in close and taking her mouth. She tastes sweet, like the apple and honey, so I lick at the seam of her lips, wanting every delicious bit of the flavor from her.

She kisses me back, leaning toward me and almost climbing into my lap. I'm tempted, so fucking tempted, to let her. Sitting on the lakeshore with Ana grinding against me sounds like a teenage dream come to life. Actually, I think we did that once. But we've grown up since then, and I want more.

Pulling back, I shift so that I'm sitting behind her, cradling her hips between my spread thighs. "What are you doing?" she moans, her head falling back to my shoulder.

I let my hand drift up, wrapping gently around her neck, guiding her to tilt her head so I have access. I lean down, sucking and nibbling along the line of her neck as I slide my other hand lower to pull her knees open. I knead her inner thighs, squeezing firmly through the soft denim. Ana lets out a gasp at the sharp massage as I get closer to her center. "Aubrey—"

"Can you be quiet, Ana? There's nobody around, but we're sort of in public here, and those sounds you make . . . those are mine, no one else's."

A groan escapes her open mouth, sounding somewhere between aroused and annoyed, and definitely loud. But luckily, we seem to be alone, for now, but that could change at any minute, even if Brad and Trey aren't due back for a while. "I can be quiet." Her voice is breathy, desperate, and needy.

I chuckle darkly. "Woman, if there's one thing you never are . . . it's quiet. But I can help with that too." I unbutton her jeans, slipping a hand in to caress her pussy. She's slick with desire, and I spread her juices up to her clit, circling it in quick, tight circles to get her to the edge fast and hard.

Her breathing hitches, and she bites her lip, trying valiantly to stay quiet but failing miserably. I move my hand from her neck to cover her mouth, watching her face for any signs of discomfort, but she seems more than fine. In fact, I think she likes it. I press harder, both against her mouth and her clit, growling in her ear. "That's it, Ana. Scream your pleasure into my hand. I'll keep you quiet as I make you come for me."

It only takes a few more swipes of my fingers across her clit before she shatters, her hips lifting as her back presses to me. I clamp her cries with my hand, the vibrations hot on my palm as I gather every one like a trophy for giving her pleasure.

She comes back to earth, and I release her mouth, slipping my fingers out of her jeans and into my mouth. She tastes delicious, and I love the way her eyes dilate and her mouth opens as she watches me lick her orgasm from my fingers. She watches raptly, then meets my lips in a heated kiss, tasting herself on my tongue.

CHAPTER 20

ANA – TEN YEARS AGO

*T*he lunchroom is normal, which means that I can almost imagine David Attenborough giving a voice-over. *As the teen animals begin to feed themselves, groups form to help protect from predators. The only question is, who are the predators and who are the prey?*

I guess it's the same in every school lunchroom. For me, my eyes immediately search the room, looking for my handsome boyfriend, who is now damn-near six foot five but finally seems to have stopped growing. At least he's easy to spot.

It's not Aubrey I see first but Declan, one of Aubrey's teammates. "Hey, Declan, seen Aubrey?"

"Draining the lizard," he says, grinning as he looks over my shoulder.

Before I can turn to see what he's looking at, I feel powerful hands wrap around my waist, and I squirm, turning to see Aubrey looking down at me. "Hey, baby."

"Hey to you," I reply before Aubrey takes my breath away with a kiss. He's daring today, slipping his tongue into my mouth as Declan groans beside us.

"Will you two get a room? Or at least give a fuck if Mr. Anderson's in the room or not?"

"Okay, okay . . . don't want you to get in trouble," Aubrey says, finding us some extra seats. "Anderson isn't going to say anything with my signing day so close. Not about a kiss, anyway."

"Hey! Guess what? Marissa and I went shopping yesterday after school and I found my prom dress!" I tell Aubrey as I take out my lunch. It's a cute dress, and I know Aubrey's gonna love it. "What about you? Need any help with your tux or anything?"

"Nope, I'm all set and ready," Aubrey says, taking out a huge beef sandwich that looks like it should feed a small village. Then again, he's working out even harder than he did during football season, bulking up for college play and it shows. "Can't wait to spin you around the dance floor in my arms, show everyone what a lucky bastard I am. I don't know why you put up with me, but I'm damn sure glad you do," he teases me, well aware that I still have occasional doubts about what a star of the school on the fast track for college glory is doing with someone like me.

I'm definitely not as nerdy as I used to be. Aubrey's circle of friends accepted me and Marissa into their fold last year when we started showing up for games and parties, me on Aubrey's arm. Well, they accepted it after a while. At first, there was some definite jealousy and petty bitchy comments, but now people keep telling me that they're voting us as prom king and queen because we're 'such a cute couple . . . so adorbs!' with actual squeals. I don't get it, but I'll admit that getting crowned prom queen and dancing with Aubrey as my king sounds like the cherry on top of our high school years, a sweet beginning to our college days together at Oregon.

My imaginary image of Aubrey and me dancing, sparkly crowns on our heads, is interrupted as I realize Aubrey is still talking.

" . . . and Gabe's going to be home soon for the baby, and I'd like him to see I'm wrapping up high school on a high note. Face it, Sweet Ana, we've got the world at our feet. Finish high school with a bang, head to a great school for college . . . and most importantly, I get to do it all with you. You're gonna be my queen, for prom and for always. I love you."

"You're silly," I murmur, blushing furiously. The things he's saying are making my insides feel like the champagne my parents let me have on New Year's Eve this year, bubbly and happy and shiny. But there's a whole table full of people listening to him wax poetic about us. I'm equally proud and self-conscious.

Aubrey, though, is riding too high to notice. "I'm serious. No one else stands a chance. Everyone loves you." He swings his arm wide, gesturing to everyone in the cafeteria.

"No, they don't. Most of these folks wouldn't even know who I am if I wasn't your girl." I say, not being modest. It's just the truth.

But Aubrey's not hearing it. Suddenly, he stands up, pulling me with him and his voice booming out across the lunchroom. "Hey everyone!" There are a few folks that echo back a greeting and all eyes turn to Aubrey as I try to sit back down, a huge grin on my pink face. I don't know what he's doing, but it's already such an Aubrey thing to do . . . impulsive, confident, and loud. "You know my girl, Anabelle Tucker, right? Just wanted to make sure you knew who you're voting for when you write her name down as prom queen. She's the best girl in the whole world, and I'm lucky enough that she puts up with me, so she damn sure deserves a crown." He laughs, and the whole room laughs with him, although I hear more than a few 'oohs' and 'ahhs' from the girls. I want to tell them that I agree with their sentiment . . . Aubrey is over-the-top and romantic and crazy. And *mine*.

I'm blushing again, his words meaning more to me than he

could possibly know, a big grin of happiness fighting down the nerves of standing up in front of the whole room of kids.

"Baby, come on," Aubrey says, leaning in to talk with me softly. "I'm your king, you're my queen. Now we're gonna make it known to the whole damn school."

He bends down to kiss me, full on the mouth in front of everyone. Suddenly, Mr. Anderson is at our side. "Mr. O'Day and Miss Tucker." His voice has that hard edge of a teacher, but you can hear the humor tickling underneath where he's pushed down his grin too. Aubrey's like that. His charm can get anyone on his side for anything, even obviously breaking the rules against PDA in school. "I think your declarations are done for the day, and perhaps it's time to get on to your next class."

Aubrey grins at Mr. Anderson, throwing an arm around my shoulder. "I think you're right, sir. We're off to fifth period. We have chemistry, right?" He says it with a wink, and at first, I don't get it, too good-girl to catch the tease. But when I realize what he's joking about, I blush again and Mr. Anderson quirks an eyebrow pointedly. Aubrey leads me out of the cafeteria, a chorus of hoots and hollers in our wake. I wave 'bye to Marissa, who's lit up like a Christmas tree and mouths 'we'll talk later' as she quietly mimes a slow clap.

Once we're in the hallway, away from the prying eyes of teachers, I stop and look up at Aubrey. "Aubrey, I love you too. I don't need some stupid crown. Just you. You're all I need."

WHEN AUBREY MEETS ME AFTER SCHOOL, I CAN TELL HE'S GOT something on his mind, probably still prom. "Come with me," he says.

"Where?" I ask, taking his hand. I don't have a car yet, so it's no big deal to get a ride with him, but Mom and Dad like to know where I am.

"Just a special place," Aubrey says mysteriously. "Tell your mom that I'll have you home by nine."

I text Mom and jump into Aubrey's truck as he takes off out of town, driving up into the mountains. For the most part, we just chat, talking about classes, the almost constant rumors that someone's going to open a ski resort up in these mountains, what Oregon is going to be like next year, and other stuff.

By the time the sun's starting to set, we're a good way out of town, and it's getting a little chilly. "Glad the heater works in this thing."

"Yeah . . . here, wear my jacket too," Aubrey says, grabbing his letterman's jacket from the back seat and handing it to me. "That'll cover you."

"From knee to shoulder," I joke, slipping it on. It is warm, though, and when Aubrey turns off the main road and down a short dirt path into a clearing, I find my breath taken away. About halfway across is a small pond, barely a hundred feet across, but it's breathtaking.

"Wow, this is beautiful," I whisper as I look out over the entire Great Falls valley. We're surrounded by nature, the darkness of the evening encroaching all around us, but below us, the lights of town are just beginning to come on. "How'd you find this place?"

"My folks used to take Gabe and me camping up here when we were kids, but we found this place a lot later than that," Aubrey admits. "One of the rare times Gabe was on leave, he and I came out here . . . hiking, camping, talking, just roughing it up and goofing off like we used to. We found this spot, and I knew as soon as I saw it that this place was special."

We walk across the field, which is crunchy with the last remnants of winter's frost, but the spring daytime sun has melted most of the ice and snow. The thin film of ice around the edge reminds me that we're up in the mountains, but Aubrey's jacket and his warm arms help me. "Thank you for bringing me here. This place . . . it's beautiful."

Aubrey nods, and we sit on a blanket, watching the sun go down and the first stars twinkle to life. "I come out here to think sometimes, and it was here I decided something," Aubrey says, looking up. "Ana, this is where I realized I was in love with you."

My eyes shine bright, remembering the first time we'd said 'I love you' to each other. It'd been quiet and soft, sweet and special. I hadn't been surprised. I knew we'd both been feeling it for a while, but the meaning in the depth of the words would stay with me forever.

"I came up here last week again, thinking about my future, *our* future. What I want it to look like and knowing that things are going to be different in college."

I hold my breath, not sure where Aubrey's going with this line of talk but able to read the seriousness of this moment in his eyes.

He takes my hand, his eyes locked on mine as he swallows audibly. "My Sweet Ana, we've got our whole lives in front of us and I imagine what that might look like every day. In every one of those possibilities, I see you, me . . . us. I know we're young, way too young to get married, obviously. But I want you to know that I see that for us. I want that."

He digs in his pocket for a second, pulling out a small black box, and I gasp, unable to hold back my shock as tears start streaming down my face. "Aubrey—"

"It's not an engagement ring, and I'm not getting down on one knee yet. But this is a promise that one day, I will. A promise ring that one day, I'll put a diamond ring on your finger and then a wedding band. And that we'll have that forever I see in my dreams." He opens the box, and I blubber all over again.

The tiny gold band has a knot at the center, the two sides coming together and weaving into an infinity knot. He takes it from the box, slipping it onto my finger, a perfect fit. And we kiss, my arms wrapping around his neck and him pulling me tight to him with his hands on my waist.

The kiss turns heated quickly, and as Aubrey moves lower to kiss along my jawline and down my neck, I finally find words. "I want that too, Aubrey. All of it. A future with you. But Aubrey, I also . . ."

He pulls back, looking at me, and the heat in his eyes gives me the courage I need. "I also want you . . . now. We've waited, but we're eighteen, about to go to college together, and promising to have a future. I want it to start right here." I move in to kiss him again, the flames reaching higher than ever before.

"Ana, are you sure? We've got forever. There's no rush." He's trying to be noble, respectful, and not to pressure me.

But I've never been surer of anything in my life. We might be named prom king and queen in a few weeks, but our life together beyond high school starts tonight. Right here, right now. Our bodies pressed together, our hearts full of love, and his promise ring on my finger. "I've never been surer, Aubrey. I love you."

CHAPTER 21

ANA

"That night was so magical," I finish. "I wore that ring for a long time. I would take it off when I was mad and yell at it for promising things you didn't follow through on, but I always put it back on. For a long time. *Too* long. It meant something to me. That ring, that night."

"It did to me too," Aubrey says, still stroking my arm. "How many times did we go back up there in the weeks before prom?"

"Had to be at least half a dozen," I reply. "Each time was better than the last."

"It was," Aubrey says, definitely remembering the visits we'd made in those weeks. We'd talked about the future, shared our bodies, our dreams, our fears. Everything, I'd thought.

I look away, breaking the force field that surrounds us every time we're close to each other. Letting my eyes scan the lake, I hear a yell off to the left. "That's Trey and Brad. Looks like our picnic is over."

We watch as Trey and Brad paddle their kayaks over to us, Ana waving them in the whole time. "Whoo, that was fun! I haven't been shaken around that much since Trey took me to a honky-tonk with a mechanical bull!" Brad says as they come ashore.

Trey shakes his head, mouthing, "Never happened."

But Brad continues, loud and excited, "And the lake! It's totally crystal clear! I swear I looked down and saw the Cockness Monster!"

"That wasn't the lake you were looking at," Aubrey deadpans. "Just admit it."

"Ooh, guilty as charged!" Brad says sassily, obviously pleased that Aubrey joked back with him. "Speaking of my monster, Trey and I had a little chat and he agreed with me."

"Agreed to what?" I ask worriedly, decidedly concerned about how this conversation is going, considering the start.

"Well, since your sleeping arrangements are *obviously* covered," he says, wagging a finger between Aubrey and me, "Trey and I are staying in the other cabin. And you're not invited."

Aubrey huffs a laugh, telling Brad, "Well, I *guess* she can stay with me."

I growl, "Uhm . . . *she* is standing right here and doesn't appreciate your talking about her like she's not."

Aubrey laughs, kissing me quickly. "It's so hot when you talk about yourself in the third person."

I laugh, his ridiculousness contagious.

I meet Trey's eyes and can tell he wants to talk with me brother-sister, so I step to the side, motioning for him to follow me. "Hey, guys? Can you two load up the kayaks and picnic? I need to talk to Trey . . . or rather, my sister's intuition tells me that he needs to talk to me."

Aubrey looks at me, checking in to make sure I'm okay, and I wave him off with a smile. Trey watches the whole exchange, but I catch the look of appreciation he shoots Brad when he pulls Aubrey off, putting him to work on getting the SUV loaded.

We walk along the shoreline, silent for the minute it takes us to get out of earshot. "Hey, Sis, I just wanted to check—you okay with all this?"

I think, then nod. "If you guys are here for fun, I don't mind. But if you're here to check on me, I'm a big girl. I don't need a babysitter, Trey."

He nods. "Fair enough. I'll admit that I mostly came up here to check on you, but I can respect that you're grown. For the most part," he says with a boyish smile that reminds me of when we were kids. "So, what's the deal between you two?" he asks with concern. "You two . . . make up?"

"Sort of. But we haven't really addressed it, to be honest. I don't really know what's going on."

"What do you mean, you don't know?" Trey presses. "It looks like you two are pretty cozy together. Hell, looked like you've been staying in his cabin . . . not yours."

"Temporarily," I point out. "It's only until his ankle's good enough that he isn't going to become fodder for the wolves or something."

"Are you saying you're just here playing nurse when you're supposed to be having some *me* time?"

Damn. He's grilling me hard. I don't really know what to say to that. The fact is, I wasn't expecting to end up in this situation, and I can't say I'm not somewhat pleased with how things have turned out, but I'm just not comfortable talking about it when I'm not exactly sure what's going on myself.

It's too new and could be over as soon as I leave.

Trey is watching me closely. "Thought so. You're not just playing nurse. There's more. And judging by how we found you this morning, a lot more."

"Has he told you why he left yet?" Trey asks when I don't say anything. "I mean, I figure if there's *one* thing to talk about, it's that."

"Not yet," I admit, thinking about our meandering trips down memory lane over the past few days. "But we're getting there. We were about to twice . . . when we were interrupted."

As if almost on cue, Brad hollers from the SUV. "Come on, use them biceps! I want to get back and have some snuggle time with my favorite wild animal!"

Aubrey grumbles something back that we miss, and Trey laughs. "I think Brad's growing on him. I've noticed with Brad, you either love him or you want to kick his ass. Although, I'll admit that sometimes, I fall into both categories at the same time."

I laugh, shoving his shoulder. "That's scarily true," I reply. "But he makes you happy, and that's what counts. I'm glad you found your person, Trey. Brad is crazy, admittedly, and not what I would've expected for you, but I can't see you with anyone else now. He's it for you."

Trey looks at me, his head tilted a bit. "Not what you expected. What did you expect? A girl? Some sweet little thing I could take home to Mom and Dad?"

It's my turn to look at him with my head tilted, knowing we've talked about this a little over the years. "Trey, you told Mom and Dad ages ago, but I knew in high school for sure. You're my brother, and we were best friends for a long time. What I meant was that I guess I expected you to end up with someone more staid and serious, a suit-and-tie kinda guy. But Brad's irreverence has made you different, happier and more confident in your own skin. And for that, I will always love him. And you."

"Thanks, Sis. He does make me happy, even when I want to stuff a sock in his mouth so he'll shut up."

I laugh. "What you two do in private is your business. I don't need to know," I say, covering my ears and shaking my head like I'm five.

"You're such a brat, Ana." Trey laughs at me. "Seriously, though, speaking of who you thought I'd end up with, I always thought you'd end up with Aubrey. I don't know what happened back then, and maybe it's not something you can forgive. Hell, maybe he doesn't even deserve it. But it killed me seeing you like that back then. So the least you deserve is an answer about what the hell happened. Maybe it'll lead to forgiveness, maybe it'll just be closure, but you've earned that."

He pulls me in for a hug, patting my back and laying a light kiss to the top of my head. "Thanks, Trey. I don't know what I'm doing if I'm honest, but you're right. I need to know."

"Okay, then I'll keep Brad on our side of the clearing tonight. A quiet dinner by the fire sounds nice, and that'll give you and Aubrey a chance to talk. Just be careful, little sis."

"I will, and I'm a bit overgrown to be 'little'," I remind him with a punch in the arm. "But I love you."

"You'll always be my little sister. Love you, too."

We walk back to the SUV where Brad is looking like the cat who got the cream and Aubrey looks like he might explode any second. I whisper to Trey, "Looks like Aubrey's falling in the 'ready to kill Brad' camp right now."

Trey winks at me. "That's okay. That's step one of his process. Aubrey will be in love with him before he knows what hit him. That's what happened to me. That's what Brad does to everyone." Trey looks at Brad, and I can see the light in his eyes. It makes me happy that my brother is so in love.

We drive back to the cabin, Brad and Trey giving me hugs as Aubrey stands by, waiting comfortably even as Trey eyes him down.

We walk toward *our* cabin, and I look back over my shoulder. "You boys be good, or else I'll send Rex after you."

Brad chuckles, and I catch up with Aubrey, who's nearly at his porch. "So they're okay? Trey isn't freaking out?"

I laugh, reminding myself again just how smart Aubrey is. "He just wants to make sure I'm okay. He did ask what we're doing. I didn't have an answer."

"What *are* we doing?"

I bite my lip, feeling that strange swing of emotions that seems to happen around Aubrey a lot, the sweetness and pain of the past swirling with the desire and connection of the present. "I don't know. Trying to get to know one another again, I guess?"

Aubrey nods. "More than trying. Doing pretty well, all things considered."

"But Aubrey," I add, taking his hand, "I think it's time that we have that talk. No interruptions this time. It's the elephant in the cabin we've been dancing around for a little too long now. I tried to avoid it, but I think I need to know almost as much as you need to tell me."

Aubrey nods and sighs. "It's been hard, and I've been afraid, Ana. Afraid of talking about it with anyone. I'd gotten to the point I thought I'd gotten over it a little. And my running off, it feels so stupid now, considering what I lost. Years, my family, my future . . . *you*."

"What made you leave?" I ask. "Aubrey, if there's going to be any chance of what I think is happening between us surviving, I have to know."

"Okay," he says finally. "Just tell me what you remember of that night, and I'll fill you in on the rest."

That night. How could I forget it? It's been etched in my memory forever.

"Okay, I remember it like it was yesterday."

CHAPTER 22

ANA – PROM NIGHT

I've been dreaming about this night with Aubrey for months. This night . . . it's all ours.

I feel beautiful. I feel like a woman.

Sure, part of it is the dress, red satin that hugs my upper body before dropping away into a full skirt with a high-low hemline, giving me an illusion of a train. Layers of mascara and glossy lips are framed by an upswept do that Marissa helped me style specifically so that a crown wouldn't disturb it. If I get to wear one, that is.

I thought about wearing white, but Aubrey says I look great in red. He says that I remind him of strawberries and all he wants to do is gobble me up. So when I saw this dress, I knew it was the one.

"You look beautiful, Sis. If you don't win prom queen, there's no hope left in the world," Trey says.

"You're too sweet," I say as I turn to him. "I'll be excited if I win, but I'm not holding my breath." Despite my casual front, I'm nervous as fuck. While I initially didn't care, standing up there on Aubrey's arm would feel so wonderful, and now I'm secretly hoping that dream comes true.

"Aubrey isn't gonna know what hit him when he sees you," Trey says.

Before I can respond, the doorbell rings and Trey runs to open it. "Mom, get the camera!" he yells.

"Hey, my future queen, your king is here!" Aubrey calls. I hurry toward the door, feeling a ball of nerves in the pit of my stomach. Aubrey hasn't seen my dress and I hope he likes it. And I can't wait to see him in his tux.

Aubrey's jaw drops as I come into view, the red rose in his hand dropping for a moment before he regains his composure. "You're so damn beautiful."

"You look handsome yourself," I manage to say through batted eyelashes as I reach him. He hands me the flower, and I feel a wave of faintness. "Thank you. I love it."

"I spent an hour at the flower shop looking for one that I thought would be as perfect as you," Aubrey says, unable to take his eyes from me, "and I'm happy to say I failed. You've never looked lovelier than you do at this moment."

His words calm my nerves, and he pulls me in for a kiss, our lips light for now because I want to preserve my makeup, but it still takes my breath away.

Suddenly, I remember we're not alone as I hear the *click-click-click* of my mom taking pictures and pull back. "So cute. Now, Aubrey, hold the flower again . . . *click* . . . now Ana, take the rose . . ." It goes on forever, Mom directing poses and taking pictures to commemorate the night.

Finally, Trey intercedes on my behalf. "Mom, they're gonna be late."

"Oh, I didn't realize how long I was taking. You kids have fun, be good!" Mom says, her voice high with a note of happiness but I can see the bittersweet tears in her eyes. Her last baby is almost done with high school and leaving in mere weeks for college in another state. All things considered, I'm happy to take a few extra pictures for her.

I give everyone a hug, and Aubrey shakes their hands, both Trey and my dad giving him a bonus glare, knowing that prom night is supposed to be special for every girl and warning him without a word to not fuck it up.

"Come on, or else we'll be late," I say.

Aubrey helps me into his truck, all freshly-cleaned for the occasion. We meet the rest of our group in the parking lot, mostly Aubrey's teammates and their dates. Marissa and Declan are the last to get there. I'd been surprised when she'd told me Declan had asked her, since they barely talk, but apparently, they'd decided to go as friends and it worked out since we're all part of the same larger group.

The prom committee did a number on the gym, turning it into an island paradise with tulle streamers along the ceiling and palm trees around the basketball court dance floor. Even the punch has little umbrellas. It's not over the top but lends a fun flair to the festivities.

Everyone's looking their best, wearing dresses and tuxes that turn even the normal into something extraordinary. More than once, I have to do a double-take as I realize just who's crossing the room. "Jeez, it's like everyone is a different person. Everyone looks amazing."

Aubrey laughs, sending a thrill down my spine. "And for every look you're giving, you're getting four or five. But there's only one that matters. I can't take my eyes off you, baby."

"Thank you, though I'm still so nervous that I'm going insane," I reply. "It just feels like a huge buzz in here tonight! Like anything could happen."

"I know. Come on, I can at least solve your nerves," Aubrey says as the DJ starts playing *Sexy Back*. Dragging me out on the dance floor, I'm quickly laughing and turned on as Aubrey moves like a cat, little touches and moves combining to send my pulse racing and my nipples tightening in my dress. "Enjoying yourself?"

"You know exactly what you're doing to me," I reply as he starts grinding behind me. I feel him press against my ass, and I gasp, looking back. "Are you popping wood back there? Careful," I say with a wink. "This is prom."

Aubrey growls in my ear. "That was my phone, but yes, I am. And you know what's coming after."

I do. And I can't wait.

The song transitions, and after a few seconds, I realize the DJ is slowing the pace down. "May I?" Aubrey asks, pulling my hands behind his neck and then settling his on my hips.

I nod, swaying back and forth with him, memorizing the moment.

As the song wraps up, Mrs. Vereen, the school's French teacher, takes the stage and grabs the microphone. "And now, Great Falls High, it's time for Prom King and Queen!"

After applause, Mrs. Vereen continues. "Thank you to all who were nominated, and all who voted . . ." she begins her speech.

Aubrey gives my hand a squeeze. "We got this."

"And now the new Queen of Great Falls is . . . Anabelle Tucker!"

I'm shocked, sure she made some mistake as the cheers start. Aubrey, though, sounds totally unsurprised. "Great job, my

Sweet Ana. Now go on up there and get the throne warmed up. I'll be right behind you."

I nod, grinning widely as I walk up on stage. Mrs. Vereen, who was a pretty cool teacher, actually, grins back. "Our new Prom Queen!"

The crowd goes wild as Vicki Washington, the student council president, crowns me and hands me my scepter. I look out on the crowd, laughing as I do my best 'Princess' wave, mostly blinded by the lights. Everyone and everything's just a dazzled dark blur in my eyes.

"Now, on to the King," Mrs. Vereen says. "This one's no surprise, but there is no doubt Great Falls High has spoken! Our new King is none other than Aubrey O'Day!"

I'm hopping up and down, clapping as the crowd cheers wildly, watching the direction he should be coming from.

The cheering continues, Mrs. Vereen speaking again. "Aubrey, come up here and accept your crown and new queen!"

The clapping starts to turn nervous as Aubrey doesn't appear, and the spotlights swing off me enough to see him talking on his phone, his face white. Before anyone can say anything, he turns, shoving people out of the way to get to the doors.

"Aubrey!" Mrs. Vereen calls out as panic grips my heart.

I don't know what I'm doing as I grab the microphone from Mrs. Vereen. "Aubrey? Where are you going?"

But Aubrey doesn't respond and disappears, the door to the gym swinging closed, leaving me just . . . stunned. Why is he leaving me, deserting me in our special moment? Everyone is looking and the crowd starts to mutter.

"Aubrey!" I call out one more time, tears starting to flow. I'm so scared, and in the back of the crowd, I can hear someone start to laugh. The embarrassment starts to set in as I realize people are openly gawking, smirking and laughing . . . at me.

I turn, running from the stage to hide behind the curtain. Vaguely, I hear Mrs. Vereen directing everyone to resume dancing in honor of their prom king and queen, and the tears fall as giant sobs rack my body.

Marissa is at my side in an instant, gathering me to her and asking the question I want the answer to as well. "What happened? Where'd he go?"

I shake my head. "I don't know. I don't know."

She holds me, rocking me back and forth until Declan comes running up. He skids to a stop near us, obviously not sure what to do with a crying girl. But he rallies. "I tried to catch him, Ana. I tried. But he ran out and squealed out of the parking lot. He's . . . he's gone."

CHAPTER 23

AUBREY

"It felt like a dagger pierced my heart," Ana says, tears falling down her face. "Marissa and Declan took me home. I called you over and over. I even went and banged on your door the next day, determined to know what happened, why you'd left me like that. It took me a long time, years, probably, to realize that something awful must've happened. I was embarrassed, maybe self-centered the way only teenagers can be, especially with all the drama and teasing about that night at school. But eventually I realized, maybe hoped, that something bad must've happened just so that it could all make sense." She shrugs. "I don't mean that I hoped something bad happened to you, but just that you'd been so excited about the whole prom thing . . . but when you ran out, you looked like you'd seen a ghost."

Seeing her pain up close, I hate myself. I could have at least mitigated this with a phone call, a letter. Fuck, an e-mail, maybe. I'd even written her several times, but she deserved more, and I'd burned them instead of sending them. I left her in agony, and who knows how long it lasted?

I only hope once she hears my side, she'll understand. I take my thumb and wipe away her tears, looking into her eyes. "I'm so sorry," I whisper, feeling wetness on my own cheeks. "I shouldn't have done it, but it all happened so fast and at the time, I had to leave."

"Why?"

I sigh. "That's gotten harder to answer in the time you've been here. Ana, I have to ask. When you saw me here, what did you think?"

Ana snorts, wiping her nose. "That I wanted to kick your ass. And that you were hot as hell."

It's my turn to snort, nodding. "Yeah . . . I knew that much. When I first realized who you were, that it was really you, I thought it was a sign that maybe it was time to, I don't know, reset everything? I've been in pain for a long time, running from a lot of shit. And yeah, the past week has been good, but I want more than that. It's why I keep hoping that we could be more again and why I'm afraid that you're never going to forgive me. Because it's taken me years to even look myself in the eye, and I'm not even sure if I forgive myself."

Ana licks her lips, sighing. "Those first few days, I wasn't interested in anything you really had to say. Honestly, I was torn between being angry and turned on. But we need this truth. I need to hear it and you need to say it. I remember checking up on you. You never came back to school, you never enrolled at Oregon, you just . . . disappeared. I checked for over a year, and then it just hurt too much to keep tearing the scab off my heart."

I take a deep breath, my heart feeling even heavier as I think about the events that set me on the path to this cabin and all the mistakes I've made. "Walk with me?"

"Where?"

"You'll see," I say, taking her hand. Rex tries to follow, but I stop him at the door. "Not this time, boy. Stay."

Rex goes over to his old Army blanket, lying down and looking at me. I'll make it up to him later.

Even with my limp, we make good time. I know the trail by heart, and my flashlight illuminates any rocks as we go around the twists and turns, following the stream once we hit it until, like we're emerging into a fantasy scene, we're at the clearing.

"Told you it was close," I say softly as Ana stops. "It was always here, but I couldn't bring you back here until now."

We walk quietly for a moment as we let the sounds of nature surround and envelope us. We reach the edge of the clear pool, and I look, seeing the same edging of ice that we'd found years ago. I spread a blanket and sit, guiding Ana to sit beside me. I hug my knees as I let the memories finally come out. "That night, I got a phone call. It nearly shattered me. It damn sure shattered my family."

"What happened?" Ana asks. "And why didn't you tell me?"

I swallow, my voice thick as I try to control myself. "I wish I had, then or after. But I was in shock and I had to get home."

I glance over and see that Ana still doesn't understand. Her face is like stone. It's like the weight that's been hanging around my neck for years, and I know if I'm ever going to get rid of it, it has to be tonight.

"So when you were up there, my phone rang."

CHAPTER 24

AUBREY – DAY OF PROM

"*D*amn, little bro, I'm going to have to take some tips from you when I get back to the real world. You're looking hella *GQ*," Gabe says as I turn this way and that in front of the camera. It feels a little stupid to be doing it at five in the morning, but it was the only time Gabe had available to get on Skype.

"Just trying to get a head start. I know once you get back here, you're gonna have me wearing this damn thing for your wedding."

Gabe chuckles, shrugging. "Yeah, well, at least I don't have to wear a tux. The Class As are good for me."

"You're going to wear blue for your wedding?" I ask, smirking. "Maybe I'll have to do green and yellow for mine someday, show some college spirit."

Gabe laughs. "Getting ready for Oregon next year already? I don't know if I see it. Show me some duck lips?" I pucker goofily and then laugh along with him. It feels good, like my brother is right here next to me, not half a world away. "So, this girl you're

195

going to prom with, she's pretty special, huh? Special enough you're picking your college with her?"

"Yeah," I admit, leaning in closer. "I know I'm just eighteen and everyone's gonna call me young and stupid, but I think she's the one, man."

Gabe holds up a hand, shaking his head. "Slow down, Aubrey. I don't want to just be lumped in with *everyone*, but you're not even out of high school yet. You've barely started your life. Don't even worry about *the one* right now. Look at me, I'm twenty-five, and despite the jokes, I still don't know if Angie and I are gonna get married. We have a lot of shit to sort out when I get home, and Lord knows, she's put up with too much with my always being gone, but we're both stepping up to see if we can be a family. But it's a big, complicated, scary thing. Being an adult, making that commitment isn't as easy as it seems when you've got stars in your eyes and the world at your feet."

"Yeah, I appreciate what you're saying, Gabe," I reply, glad that he feels like he can trust me with this sort of talk. I know Mom would shit herself if she heard Gabe say he wasn't a hundred percent convinced about marriage. "But I don't know. I can see myself spending the rest of my life with Ana. Actually, I can't see myself *without* her."

Gabe narrows his eyes but nods. "Okay, man. Just do me a favor —don't worry about that right now. There's no rush. Just have fun with her and kick ass at Oregon. The rest will come when it does. I don't want you to limit yourself and end up getting hurt."

I laugh. "Me, get hurt? You should worry about yourself. You're the one in a warzone."

Gabe laughs. "Just a little longer and I'm out of here. Back to my family, Angie, and my unborn son. I've been saving up my leave time, so I should get a good couple of weeks after he's born."

I smile at the thought. Having Gabe around, holding the next generation of O'Days, sounds pretty awesome. "You and Angie making plans for the baby?"

Gabe tries to hem and haw for a moment before grinning. "Actually, we are. We haven't told anyone this yet, but we're gonna make him a junior . . . little Gabriel O'Day Jr. But don't tell Mom and Dad that. I wanna see their faces."

I smile wide. "No fucking way!" I shake my head. "You know Mom and Dad are gonna flip the fuck out, right?"

Gabe's smirk is obvious, even through the digital static taking over the screen. "I know. It's gonna be great."

We both laugh again, the feeling so familiar, and I realize how much I miss his being here for daily chats. "So listen, I've gotta go, back on patrol in fifteen, and I gotta hit the head before I report for duty. But you have fun tonight, man. Prom is a big fucking deal, so make sure you do it right."

"Will do, Bro. Next time you see me, I'll wear my crown and you can call me King Aubrey."

He snorts. "Doubtful. But you should definitely wear the crown so I can give you shit. Love you, Brother."

"Love you too. Be safe," I answer just as the call disconnects.

After I close Skype, I shake my head, tears burning my eyes. It's always good to talk to Gabe, but when we hang up, it hits me how long it's been seen I've actually seen him in person. As hard as that is for me, I know it's a million times worse for him.

But for now, it's time to get my 'A' game going. I've got about twelve hours until I pick up Ana, and my day is packed with a trip to the barber's, a stop at the florist, and a detailed wash for my truck.

But none of those places open for another couple of hours, so I fall back into bed for a short catnap, knowing it's going to be a late night, full of fun with the prettiest girl in the world on my arm.

I GIVE ANA'S HAND A SQUEEZE AS MRS. VEREEN'S SPIEL COMES TO an end.

I'm probably the least surprised person in the room when Ana's announced as the winner, and I give her a kiss on the cheek. "Great job, my Sweet Ana. Now go on up there and get the throne warmed up. I'll be right behind you."

While the DJ plays some cheesy music, I watch as Ana walks to the stage, a stupid grin on my face as I wait for my turn. I feel a buzzing in my pocket, and realize I've left my phone on. Whoever is calling is going to have to wait. This is my moment and I'm not missing it.

But my phone keeps buzzing, damn-near going apeshit. Finally, I pull it out to see that it's a call from Mom . . . and she's not taking voicemail for an answer.

My heart skips a beat, and a dark sense of dread creeps over me. Mom knows how important tonight is. There's no way she'd call multiple times if it wasn't an emergency. Plugging one ear with my finger, I hit the pickup button. "Mom?"

"Oh, my God, Aubrey! We need you!" she screams so loudly I can hear it over Mrs. Vereen's blathering. "Come home now!"

"What . . . what's wrong?" I ask, scared at the desperate plea in her voice. "Mom?"

"Your brother. There was an explosion and he's missing! They think he might . . . he might . . . Aubrey." She's hysterical, crying in my ear.

Dimly, in the back of my mind, I hear Mrs. Vereen announce my name, and I know around me, people are clapping, the noise annoying as I try to listen to my mom's sob-filled words. But all I can think is ...*Gabe. Not Gabe.*

Without thinking, I turn, shoving people out of the way. I can hear someone scream my name, and I think it might be Ana, but it doesn't even register. *Nothing* registers.

I BURST IN THE FRONT DOOR, EYES WILDLY LOOKING AROUND FOR my family. I hear hysterical sobbing coming from the kitchen. "Mom? Dad?" I say, running that way.

They're sitting in the floor, *on the cold tile*, I think nonsensically. Dad's holding Mom, who's buried her head in his chest. They both look pale and their faces are awash with tears. Mom cries louder, opening her arms to me, and I rush forward, collapsing to my knees with them too. We hold each other for a second, the assurance that we're here, together and real, a drop of support in a tornado of 'what the fuck'.

"What happened?" I demand.

Dad points at the letter on the table, and I reach over, my fingers trembling as I pick it up.

From the desk of Lieutenant General Donald Shaw, Commander, JFAC Afghanistan.

Dear Mr. and Mrs. O'Day,

It is with a heavy heart that I must inform you that your son, Sergeant Gabriel Ryan O'Day, has been reported missing in action. His patrol was ambushed by enemy combatants at 2330 hours local time, and by the time relief units ...

The paper slips from my fingers to flutter to the floor, where it lands half-folded, the Army crest on top still visible. My heart feels frozen in my chest, and I sit back on my ass, my head in my hands and my elbows on my knees as I stare at the letter like it's evil incarnate. "There's gotta be a mistake. I–I just talked to him early this morning!"

Dad shakes his head. "The chaplain team left a few minutes before you got here. They said . . ." Dad chokes out before a sob tears from his throat, "They said that there is still hope, but I asked and—"

I can read between his words and shake my head. "No. Gabe's a fighter. He's got Angie and the baby. He's gotta come back."

Mom keeps crying hysterically, muttering over and over . . . *my baby, not my baby*. I can see the truth in Dad's eyes. "I'm sorry, Son. They said with the location of the ambush, they'll likely never find his body. For now, he's MIA."

"Oh, my fucking God," I whisper, feeling like this is a nightmare.

It's gotta be. This is just a bad dream after talking on Skype, and I'm gonna wake up any minute to get ready for prom. But it's not.

I feel the world spin but try to hold on, to be strong for Gabe. "So, what do we do?"

"We just have to wait," Dad says. "His unit will conduct search and rescue operations, and we'll . . . we'll wait."

I nod, silently disagreeing with what Dad's saying. I can't wait around doing nothing. Gabe's not dead. I have to believe that Gabe made it out. He's resourceful and the toughest mother-fucker I know. If anyone could survive a situation like that, it's my big brother. I wish there was something, anything I could do. But I'm fucking useless, sitting in the floor with my parents a million miles away from him.

I scoot closer to Mom, placing my arm around her shoulders.

"Just hang in there, Mom. Gabe is gonna be fine. We're gonna hear from him soon."

Something about my touch seems to strengthen her some, and she wipes at her eyes. "This can't be happening. I refuse to believe it."

The phone rings, and all of us freeze, a hope that there's been some mistake taking root for a split second before Dad checks the caller ID and answers, "Angie?"

Oh, God. Angie. She must be going crazy too. "Does she know?" I ask Mom, who nods.

"Yes, your father called her while I called you."

Dad is listening intently. "Okay, yeah . . . understood. We're on our way." He hangs up, taking a steadying breath as he turns to us.

"That was Angie's father. After I hung up with her, she was understandably upset. She's having some contractions, so they're taking her to the hospital for observation. He . . . uh . . . well, he recommended we come. Now."

Mom gasps. "No! Not the baby too! That might be our only link to Gabe!" she cries out, giving voice to our deepest fear. That Gabe could be dead. That his unborn son might be the only piece left of him in the world beyond the memories in our hearts.

CHAPTER 25

AUBREY

"I'm so sorry, Aubrey. That's horrible," Ana whispers, shaking her head. Tears stream down her face, and she shivers, partially from the cold and partially from the feelings the story stirs up. "I–I never knew, Aubrey. Oh, God, that's just terrible."

I nod, feeling tears burn my eyes. "It was awful. We left right then. I remember it being such a mad rush. I dumped my school backpack in the floor and threw a change of clothes in it and ran out the door. Angie and her family were a state away, so we went to the airport and showed up to the hospital ready to help however we could."

Ana looks hesitant but asks anyway. "Angie and the baby? Are they . . . okay?"

I shake my head, looking up at the stars and preparing myself for the next part of the story.

"No. Angie was in preterm labor, and they couldn't get the contractions to stop. We stayed at the hospital for days, a week or two maybe. Basically, holding vigil, praying and willing everything to be okay. It didn't work. Angie lost the baby." The words are foreign on my tongue. I don't think I've ever actually said them out loud, and the pain burns fresh at the lost piece of my brother.

Ana gasps, the sound breaking me from the memories of the past that threaten to drag me back down. "No. Oh, my God. I'm so sorry. Angie?"

"She's okay . . . now. She wasn't for a long time. And she had to pull away from us for a while to heal. I think she felt so much guilt even though none of it was her fault. It was just a lot of loss for her all at once, and whatever she needed to do to stay sane, we understood and gave her some space. I think she talks to my parents every once in a while. I'm not sure."

"You don't know? What about you in this whole story?" Ana asks.

As bad as the first part of this story is, it was largely beyond my control. The next part? It's *my* fuckup . . . *all mine*. I hope Ana can forgive this part.

"So, when we were waiting in the hospital, I felt so useless. I couldn't save Gabe, I couldn't save his girl, I couldn't save his baby. And I know that's stupid. I was just a kid and none of it was my responsibility. But I felt this pressure deep inside, this need to do something. To make Gabe proud, help him, or maybe help some other family so they never had to go through this like we were. So I . . ." I gulp, not able to say the words that turned my path so sideways.

Ana reaches out, touching my hand. I look to her, seeing that her eyes are soft and teary, waiting and ready for whatever I'm going to say without judgment. I can't hold her eyes when I say it, letting my gaze drop. "I enlisted."

"What? Aubrey, you were in the military? I had no idea!" Her shock is palpable, as real to me as the weight I've been carrying on my shoulders for so long.

"I was. Did one tour. My parents were . . . less than thrilled. Actually, they tried to undo it, but I was eighteen and I'd already signed. They'd lost, or possibly lost, one son to the military and had no desire to risk their other. But I needed to do it for Gabe. We had a huge blowup fight because they didn't understand, said I was being impulsive and stupid. They were probably right, but it was ugly, all of us taking our grief out on one another, unable to handle Gabe being MIA. We've never been okay since then, rarely talk, actually. Carlotta is the only family I interact with anymore."

Ana bites her lip. "I remember your family as so close-knit. When you disappeared that night, I tried to track you down, but your whole family was gone. No one knew what had happened. You just never came back, not for classes or graduation, and you never enrolled at Oregon. When a moving truck showed up to your house, the whole town was talking, and I interrogated the movers, but they didn't know anything."

"Yeah, there was some Senator's son who was all over the news about that time, so a military loss wasn't exactly hot for the media. As for the house, that was over the summer, right? I was already gone by then. I think Dad just hired it out because Mom couldn't go back to that house, said Gabe was in every wall and piece of furniture and she couldn't bear to look at it all. As far as I know, they've never been back to Great Falls. I go as little as possible, just for work, mostly. Too many memories there."

Ana flinches at my words. "There are a lot of good memories there too, Aubrey," Ana says softly.

Flashes of memories overwhelm me . . . Gabe and me sledding down the big hill when we got fresh snow, my family watching fireworks on the fourth of July, camping in the backyard with

Gabe when we were little and here in the mountains when we were older. There's also Ana . . . our first date after I won the game for her, the way she'd light up every time she saw me in the hallways like she was surprised I was talking to her again, the fumbling way we'd learned about each other's bodies, the intensity with which I loved her, sure and certain the way only an untested teenager can be.

"I know, I just couldn't go back. I did my four years, saw and did shit I never would've imagined, which sometimes made me feel closer to Gabe and sometimes made me feel even further away from the boy he knew and loved. I kept thinking he was going to pull some Rambo-style shit and come busting out of those mountains in a helicopter. Never happened, and eventually, they declared him Killed In Action. When I got out, I was lost in a dark hole, didn't care about anything or anyone because the world just didn't feel right without Gabe in it. So I bounced around a bit, ended up selling cars, something I never would've imagined. But I was decent at it, my lack-of-fucks-given attitude surprisingly coming across as no-nonsense, which put people at ease. But when I got the chance to buy this place, I jumped at it, escaping my job, escaping my past, escaping my life."

Ana lets out a surprised laugh, light and bright in the heaviness of the air. "A car salesman? I don't mean to be rude, especially considering everything else you just said, but that's definitely not something I ever thought you'd do."

I laugh a bit too, a welcome reprieve as the tension breaks.

Ana shakes her head, sighing hollowly. "I can't believe this, Aubrey. And I thought I went through hell. I wish I could've been there for you. I would have understood. I loved you."

I pick up a pebble and toss it into the pond, watching the ripples spread in the moonlight. "I should have told you, first thing. But after I waited too long, I didn't want to ruin what we had with the person I'd become. I truly hoped you'd moved on and had a happy life, all the things we'd wanted and dreamed of, with someone able to give you that. Because I couldn't."

She takes a deep breath and looks at me, her eyes filled with more than sadness but also hurt and anger. "All the ignoring in the world won't make a heart heal faster . . . or an ankle," Ana says. "Is that what you're doing to yourself? Isolating yourself to take the pain inside and punish yourself?"

"For a long time, I definitely did that. I distracted myself with work and pain." The admission is a truth I hadn't fully realized until it popped out of my mouth.

"And now?"

"I think I'm doing better now. Seeing you and being with you have given me a passion for life again. I want you, Ana. I want to be with you. I've been given a second chance, and I'm not going to let go this time. I'll do whatever it takes to make it happen," I say, strength and determination filling my voice.

"But before I got here? Were you still stuck in the past or were you doing well? I think we both know the answer to that, Aubrey," she says, and I can feel the distance between us even though we're sitting inches away from each other.

"Ana—"

"I just . . . that's a lot of pressure, Aubrey. I haven't seen you for ten years, and now that I know what happened, I'm not as angry as I was. I understand, I do. But like we said, we're different people now, and I don't know if I'm this saving angel you want me to be. I'm not your Sweet Ana, the kind, giving, trusting girl who loved you with her whole heart." Her voice has a tinge of sadness, the loss of that innocent girl apparent in her eyes.

I shake my head. "But you are. You stepped right up to help with my ankle, saving me from my own stupidity. And I know you feel this too." I take her hand, pressing it to my chest, letting her feel the steady thump of my heart, knowing that it beats for her. "My heart . . . it's always been yours. You can't tell me that's not true for you too, that it's not why you're still alone."

"I just don't know if that's where I'm at yet. I want this. The little girl in me wants this so fucking bad, Aubrey. But a week ago, you didn't want me here, then you wanted just casual, and now —" She's holding up her fingers as she lists the supposed progression of my feelings, but I interrupt her.

I grab her hand, locking my fingers through her raised ones and pressing them to the blanket as I push her down to her back, looming over her. My voice is hard, leaving no doubt. "I *never* wanted casual. From the moment I saw you, I was all in, scared as fuck that you'd run, and fighting my instincts to lock you in my cabin and never let you leave, force you to listen to me, and understand. To forgive me. I tried to be casual so I wouldn't scare you."

Her eyes flash fire, but I don't know what it is . . . anger, maybe? "I'm not scared of you."

I reward her, or maybe it's punishment, I'm not sure, but I take her mouth, devouring her, needing to reassure myself that she's still here, hasn't run away yet after hearing what happened all those years ago. She kisses me back, her tongue fighting with mine, giving just as aggressively as I am. When she relaxes, the fight draining from her, I pull back slowly as I watch for signs she's feigning. I press my forehead to hers, the puffs of our heated breaths mingling in the cold air around us.

"See, Ana? It's us. Nobody else does that to you, I know they don't. It's supposed to be us. It was *always* supposed to be us. I fucked it up, and I'm so sorry, but I swear, I'll make it up to you."

She bites her lip, tears streaming from the corners of her eyes to run back into her hair as she shakes her head. "Aubrey, I need time. I gave you everything and you took ten years. You left me alone, confused, feeling like I wasn't enough. After a while, I knew that something had happened, and I could've helped you, would've helped you with anything. But you didn't let me. And now, you want me to just turn on a dime and bring back these emotions like no time has passed. I just . . . I need time. Please."

It's the *please* that does it. Ana shouldn't have to plead, not to me, not for anything. I sit back, letting her hands go after I help her sit up. "Okay. Time? Take whatever you need, Ana. Because I'm not going anywhere. I'm here . . . right here for you. And I'm not letting you go this time, not for anything." It's a promise, a new one. I don't have a ring, but it's just as serious of a commitment as the last promise I made her. And I intend to fulfill it, along with the previous one, however long it takes.

Ana stands up, offering me her hand. "Can we go back? I think I'm going to stay with Trey and Brad tonight. I need to get my head on straight, do some thinking. Everything you've told me tonight . . . it's a lot to process."

I take her hand, flipping it over to kiss her palm. "Do you know how to get back? I'd like to stay here a bit, maybe talk to Gabe." I look over at the lake, a memory coming like a shockwave of the time we went fishing right over . . . there. A small smile hints at my lips as I remember how he'd told the story over and over again, the fish getting bigger every time.

Ana looks skeptical, her eyebrows furrowed. "Are you sure you're okay out here by yourself? I can get to the cabin just fine, but I don't want to leave you if you're upset."

"I'm fine, but like you said, it's a lot. And it's been a while since I've even *thought* about some of that stuff. Saying it was a first." I give her a slight smile, hoping she sees the difference she's made in me after such a short time. I know I was a grumpy asshole, more grunts than words, as Carlotta always reminded me. But tonight, I've spoken more words than in the ten years before combined, and each one was from my heart.

As Ana walks away, making her way carefully back toward the cabins, I turn my face to the sky once again. "Hey, Gabe. How you doing, big brother?"

CHAPTER 26

ANA

*C*limbing the porch steps to the rental cabin, I don't hear much inside, but I knock just in case because I don't want to interrupt Trey and Brad the way they did me and Aubrey.

Brad grumbles as he opens the door, "Bitch, you are interrupting hot tub time so this had better be some good shit—" He stops abruptly when he sees the expression on my face. He immediately scoops me into his arms, pulling me inside. "What's wrong, baby girl?"

I shake my head. "Brad, do you mind if I talk to my brother alone for a minute?"

Brad's worried by the look on his face, but he nods, giving me a kiss on the cheek. "I understand, honey. Listen, I'll go hit the hot tub by myself, leave you and Trey alone. Just get me when you're done."

I walk over to Trey, sagging down onto the couch as he scoots up next to me. "What's going on?"

"I had a talk with Aubrey. You know, *that* talk," I say quietly before I tell Trey the whole story. It takes me awhile, and there's more than once when I have to stop to wipe at my eyes. "I knew it had to be bad, and I had a lot of time to run over the possibilities, but it still caught me by surprise."

"Damn," Trey says softly, opening his arms, and I curl up in them. It reminds me of when Aubrey left the first time and Trey held me plenty of times as I cried my heart out. "I guess everyone has their way of dealing with things. Maybe we should've pieced things together? At least had a clue? I don't know, I never heard anything about Gabe. With Aubrey, there were dozens of rumors, so you never knew what was real and what was complete bullshit."

"Yeah, but none of the gossip said his family suffered an unbelievable tragedy and splintered into a thousand pieces," I whisper.

I think back, about my first year at college, how hard it was to get through it. I didn't go to Oregon, couldn't stomach it, even if I did check as many different campus groups and teams as I could find to see if Aubrey was listed as a member. All that time, I'd thought I'd had it so hard. But Aubrey . . . he'd been the one going through hell. But time did help a little bit.

I hug Trey harder. "Jesus, Trey, why couldn't he have told me? Why couldn't I figure it out? I would've waited, would've supported him through whatever he needed to do."

Trey thinks, then clears his throat. "When I first realized I was gay, I felt so . . . alone, scared. I wanted to tell someone, but I couldn't."

"You could have told me. I wouldn't have judged you," I reply, and Trey nods.

"I know that now. But I'd be lying if I said there weren't stupid fears keeping me from admitting it even to myself. I kept saying I was just looking for the right girl. I had to come to terms with myself before I could come to terms with the rest of the world.

Some people are different. They just show their shit to the world and adjust on the fly, letting the whole world watch every step and misstep. I couldn't, but I still loved you, even when I couldn't say anything to you. Sometimes, you just need to find yourself first."

He hugs me again, stroking my back. "Is what I'm saying even making any sense? You going to be okay?"

"It's not quite the same, but I get what you're saying. And I don't know. I don't know what to think," I admit, pushing forward and sitting up more. "Should I take meeting Aubrey again as a sign that maybe we were meant to be together? Or has there just been too much time, too much pain? When I first got here, the answer was simple and I wanted to leave everything in the past. But then things were a little different as we talked and hung out. And tonight . . . I feel like the walls finally came tumbling down, and we were left naked and exposed, and I'm not sure I'm strong enough."

"You're one of the strongest people I know. What makes you doubt that?"

"Because he's right. There are some wounds that you can't heal. They change the landscape of your soul, making you different than you were before. And while Aubrey seems to be doing better, I'm not sure if he's for real or if it's just a reaction to a blast from the past, a chance to reset his path to the one he wanted before it went to hell in a handbasket. And I'm not sure I can fix it, even if I wanted to. I mean, look at us. We live in two different worlds, two different people. I'm a nurse who works down in town, and he's a loner with a lot of baggage, hiding in the mountains. How do we have a future?"

"I don't know Ana. I'm just worried about you. I don't want you to wind up hurt again. And honestly, I don't know if you'd hurt more with him or without him." He pauses and looks out the window at Aubrey's cabin. "By what you're telling me, Aubrey is a man with a lot of demons. I think you deal with enough of that at the hospital and don't need to take that kind of weight on when you get home. But then I picture you without him, what that life could look like. You've been happy the last few years, truly happy. But could you be happier with him?"

"I don't know! I'm just so mad at him for not coming to me when we both know I could've helped him."

Trey strokes his chin and looks down at me, preparing me for a bit of sage wisdom. "Who are you to judge his way of dealing with a tragedy?" Trey says quietly. "Who knows how we would act if we were in his shoes? If I lost you . . . dear God, Ana, I don't know what I'd do, and I'm thirty. How do you think I would have acted as a teenager?"

I stop, wanting to protest, but I can't argue. I really don't know. "I guess you're right. Still, I can't help but think about what could've been."

"You just heard the truth," Trey advises. "You didn't expect him to tell you and then just forgive and forget, did you? You had it right. You need to give it some time."

"So, what should I do?" I ask, afraid of the answer.

Trey gets up, coming over to look me in the eye. "Besides letting it all sink in? What does your heart tell you?"

I cross my arms, shivering as an invisible chill wind goes rippling down my spine. "My heart tells me that I still have feelings. But my mind tells me that this could end up being a bad thing for both of us. If it doesn't work out, at least I have a support system. It'd destroy him . . . for good."

Trey nods. "I think so too. Ultimately, it's your decision. But in my opinion, you did the right thing to tell him you need space to process your feelings. Who knows? In a day or two, you may be ready to talk things out and see where you are then."

I nod. "You're right, and that's what I told him. I'll give us both space to process feelings and make sure we're not saying things we don't mean."

Trey nods, pulling me in for a hug. "Whatever you need, I'll be here for you."

"I know," I reply, hugging him back. "For now, though, I think what I need is to go to bed. Thank you. I love you, Trey."

Trey gives me a final big squeeze then punches me lightly in the shoulder. "Love you too."

THE NEXT MORNING DAWNS BRIGHT AND CLEAR, IN DISTINCT contrast to my mood. I'd lain in bed for hours last night, thoughts swirling like a tornado. Mostly, I'd cried for the boy I'd loved whose whole life got swept away at once, leaving him a man with scars peppering his mind and heart. But I'd slept eventually, deep and restful, my body exhausted after the mental calisthenics. Now, in the light of day, I feel a little better, cleansed maybe, after ten hours of uninterrupted sleep and a lot of processing.

What I decided is that the past is the past and I can't change it, which admittedly sounds a little 'duh' but was a hard thing to accept alone in the darkness last night. I'd spent way too much energy wishing I had a magic wand that I could wave around and change the terribly tragic things Aubrey went through and miraculously make them better and heal those scars. But I can't. That's not in my power. As for my past, while I'm angry at being left in the dark for so long, I'm going to have to let that disappointment go because wishing it wasn't so won't make that true either. Letting those feelings fester might even prolong this hurt, fresh and new to me even though it's been ten years since it all happened.

But no matter what happened in the past, I can do something about now . . . about who he is, who I am, and who we may end up being. I just need, well, I need more time.

Getting up, I pad out to the wonderful smell of bacon and fruit, seeing Trey and Brad sitting down to breakfast. They're both looking at me with questions in their eyes, questions I don't have answers to yet, so I deflect. "Well, I see we've got good and evil all in one meal."

"You know it. But I'm too cute to go to hell," Brad says with a smile. "How'd you sleep, honey?"

"Not bad, considering. Once I fell asleep, I think everything just shut down," I admit. "You guys?"

"Well, it ain't the Ritz-Carlton, but it'll do in a pinch." Brad winks. I appreciate his humor, knowing he's doing it intentionally for my benefit.

"You two got anything planned for today?" I ask as I chew on some bacon.

"I thought you might like to be alone today, so I figured we'd go on a long hike and give you some privacy. But if you need us, you're welcome to come along or we can all stay here. Whatever you need from us, we're your guys," Trey says, reminding me again why he's the best brother a girl could have.

I nod, thinking about it. I know Aubrey is probably going stir-crazy in his cabin, wondering what I'm going to do. And while escaping for a bit for a hike sounds like fun, it's delaying the inevitable. And I've been doing that enough lately. It's time to face the music, or at least face Aubrey to let him know my thoughts and feelings. That's what I would've wanted from him, back in high school and now, so I owe it to him to do the same. "No, you two go ahead. I think I'm gonna check on him, maybe talk a bit more."

Trey narrows his eyes, evaluating me for something, and then he hums, "Good girl, Ana. You can do this. Remember, you're the strongest person I know." He looks proud, and I sit a little taller, his support boosting me up.

Brad snaps, "Is that even in question here? Because you are, by far and away, the epitome of a strong bitch. Able to take on growly mountain men in a single bound, more powerful than a whole flock of divas, and faster than . . . wait, are you fast at anything? I usually think of you as the careful type, you know the ones who do the speed limit even when there's no one around like a good Girl Scout. But that's okay, girl," he says, pointing at me. "You do you, because you are fierce. Embrace it."

It's Brad's version of a pep talk, and surprisingly, it works, even if I tease him a little bit about totally shredding the *Superman* slogan.

It makes us laugh, and even after the guys head out on their hike, the words help me as I get dressed to walk across to Aubrey's cabin.

I knock on the door, nerves fluttering in my belly for some reason. When Aubrey opens up, the butterflies churn in a frenzy. Rex wags his tail as he sees me, and I use him as a distraction, reaching down to pet his head and taking the moment to breathe. "Good morning," Aubrey's voice grumbles above me, the lack of sleep apparent in his voice.

"Good morning," I reply, trying my best to ignore the silent question in his eyes for now. "I came to check on your ankle."

Truth is, I kind of want a reason to see him, even if I haven't made any decisions and it's under the pretense of looking at his ankle. It's been over a week, and it's healing well. Unless he re-injures it, he doesn't really need me. We both know that, but he lets me keep up the charade.

Aubrey nods and walks over to his big chair. "Stiff right after waking up, but it seemed to be loosening some as I made breakfast."

Staying professional, I look at his ankle. "Main thing you need to work on is range of motion. Here's a trick to help you keep mobility. Every few hours or so, use your big toe to write the alphabet in the air, moving your ankle through every plane of motion."

"I understand," Aubrey says, starting to trace letters. "Like that?"

"Yep, just gotta do it a little longer, the whole alphabet," I reply as I start to rewrap his foot. "Let it heal all the way before you start back to your crazy shit like wood chopping again." It's a lame attempt at a joke, but it's all I've got.

Aubrey chuckles, smiling a little. "I'll try. So, uh . . . get much sleep?"

"I did," I reply, feeling an awkward silence descend between us. Actually, it feels like there's a canyon between us, me on one side facing away from him, and him on the other side, silently begging me to turn around and come to him. I can tell Aubrey wants to talk about our feelings, but I'm not sure if I'm ready yet. I'm just . . . afraid and confused. "How 'bout you?"

"I slept some. But it did feel . . . strange," Aubrey admits. "I've slept in that bed alone every night for years, but last night, it felt empty without you by my side."

I flinch a bit, knowing he didn't mean it to sound accusatory but feeling the sting anyway. Aubrey sees the movement, though, jumping in. "I'm sorry, Ana. I'm trying to be honest, transparent about whatever I'm thinking, whatever I'm feeling. You asked for that last night, said I should've told you what happened back then, so that's what I'm doing until you tell me differently. And the truth is, last night, I missed you."

"I appreciate that, really, I do. I spent hours thinking about everything you said, and I considered a lot of things. I kinda feel like we were rebuilding something here these last few days. I don't know if it was a future, but it felt like . . . something. But we built it on a faulty foundation, one with secrets and some seriously life-changing shit. Now that the foundation has been rattled, it seems like the rest is tumbling down. And I don't know if I should stop the collapse or try to save it. God, I am a saver, Aubrey . . . but I don't know if that's the right thing to do here. Maybe we should just go our separate ways and build a future that's easier, with fewer cracks in the structure, even if that's with someone else. I mean, wouldn't it be easier for you to not have to keep apologizing for something you did or didn't do ten years ago? Someone you could just start fresh with and be who you are without this pull to be who you were?"

Aubrey looks angry, his jaw tight and his eyes hard. "No, it would not be easier. You're it for me, Ana. You always have been and you always will be. I'll apologize as many times as I need to, wait as long as you need. But the only future I have is with you or alone. That's not to put pressure on you, but it's the goddamn truth. I like . . . hell, I fucking love that you remind me of who I was. That once, I was whole, but I shattered a million times over. But those little cracks made me who I am now, and if you'll let me, I'd like to see if you can love me when I'm broken the way you did when I was solid."

I can see the changes in him, highlighted in stark relief against the boy in my mind. Where he was once carefree, joking, and easygoing as we foolishly planned a future together, he's now jagged, hard, and unyielding. And his desire is focused on owning me once again. Not desire in the physical sense, although there's always that chemistry sparking between us, but the desire in his heart to be mine and for me to be his.

I search his face, my eyes tearing up at the raw vulnerability there, but it's underscored by the fierceness of a predator. Brad had called me fierce, but he's never seen Aubrey on a mission.

He's a sight to behold. "Aubrey, I can't pick up where we were ten years ago. Hell, I can't pick up where we were yesterday. Things are different. We're different. I'm so sorry for what happened to you."

I shake my head, his story still fresh in my mind, sad and tragic, but reminding me again that he could've contacted me at any time. He knew where I was or at least how to get ahold of me, but he didn't. This whole scenario could've been different if it'd happened ten years ago, five years ago, even weeks ago if he'd reached out to me. But instead, fate intervened and he was *forced* to deal with this. I deserve more than that. I'm worth his wanting me and wanting to make this right because he felt it was time.

I turn to leave, hustling toward the door before I turn into a mess because I feel another ugly cry coming on. But I hear Aubrey rising quickly, his chair creaking as his weight leaves it. "Ana, wait."

I don't stop until his hand catches my arm and he spins me, wrapping his arms around me and holding me close to his body. It feels right, it feels like home, but home shouldn't come with this much heartache, should it?

Aubrey tilts my chin up with gentle fingers. "Ana, you said our foundation is cracked. What if we don't fix it? What if we build a fucking new one, right next to it? One built on the truth, on our love, on who we are now. Build a new us, a new future without totally letting go of the past. I don't want to lose that completely, because I love that we have that, but I want to build a relationship with you for the future."

I sniffle, the tears threatening to spill as I shake my head. "I don't even know how to do that." It's not a no.

Aubrey smiles. "That's okay. I do. I got the prettiest girl in the whole school to go out with me once, using my charm and good looks. I can do it again. Let me do it again, Ana. Let me make you fall in love with me again."

I press my cheek to his chest, asking myself if I'm strong enough for this as he wraps me in his arms. I bite my lip, making the decision that feels simultaneously like the easiest thing I've ever done and the hardest. I nod against his hard muscles, and I hear his heartbeat pick up the pace.

He squeezes me tightly, laying a light kiss to the top of my head. "Thank you, Sweet Ana. I promise . . ."

He doesn't say what he promises, just lets the words hang around us like a cloak of intention.

FOR THE NEXT FEW DAYS, HE HOLDS TRUE TO HIS WORD. I COME BY every morning to check on his ankle, and he's charming and sexy as fuck, which makes me insane.

He brings me flowers, wild ones he picked out in the field himself. I'd yelled at him for walking so far on his almost-healed ankle, but it'd been half-hearted as I buried my face in the bouquet, inhaling deeply.

He warms up stew for our lunch, setting the tiny table in his kitchen for two, even lighting a candle.

He tells me story after story about his time overseas, how he'd realized fairly quickly that he'd done it for the wrong reasons but was determined to serve proudly and complete his commitment. He feels like he at least honored Gabe with those years.

Yesterday, after whipping through his alphabet exercises with such speed and accuracy that the letters would likely have been legible if he'd held a pencil between his toes, he'd told me that he needed to work. I'd tried to veto it, telling him that he needed a few more days when really it was that I needed more time with him. But he'd sheepishly said that it couldn't wait and one of his customers needed the wood. I'd compromised and agreed that he could do it if he let me help. It'd turned into a comedy of errors as he tried to teach me to swing the axe. Ultimately, I'd done the bending and picking up of the logs, moving them from a pile of unchopped to the neat pile of chopped wood while he did the axe swinging and stayed in one spot. It wasn't a perfect assembly line, but we managed with a lot of laughter. It'd felt good, like we were a team again.

Basically, his plan is working. He's charming me, seducing me into liking him once again. Well, I never stopped liking him, but I was mad at him. I guess he's seducing me into not being angry anymore. His apology rings loud and clear, both in his words and more importantly, in his actions. Now, those actions seem more directed toward wooing me than apologizing.

The days have flown by, and I'll admit that we're back to something less adversarial and more akin to friendship, albeit with those blazing sparks we always seem to ignite. It feels like us in the past, just older and wiser.

I've seen the flames in his eyes, watched as he traced my body with his gaze, knowing he's desperate to be inside me again. I want that too. But I need more. I'd told myself that we could be casual while I was here on vacation, but I know, deep down, that was never true. This time, I'm being honest with myself. If I go there with Aubrey again, it'll be a sure sign to us both that this is happening, that *we* are happening. I need to be sure before I give in to that, but he's making it so fucking hard right now.

He's shirtless, tossing a stick for Rex over and over, his muscles flexing and stretching. I'd almost think he was putting on a show just for me, but it seems so natural, goofing off with his dog. Even so, as I sit on the back porch, I can feel myself getting aroused, the slickness between my thighs testament to the power Aubrey has over me. I scissor my legs, readjusting on the seat several times, trying to get relief while at the same time forcing the dirty thoughts deep down.

Aubrey approaches the porch, and I can see a sheen of sweat covering him. I watch a single drop of sweat trace down his neck, getting absorbed by the soft hairs on his chest, and I feel cheated, wish I could've licked it up. *Damn it, Ana . . . bad girl. Slow. You're taking this slow. On fucking purpose*, I remind myself.

I look back to Aubrey's face to see that he's smirking, obviously busting me and my appreciation of his body. He jerks his head to the side. "Come on, let's get a glass of tea. I'm thirsty."

As he walks past me, I can't help but think . . . *me too*. In the kitchen, I collapse to a chair as he pulls out two glasses and a pitcher of tea. He pours one for me, setting it in front of me, then one for himself. He leans against the counter, eyeing me as I drink the whole glass down in one big gulp. "Guess I was thirsty too," I say, laughing, but we both hear the flirt in my voice.

"Ana . . ." Aubrey's tone is darker than it has been the past few days. It's his bedroom voice, the one I know so well, and that instantly makes me wet. Well, wetter. The tension in the room is thick in the few feet between us, and I see the bulge in his pants getting larger.

"I know, Aubrey. I feel it too," I say, my voice breathy, but look at me being all honest and shit, not hiding like I want to. "But we can't. You know it'd mean something, and we're not ready. I'm not ready. Hell, I'm leaving in a few hours to go home."

He growls, "I know. And watching you drive down the mountain is going to be one of the hardest things I've ever done, and that's saying something. But this isn't over when you leave. I'm still chasing you, whether you're next door or in Great Falls. We're still doing this."

That shuts me right up. I guess I had thought this had a deadline, that if I wasn't head over heels by the time Trey and Brad were ready to go, that'd be it. A valiant effort, but futile in the end.

I'm silent long enough as the realization hits me that he continues, "I know you're not ready, and the next time I bury myself in you, I don't want there to be any doubt for either of us. But there are other options. Remember the shower when you first got here?"

My eyes snap to his. Is he saying what I think he's saying? He wants to watch me? That's not something I do in front of people, other than that time, and I hadn't known he'd been there. But I remember his telling me how he'd jacked off in the woods, how I'd wanted to see that.

The question must be in my eyes because Aubrey nods slowly then moves a hand to cup his cock through his jeans. Every action is in slow motion, like he's scared I'm going to bolt. I might. But as he presses his palm to himself, I might not.

"Aubrey," I plead.

"Need me to start it, Sweet Ana? I can do that." He unzips his jeans, slipping them down over his ass and then freeing his cock. It's jutting up proudly, hard and ready with a slick drop of precum pearled at the tip. He grasps his shaft, stroking slowly. "This is what you did to me that day in the shower. You had me jacking off in the woods. Never done that before, but I couldn't help it. You were so beautiful, so fucking sexy. You still are. Can you show me?"

His movements start a rolling heat at my core, and his words are the match, lighting me on fire. With a groan, I unzip my jeans and slip them down and off, my panties following and leaving me bare-assed on Aubrey's kitchen chair.

"*Fuck*, Ana. I can see how wet you are from here. Spread your legs and show me more." His voice is gruff, a demand allowing no doubt to creep in, and I'm thankful for that.

I do as he instructed, prying my thighs wide open and tracing a finger down to my pussy to gather my juices and spread them up to my clit. I toy with myself, drawing circles one way and then the other, loving the way Aubrey's breath hitches as I change direction. I match his pace, moving along my clit as he strokes himself. "Yeah, Aubrey. Show me too."

He groans, squeezing tight at the base of his shaft. "Not yet . . . fuck, not yet. I'm memorizing this. Every swipe of your fingers, every sigh you make, every expression of pleasure on your face. Not because I won't see them again, because I'm going to. I'm gonna see you lost in me again when I'm balls-deep in that pussy. But this is the moment. Right here, this is the moment you admit to yourself and to me that we've got a chance. That this is more than these two weeks. I'm coming for you, baby."

My eyes shoot to his cock, ready to watch the cum burst from it and coat his hand. "Mmm, not like that, although I'm close, fighting it off. I mean I'm coming for you in that I'm chasing you. Forever and always. Wherever you are, however much time it takes, I'm coming."

This time, he can't hold it off, and I watch as the jets shoot out, dripping along his hand as he bucks. I speed up, giving my clit a few sharp smacks with my flattened fingers. "Oh, God, Aubrey," I cry out, falling off the edge into bliss.

Outside my bubble of sparkles, I can hear him. "Fuck, baby, that's it. Come for me, Ana. Smack that pussy for me." I do it, again and again, another orgasm beginning before the last one is even finished, and my body shakes as the waves rush through me. I'm thankful I'm sitting because if I'd been standing, I don't think my legs would've held me.

I'm sprawled out on the chair, legs wide and back hunched as my head lolls to the side. When I can finally open my eyes, Aubrey's gaze is locked on me, his hand slowly stroking his softening cock.

When our eyes meet, he takes one step toward me. I feel the wall between us resurrect . . . just a little. It's not solid and made of brick, but it's there, paper-thin like a shoji screen. He must feel it too. He's still taking the few steps toward me, slow and easy, giving me time to stop him or to bolt, but I don't. I try honesty instead. "Aubrey, I can't take anymore. Physically or emotionally. I can't."

Aubrey stops right in front of me, pulling my hand from between my legs and bending low to catch my fingers in his mouth. His tongue sweeps all along their length, finding and sucking every drop of my cream. My breath catches, my jaw dropping. Aubrey moves his fingers, coated in his cum, and shoves two fingers deep in my mouth, almost choking me. It's not gentle. It's not a question. It's a silent order. *Suck my fingers too.* And fuck, I do it. I do it and I love it.

When we're both clean, we get dressed again. Aubrey doesn't push for more, though I know he wants it. I do too.

"I should probably go," I say awkwardly. "Trey and Brad were planning to leave by two so that we're home in plenty of time for dinner."

I walk toward the door, and Aubrey follows me, placing a hand on the doorknob so I can't open it. "Ana—"

"Don't," I cut him off, scared of what he'll say. If he asks me to stay, I will. But I don't think I should so I don't want him to say a word.

His face pulls taut. "Not that. I understand and I'll wait. I just wanted to say this . . ." And he takes my mouth in a passionate kiss, holding my chin and not letting me escape. It's everything, our childish dreams, our adult desires, our scary hopes for the future, all mingled together in a kiss that tastes like a combination of our cum. When he pulls back, he cups my cheeks. "Let me know when you get home so I know you're safe. Please."

The irony of that statement isn't lost on either of us, but it feels petty to bring it up. It's a sweet request and so I agree. "I will. Stay off your ankle."

He grins, the lie intentionally obvious. "I will." And then he opens the door for me and lets me leave. I'll admit that part of me wants him to stop me, to keep me here and force me to listen like he said he wanted to do weeks ago. But I need to choose this, choose him as he is now, not be forced into a relationship with him by our pasts or his demands. Still, walking out that door is hard, especially when I hear him from behind me. "I'll see you soon, baby. I love you, Sweet Ana."

I don't answer, the tears already spilling. I go out and get in the SUV, and as we pull off, I stare at the cabin, feeling sadness, anger, and loss, but also hope, love, and faith. I came here expecting a recharge and instead confronted the unexpected and got answers to some of the questions that had shaped my early adulthood. I don't know if Aubrey meant it, if he's going to keep chasing me into the city. What does that even mean? I can't imagine Aubrey, huge and wielding an axe as he struts along Main Street like he used to. No, I'm afraid that once I'm gone, he'll revert to his grumpy mountain man self, wild and untamed . . . lost to the woods, to time, to me.

As the cabin disappears into the trees, I turn away, wiping a tear from my eye, leaving Aubrey in my past. For the second time.

CHAPTER 27

AUBREY

*R*ex whines next to me. He knows something is wrong. Sighing, I pick up my bowl and look at the half-eaten pile of old stew before I set it down on the floor. "Go ahead, Rex. I'm not hungry."

It's been hard the last few days. I wanted Ana to forgive me so much, I think I'd built it up in my head unknowingly like some sappy romance movie. Like she'd wrap her arms around me when I told her all the ugly, stupid shit I'd done, brush my hair back, and tell me it was okay and that she still loved me.

Hell, I'd watched as the SUV had pulled away, hoping against hope that I'd see the brake lights tap on and then the door would open and she'd be running back to hop into my arms and smother me with kisses.

But neither happened. Not even when I'd waited by the door, telling myself that when she hit the main road, she'd realize . . . or when she got to town, she'd miss me . . . or when I wasn't at her house, she'd come back to mine.

Ugh, I growl to myself. I'm going fucking nuts around here without her. She'd called just like she said she would when she got home, but that was three days ago. She'd sounded so far away that I'd gone up to the lake that night just to look out over Great Falls. I'd wondered if one of the lights in the town far below was hers. I'd talked to Gabe a bit too, but he basically just called me a dumbass and told me to go get my woman.

I'd agreed with him, but she'd said she was working the next few days. She probably wouldn't want me just showing up on her doorstep without an invitation.

So I've been alone, just me and Rex. He keeps sighing, staring at the door and walking around like he's looking for something, or someone. I didn't think they'd hit it off too well, just a few pats here and there, but he acts like he misses Ana too. "I know, man. I'll get her back though." He huffs at me and turns three times, lying down on his blanket with his eyes glued to the door, keeping watch. "Good boy," I praise him. He doesn't even look at me.

But I've been keeping busy, returning to my usual routine and taking it easy on my ankle. I've even done that alphabet exercise a few times a day. It seems to be helping, the letters getting easier and bigger as the range of motion returns fully.

I cleaned the other cabin, both hoping no one ever rents it again and wishing someone would so that I'd have company nearby to visit with. That's strangely odd for me, but the truth. The silence and solitude that used to be my sanctuary feel empty without Ana here. I don't know how she did that in two short weeks, but the whole mountain feels desolate without her.

Rex and I cleared two huge trees and took the cords of wood into town for deliveries today. The trip was early for my customers but they were pleased to see me and didn't ask too many questions when I'd told them I had business in town and thought I'd make it a two-fer. I didn't have business in town, just needed something to do.

And then I'd driven back up the mountain. Alone. Again.

CHAPTER 28

"*D*r. *Chen, please come to Radiology. Dr. Chen to Radiology.*"

I sigh, closing my locker and double-checking that I have all my stuff. ID, penlight, stethoscope. Guess I'm ready for my shift. But the reality is, I don't want to be back at the hospital.

"Hey, don't worry," Abby, one of the other nurses, says. "Last time I took two weeks off, I was all sorts of discombobulated when I came back. You'll be good by end of your shift though. It all comes back like you never left. Just take it easy."

"Yeah, well, this might be the first time I actually hope something interesting happens," I reply with a small chuckle. "I'm not saying something bad. Just . . . you know, I want to stay busy."

"Just remember," Abby, who's our resident weirdo even on her best days, "when the zombie apocalypse starts, we're going to be the busiest people in town. Stay alert, stay alive." She presses her fist to her chest over her heart in some misguided notion of a salute.

I laugh. At least her quirkiness is good for that. We start shift, but I'm not expecting any zombies or even anything out of the ordinary.

I grab my checklist and med cart, starting my rounds. Everything's normal, and Abby's right, I'm starting to get back into the routine when I come to Eleanor's room, a smile crossing my face at her insistence that I needed a vacation. I wonder what she'd think about how that advice ended up.

There's a new patient assigned to the room, Mr. Benson, who's recovering from a hernia surgery that was complicated by his high blood pressure. "Hi, Mr. Benson. How are you feeling?"

He winces as he adjusts himself, complaining, "I'd be better if I wasn't stuck in this hard bed. How do they expect anyone to rest in these things? Oh, and I could eat. When can I get some real food?"

I check his chart, giving him my best professional smile and letting the grumpiness roll off me. Some patients do this . . . their fear and nerves turn them into demanding children. It's all part of the job. Smile and reassure. "Don't worry, you'll be getting your dinner soon."

I finish my round and go back to the desk, where Abby's on the computer. Mr. Benson's call light is already on. "He's not quite as charming as Eleanor was, huh?" I ask Abby.

"The funny lady in 1264?" Abby asks, looking up. "She left before your vacation, right? Oh, that reminds me. She sent donuts to the whole floor, and there was something for you."

"For me?" I ask, surprised. "Really?"

Abby nods and roots around in the desk for a moment before pulling out an envelope. "Here, I knew I put it somewhere."

I bite back a comment that Abby could have just put it in my staff mailbox, but that's Abby. Taking the envelope, I find a quiet corner of the nurse's station and open it, finding a single sheet of paper inside written in spidery, slightly shaky script.

Dear Nurse Anabelle,

Thank you for your sweet care and laughter during my recent stay. It was perhaps the only thing—besides getting down to Occupational Therapy to look at Dr. Greene—that kept my spirits up around here.

I've decided that life is too short to sit on my ass during my so-called golden years. So I've decided that, even though I'm 71 years old, I'm going sky diving. And if these old bones can handle that, I'm going hang-gliding in Arizona. I saw on TV that they do something called a tandem ride where I just get to hitch along and the teacher does all the hard work. Sounds great to me. I'm going to kick this year in the ass!

If you'll let an old lady leave you some advice, it's this. I spent too many years when I was young talking about all the things I wanted to do and not doing them, for one reason or another. Well, enough of that!

Whatever you do, live your life to the fullest because you only get one and you never know how long or short it's going to be. Go laugh, party, tear the house down. Cry, have your breath taken away. But most importantly, love. Love with all your heart. It's worth it. You'll find your life a lot better when it's your turn to be 71.

Good luck.

Her signature is scrawled at the bottom, and as I fold her letter and slide it back into the envelope, I smile slightly.

"Crazy old bat," I murmur with a smile, but it's a loving comment. I sit back for a moment, thinking about what Eleanor said. Live my life to the fullest? Have I really been doing that?

I know I was the past two weeks. Being with Aubrey, I woke up every morning looking forward to the adventure the day would bring and went to bed every night fully satisfied in every way. I was . . . happy.

Love with all your heart. Live to the fullest.

Okay, Eleanor. Your last advice worked out pretty well for me. Let's see what else you've got.

CHAPTER 29

AUBREY

*T*he sun is unseasonably warm, and I've already peeled off my flannel as I let my muscles warm up. Rex lies by the porch, his tongue lolling as he pauses after chasing a squirrel around for the past few minutes, and he looks content as we get back into our routine.

Honestly, I'd like to take a break. My shoulders ache and my forearms are trembling from the chopping I've gotten done so far, and nothing sounds more inviting than just kicking back in my chair and sipping on some spring water. But if I stop, I just think about Ana, kicking myself for letting her go and having to hold myself back from storming into town to chase her down. I'm not sure that's a bad idea, if I'm honest, but I'm not sure it's a good one either, so I'm trying to hold off on going full-caveman for now.

So I chop and chop and chop some more, filling a big order for one of the bar-b-que places in town who's hosting their annual cookoff. One whole cow and two pigs do not slow-smoke themselves, and they ordered a truckload of wood. A good thing for me, personally and professionally, but it's killing me physically right now.

The aches in my shoulders and back don't replace the ache in my chest since Ana's left, and this morning, for the first time in a long time, Rex had to chase me out of bed after sunrise.

"I really, really should have gotten that log splitter old Earl in town offered me last time I was at his feed and seed," I grumble as I set another log. Even though it wasn't powered, letting gravity and a forty-pound weight do the splitting for me sounds really good right now. "But no, I had to be Mr. Macho. Rex, I think I'm a fucking idiot."

Rex looks up, thumping his tail twice before getting up and going for a drink. I chuckle darkly, thinking he's right . . . and that I'm an idiot about more than just log splitting.

The fact is, I let Ana go. It's been four days, and while I'd told myself to be patient, especially for the days I knew she was working, the two additional days have just about killed me. I've left a *Good Morning* text each day, nothing big, but she didn't even send an emoji back to those. I can't help but feel like that's a bad sign.

"Maybe it's for the best," I tell Rex as I go around picking up the split lengths of wood and taking them over to my old work truck. The bed's about half full, and I need to get the restaurant at least three bedloads before next week. Tossing the lengths in, I know if I can get a move on, then maybe, just maybe, I'll be able to make it.

Dusting off my hands, I go over to the water spout, grabbing my tin cup. "You thirsty, boy?" I ask Rex.

He wags his tail, tilting his head, and barks once.

I down the rest of my water and refill my cup, tossing the water into the air as Rex jumps through it, biting and barking like the water is a living entity. I do it again and again, laughing at his antics, thankful for the levity.

A loud rumbling fills the air, and I look toward the trail, wildly hoping . . . but it's Carlotta, driving up in her ATV. Rex, of course, smothers her in kisses and doggy licks as soon as she gets off. "Hey, Car."

"Ew . . . you're wet! Stop it, you big lovebug!" Car says, fending off Rex before coming over. She's surprised when I come over and give her a hug, patting her on the back. "Well, now, what's this about?"

I shrug, not admitting that I've missed human contact the past few days. Car, though, being her normal self, doesn't let it go. "I see. Does this have something to do with your first guest at the cabin?"

I shrug again, picking up another armload of logs and dumping them in my truck.

"Aubrey?" she asks in that tone of hers, crossing her arms and tapping her foot. "Put the logs down and answer me."

I toss my armload in the truck, turning back to her. "I've got work to do if I'm going to get this order filled. So either give me a hand or leave me alone." Fuck. I can hear it. The short, clipped words, needlessly harsh, and the virtual growl to my tone. Without Ana to soften my edges, I'm back to being a grumpy asshole, falling back into easy habits to shut myself off.

She stares at me, then sighs in exasperation. "You screwed things up with her, didn't you?" When I don't answer, she stomps her foot. "You fucking fool, Aubrey. We don't always get second chances. If you get one, don't let it slip away."

I turn away, grabbing another couple of logs. "It's none of your business."

"Bullshit," Carlotta retorts. "You're family. Of course it's my business, especially when you *need* her."

Anger stirs my chest as I turn to her, my eyes full of fire. I don't need shit from anyone when I'm doing a pretty damn good job of my own self-crucifixion.

"I might not know a lot, but that's one damn thing I do know!" I explode, throwing the chunk of log in my hand toward the woods, watching as it flies before tumbling across the ground. I turn back to Carlotta, who hasn't moved. My voice is softer when I admit, "I know that more than you realize."

She sighs and comes over to me, putting a hand on my chest. "I only want what's best for you, Aubrey."

"I know. I've just been beating myself up and don't really need it from anyone else. I know you mean well."

Carlotta steps back. "Why the hell are you still here, Aubrey? If she means that much, you need to fix it right. Go get her!"

"And if fixing it right means she and I . . . don't end up together?" I ask, scared to voice the fear in my gut. Maybe she got home and realized her life was better without me? Maybe she's home in her apartment, feeling pity for the beast out in the woods who can't get over things that happened a decade ago?

Carlotta pats me on the back. "I have faith in the power of what you feel, Aubrey. Think about it."

Carlotta sticks around another half hour, helping me load the rest of my logs to make my truck three-quarters full before she leaves. I wave as she pulls away on her ATV and I go back to work. Lifting my axe over my head, it trembles before I let it fall to the ground and I slump down onto my chopping block, my head hanging.

Truth is, Carlotta's right, as she often is, and she's pretty damn stubborn. I'm a miserable fuck as it is, and if I don't try to make it right, I'm going to be worse. But I don't know how. There are so many emotions between us, and if there's one thing I'm real fucking good at, it's avoiding those things like the fucking plague. But for her, I'd work it out . . . share and talk and shit.

But even if I could get her to give me a chance, how do we make the logistics work? She lives in town and my home base is here. She's not gonna leave the job she loves, and while I'm doing better, I need the solitude out here. I'm just not cut out to be a city guy in a suit and tie, surrounded by hustle and bustle. Not anymore. I'd go crazy.

But I'm going crazy without her, haven't slept in days. I even found myself dozing with her pillow in my arms, face buried in it to keep her scent around me. I miss the little things, the way her nose flares when she's mad, the softness of her skin against mine, the way just being around her feels like a dose of sunshine straight to my heart.

It was that mental, physical, and soul connection that was as necessary as air . . . and now I'm floating in space again and trying to figure out how to survive when I can't fucking breathe.

Rex whimpers, and I look at him, knowing Car's right. I have to do something to fix this somehow. There's no way I'm going to end up some hermit that lives out in the middle of the wilderness, unbothered by the sheriff simply because I'm too damn ornery, only to die lonely and alone, my body some snack for the pigs or wolves. At one time, I wouldn't have minded that. Could've sold it as dust to dust or some life-cycle bullshit.

It's a fucking scary thought. I go inside the cabin, and something has me reach under my bed. I haven't looked at it in years, not since I put it away, but Gabe's duffel bag was delivered home after he went missing, along with a few letters that the mail hadn't brought yet. I'd tossed them inside, intending to read them one day. Or not. For some reason, I'm drawn to it today, willing to revisit my big brother and his life before it was cut so short.

I pull the bag out, looking at the old, dusty nylon with *O'Day* written on the side in permanent marker.

It's clipped closed and I open it. "I could really use your help, Gabe," I whisper as I reach inside. I root around, just trying to find some hope. I feel my hand bump against his medals, his dress uniform, and the bundle of letters. I discard them all, my hand finding a piece of cloth that I take out, and I realize I've snagged one of Gabe's old ACU pants. It seems like an oddly personal item, but I can't help but hug them, knowing he wore these day in and day out on so many adventures, both good and bad. I did the same in my ACUs. Out of habit, I ranger roll them to stuff them back into the bag. But a crunching sound grabs my attention. Curious, I quickly search the pockets and finally find a folded-up piece of paper in the knee pocket.

I unfold the letter and see the date. It was written the day before our last Skype talk, and I feel like the heavens have maybe opened up to me as I read.

Dear Little Brother,

I know, I know, stupid for me to be writing you when I'm going to be Skyping you tomorrow, or when I can send an email a lot more quickly. But, situations being what they are, I'm currently stuck on guard duty in a foxhole surrounded by sandbags, and the closest computer is about two miles away.

I wanted to take a moment to tell you that I'm proud of you. When I enlisted in the Army, I was a mess. Mom won't tell you, she thinks I shit rainbows, but I'd gotten into drinking, hanging with some people I wasn't supposed to, just stupidity like that.

So I enlisted in an attempt to straighten myself out. And the Army's been more or less good for me. Some of us mature later than others, I guess. That's what our Sergeant says, anyway.

But you seem to be doing pretty well, nothing too crazy. Unless Mom thinks you shit rainbows too and doesn't know about your wild side?

I'm hoping not because that'll mess up your scholarship, man. And I've told everyone about your getting that letter. I'm so damn proud my baby brother got a scholarship to Oregon! Hell, to anywhere. That's your ticket.

I've had a lot of time over here to read. It's better than getting drunk or jacking off to porn. And I've learned a few things, even if I'm not a college douchebag.

And I want you to do something I didn't when I was 18.

Seize the motherfucking day. Carpe the fuck outta that diem.

The world's a scary place, Bro. I've seen shit I shouldn't, that no man should see. And what all this has taught me is to live. Go for the long-shot, take the chance, risk it all, because you might not have tomorrow.

And if you lose . . . fuck, man, we all lose. But at least you lose as a man. You go down standing up. I know you well enough to know that you can live with that.

Hope that helps you next fall . . .

All My Love,

Gabriel O'Day

CHAPTER 30

ANA

"So I told the lady, and I use that term loosely, if you don't get this raggedy ass mop of a wig off your head, I will not be doing your makeup," Brad says as he, Trey, and I relax in a booth at our favorite after-work bar, which happens to be inside the Great Falls resort. It turns out those rumors were true and someone did eventually build a ski resort in our growing little town.

I'm glad some of the other rumors weren't true. Now that I know what really happened with Aubrey's family, some of the wilder tales seem almost disrespectful and salacious.

It's my first day off since getting back to work, and it feels good to have a little bit of relaxation, especially when I'd been sweet-talked into picking up a shift for another department. After my vacation, I've worked over thirty-six of the last seventy-two hours and then slept the rest of the time away, my body seemingly not used to the pace after a couple of weeks off. Actually, now that I do the math, I think I've been home for four days . . . and I slept until six tonight, only waking up because Trey promised me tapas and wine and threatened to kidnap me to get me out.

Brad, of course, is giving zero fucks about my exhaustion as he entertains us and probably half the patrons with his monologue. " . . . and she, get this—she actually snapped at me. *'I'm paying you to do what I want, so do it.'*" Brad mimics a high-pitched, bitchy woman before returning to his slightly less-high, bitchy man voice. "Can you imagine? She thought I was some peon that she could boss around? *Not* how this works, sweetheart. So yeah, I'm not doing that wedding." Brad's a makeup artist—actually, he usually says it like *ar-teest*—who moved to Great Falls from Hollywood and has crazy story after crazy story about celebrities. He does tons of weddings for the resort these days and will tell his clients up front that there's only room for one –zilla and it's him, Bradzilla. No bridezillas, no momzillas, no bridesmaid-zillas. I'm not sure that last one is a thing, but Brad makes sure to cover all the bases because he's rather persnickety about his work and the results speak for themselves.

I laugh a little, the story outrageous enough to penetrate the fog I'm living in. I take a sip of my wine, barely tasting the sweet Moscato.

While having a day off helps, I've been in a funk ever since I left the cabin. I love my job, but even returning to work has done little to lift my spirits, and I'm now physically, as well as mentally, exhausted. But I don't say anything. I don't want Trey and Brad to feel more put-upon than they already are.

"So what happened?" Trey asks, smirking. "Let me guess, you two had a professional discussion, where you made suggestions about other hair options and she listened politely?"

"Honey, please, you know me," Brad replies. "I spun that chair right around and *invited* her to kick it . . . right out of my salon. And she did, with the weakest little hair flip I've evah seen." He flicks his imaginary hair, tossing his head. "I don't need –zillas like that. We're too booked as it is. Two words. High. Demand."

Trey snorts, sipping his beer. "You know, Brad, a little modesty would go a long way."

"I *am* modest. I'm the baddest bitch makeup artist this side of backstage at the Oscars!"

I stifle a sigh as I tune out Brad and Trey's bickering, letting it become nothing but background music as I look around the bar. It's got beautiful wood paneling and marble accents, and the brass along the bar top gleams in the soft light. I find my eyes scanning, looking for something, and my gut does a flip-flop when I see a tall and wide guy with a beard at the bar, but then he turns. It's not Aubrey. Fuck, I'm looking for him. Here, at a bar in Great Falls, as if he'd come down off his mountain for anything. For me.

I take another sip of wine, closing my eyes for a second. Not to doze, but just to focus my mind. I miss him, that much is obvious. Mrs. Smith's letter has been bouncing around in my head, taking root in my thoughts and making me think that maybe we could find a way. It's worth trying at least, because I've never felt like this about anyone, before or after Aubrey. Although, there was never really anyone after Aubrey, just casual relationships and fuck buddies to pass the time. But Aubrey's had my heart so long, it's his. Always has been. And his is mine.

"Uhm, hey . . . Ana?" Trey's voice is hushed as he tries to wake me up, seeing my closed eyes.

I shake my head, holding up a finger. "Shh, not sleeping. Having an epiphany. Hold, please."

I can hear the smile in his voice. "Well, you might want to do it faster. I'm not sure if he's gonna run for the door or run for you."

I crack an eye at his cryptic words, "Huh?"

Trey points toward the door, and Brad is literally bouncing in

247

his seat, arm waving high as he yells out, "Yoohooooo! Over here."

To Aubrey.

He's standing in the doorway, looking uncomfortably out of place in jeans and a flannel, but also like an apex predator in the swanky bar. His height and width clear a path before he even moves toward me. And his eyes are locked on mine, targeted in on me like a heat-seeking missile on a mission.

I'm frozen for a second until Brad tells me quietly, "Girl, you'd better get your fine ass out of that seat and greet your man properly or I'm going to do it for you." He's kidding, of course. He's ridiculously and obnoxiously head over heels in love with my brother, but it's the kick I need to move.

I stand up, and that seems to answer some question I didn't know he was asking because he moves faster now, cutting the last bit of distance in just a few wide strides. He grabs me, lifting my feet from the floor, and I fight the urge to wrap my legs around him, chanting *PDA . . . PDA . . . PDA*. I'm not sure if I'm cheering for it or against it.

But I forget when Aubrey meets my lips with a searing kiss, his mouth hot and minty like he was preparing for this kiss. *For it.* I'm definitely cheering for PDA as I kiss him back, letting my legs wrap around him to hold tight.

He's trying to talk in between kisses, words and smacks intermingled. "Ana . . . I love you . . . missed you . . . fuck." I just mumble back, humming agreement with whatever he's saying, just damn glad he's here. For me.

Trey clears his throat pointedly and Brad shushes him, the noises breaking my reverie a bit as I peek over my shoulder. Trey's eyes are locked on Aubrey as he slides a keycard across the table. "Room 1904, mountain view. Not that I think you're going to care in the least."

Aubrey reaches for the card, a smile on his face, but Trey holds it in place with one finger. "Don't hurt her," he says, his voice hard and threatening.

I have no idea what's happening, how I got here. "What's going on?"

Trey cuts his eyes to me. "You don't hurt him either, Sis."

Before I can answer, Aubrey does a little bounce that moves me higher on his body and turns to walk away, carrying me from the bar that I'm never going to be able to step foot in again. Aubrey yells over his shoulder, "Thanks, Trey. For everything."

We kiss our way up the elevator. I don't know if there were other people in there or not. Didn't care. And when we get to room 1904, Aubrey fumbles with the keycard for a moment before striding inside, kicking and locking the door behind us.

He sets me on the bed and kneels at my feet. "Fuck, Ana. Okay, I don't want to mess this up. Just bear with me."

I cup his face, catching his attention and then his lips with mine. "Aubrey, breathe. Just talk to me."

He nods. "I tried, I really tried to give you space and time like you asked for. But I can't do it anymore. I love you, Ana. You own me, heart and soul. It's not a pretty gift anymore, not shiny and unblemished like when we were kids. It's full of nicks and scratches, dents and cracks. But it's all I have, and it's yours. If you want it. Fuck, say you want it, want me."

The plea is thick in his voice, the fear that I'll actually deny him real in his mind. But I wouldn't, couldn't deny him . . . us. "I love you too, Aubrey. I've missed you. I don't know how it'll all work out, but I want it to. I'll do whatever we have to because you have my heart too."

I can see the light in his eyes flare, overshadowing any darkness there with our love. And he hugs me, pulling me tight to him and gathering me in his arms as he presses his cheek to my breasts. It's Aubrey at his most vulnerable, his relief a physical release as the weight of tension leaves his body.

After a moment, he begins to nuzzle my chest, his grizzled cheek teasing along the fullness of my breasts. My nipples harden in my bra, begging to get closer to Aubrey. His mouth is right there . . . so close. If only there weren't so many layers of clothes between us.

Aubrey growls as I arch my back, pressing for more. "Wait. Ana, baby . . . I told you that the next time I took you, there'd be no doubt that you're mine." He fumbles with something in his pocket and pulls out a black velvet box just like the one from before.

I gasp. "Aubrey, is that what I think it is?" I have a flashback to his opening a box like this and giving me a promise ring. The ring that's still in my jewelry box at home, a precious memento even when it was too painful and seemingly meaningless to wear it.

He opens the box, and it's gorgeous, sparkly infinity loops on either side of a center solitaire. He pulls it out of the box, holding it up as though it's the precious thing he's giving me, but I know better. The ring is a symbol of so much more, of what he's really giving me—himself, his heart, a future.

"Sweet Ana, once upon a time, I made a promise to you that I was going to get down on one knee and give you a diamond ring and that then I'd give you a wedding band and the future we dreamed of. It took me a hell of a lot longer to make good on that promise than I thought it would, but here we are. Anabelle Tucker, will you marry me?"

I'm a blubbering mess, tears running down my face as I sniffle grossly, but Aubrey doesn't seem to mind as I nod, repeating on a loop, "Yes. Oh, my God, yes. Yes, Aubrey!"

He slips the ring on my finger, and we seal the promise with a kiss. We made it, the road longer and more winding than we'd planned, darker and lonelier than we'd wanted, but it got us here, right where we should be.

We kiss again, slowly stripping the clothes off each other as we stretch out on the bed. I lie back, Aubrey looking down at me with so much emotion burning in his eyes. "There's nothing I've wanted in my life more than this moment."

I cup his face, and he leans down, kissing me tenderly before trailing kisses down my throat to my breasts, nuzzling and sucking until I'm swimming in warm sensations. I run my hands through his hair, biting my lip as I push him down. "Please, Aubrey."

He rumbles, kissing a trail down my belly as he moves down, smirking as he reaches my mound. He pauses, looking up at me and licking his lips. "Tell me when you've had enough."

I chuckle, nodding as he lowers his tongue and licks the entire length of my pussy, teasing my lips and making me gasp. Aubrey's never been this tender, this gentle, and it adds a whole new flavor to his lovemaking, sending chills up my spine even as he makes my toes curl.

With quick, passionate licks, he teases my pussy open, licking deep in my folds until I'm left gasping, moaning in need for a release. "Aubrey . . . please."

"Always," he rumbles, withdrawing his tongue to suck on my clit. I cry out, my first orgasm jolting my spine as he traces love letters on my sensitive nub. Instead of stopping, though, he speeds up, sucking and feasting on my clit. "Mmm . . . I'm doing this again."

"And I'd let you do this the rest of our lives," I promise him as he cups my ass, holding me to his hungry mouth while I grind my soaked pussy against his mouth and tongue. Aubrey's answering growl of pleasure tells me all I need to know, and I abandon myself to his tender ministrations.

Aubrey transcends the bonds of sex, each stroke infused with energy and warmth. Every inch of my skin can feel the ripples his tongue is causing in my body, and he never seems to repeat a stroke, dancing around my clit before dragging long licks over the tip and then diving deeply down into my pussy again.

My second orgasm builds deep within me as Aubrey draws me along, letting it build and build without pushing me over the edge. I moan his name again and again, biting my lip as he brings me trembling to the edge before backing off, only to repeat it again. "Aubrey, I need you."

He suddenly withdraws his tongue and sits up, spreading my legs and sliding his cock deep within me as he looks in my eyes. The sudden wonderful stretching sends me over the edge, and my pussy squeezes him, my breath taken away as I clutch at his shoulders, coming hard around his cock.

"That's it, Sweet Ana," Aubrey whispers, grinding his cock deep within me and sending fresh waves through my body. "You're mine forever . . . and I'm yours forever."

He pulls back, lowering his mouth to kiss me before thrusting in again, a long, slow thrust that makes my heart stop. It feels so good, even as it lets my body recover from my last massive orgasm. Our bodies press against each other, skin to skin with no space between us as we slowly, tenderly give ourselves to each other.

Time has no meaning, and my brain loses the ability to even make words as everything becomes emotion, feeling, colors, and sensations. I can feel Aubrey's cock thrusting in and out of me, the bass thump of our heartbeats as we promise each other with more than words ever could to be there for each other. I take all the years of pain, the last vestiges of his survivor's guilt, and his regret over leaving me, and I wash them away, swallowing them before they dissolve in the love that we make between us. Healing him, healing myself, healing us.

I don't know who comes first. We're so joined, not just in body but in mind and spirit, that it doesn't matter. I do know that my body clutches at Aubrey's as he fills me with his warm seed, and that when it's all over, tears of joy stand in both of our eyes.

Aubrey sighs in pleasure as he lies back, and I climb on top of him, resting my head on his massive chest as he holds me in place. "I'm looking forward to tonight and tomorrow, and every day after now," I whisper, running my fingers through the light dusting of hair on his chest. "Because I think it's always going to be like that from now on."

"Really?" Aubrey asks, chuckling. "And if you just wake up one morning wanting it hard, fast, and dirty?"

"That'll be good too. I like you wild, the untamed beast that owns me with power and demand, but I like this too, the softer side of you that owns me with your heart."

"Either way, you're mine," he growls, letting the possessive beast come into his voice a bit. It sends shivers down my spine. I like it. And I love him.

EPILOGUE

ANA

*T*he sun feels good on my skin as I slip into my dress, looking down at the satiny white silk as I run my hands along my curves. "I can't believe this is happening. That's weird, right?"

Brad hums, "Nope, not at all. You'd be surprised the variety of responses brides have to their wedding days. Some are so Zen, you'd think they're overdosed on Xanax. Others are so nervous, you wish you could give them one. Then there are the freak-outs, the angry ones, the perfectionists, and so many more. I think a happy disbelief is pretty tame by comparison." He's rambling, but it soothes my nerves. I'm pretty sure that's why he's doing it.

He's spent the last two hours on my makeup and hair, even though I'd begged him to keep it simple and subtle. Turning to look in the mirror, I see that he's a fucking miracle worker. I look . . . beautiful. Like a bride, sweet and rosy and happy. It'd felt like a lot when he was layering it on, but the effect is a nice balance that highlights my features without looking overdone. He'd wanted to bring his co-owner at the salon to do my hair, but I'd balked at that, telling him to just throw it up in some version of an updo and it'd be fine. But he's outdone himself there too, giving me soft sweeps of hair with tendrils dripping down my neck. I look casual but somehow intentional. Combined with the graceful drape of my dress, it's exactly what I wanted.

Aubrey and I had decided to keep the whole wedding simple and easy, and soon. We especially wanted it soon. Once we found each other and worked out all the baggage from the past, we couldn't wait to get started on the life we'd planned so long ago. We'd wasted enough time.

We've made some adjustments, of course, mainly centered around our jobs. I'm working three twelve-hour shifts per week now, no longer covering for anyone and everyone at the drop of a hat. I keep the shifts on back-to-back days so that Aubrey and I can stay in town at my apartment. Well, it's *our* apartment now. Aubrey uses those days to run errands in town, check in with customers, and scout out new customers for his wood delivery service. The other days, we escape to our cabin on the mountain, working together to chop wood for the orders but spending plenty of time exploring the woods and each other. The rental cabin has been busy too. Brad put the word out in his salon and that's all it took. Those funds have helped cover costs as well.

All in all, it's busy and full, but the best of both worlds for us . . . a little bit of city-living and a little bit of country-living. So far, it's working well.

As I stare in the mirror, Brad flits around me, making little adjustments here and there until he finally stands back, taking me in head to toe. "Perfection. I am a fucking genius!"

I laugh. "And so modest. I'm assuming you meant to say that I look good?" I ask, one eyebrow raised.

"Good? Pshaw, girl . . . I don't do 'good'. You look stunning, and

Aubrey's gonna faint away when he sees you. Lord knows, you two have waited long enough for this. You ready?"

I nod, tears hot at the corners of my eyes.

"Oh, hell, no. Stop that shit right now, bitch," Brad chastises me, fanning and blowing in my face. It works, the tears stopping. "That's better. Alright, everyone's waiting on you. We can still make a run for it if you want though. I'm ride or die for Team Ana, just say the word."

I laugh, swatting at Brad's tuxedo-covered shoulder. "I'm not going anywhere but down that aisle to Aubrey."

"Just checking. I may not be the Man of Honor, but I've got you, girl." It's a tiny dig because I think Brad had really wanted to be my Man of Honor, something I'd never even heard of, but Aubrey and I have taken the rustic simplicity to the max. No groomsmen or bridesmaids, just a small gathering of witnesses here at our cabin, where so much of our story has happened.

This pond has seen our past, our present, and will see our future. I didn't want to get married anywhere else.

Brad and my dad walk with me to the edge of the clearing, just behind the tree line. Brad leans in, kissing my cheek and whispering, "People usually say 'knock his socks off' but who cares about socks? Knock his whole damn tuxedo off. I'd pay good money to see that." A laugh bursts out, and I cover my mouth to quiet it. Brad winks, looking my face over one last time. "Perfect . . . there's that fresh blush you needed. My work here is done."

He turns and walks into the clearing. I hear a snap and music starts playing. I look to my dad, who's smiling at me. "Anabelle, I wasn't sure about Aubrey when you two were kids. He was awesome, but you were so serious, so young. I know this time apart has been hell for the both of you, but I think it's made you more mature, readier to tackle life together. I'm so damn proud of you, honey. I think you've picked a great man, and even better, I think he's picked an outstanding woman."

I duck my chin, his words touching me. "Thank you so much, Dad. And I appreciate your accepting Aubrey back into the family. I know it wasn't easy because you all dealt with the fallout from before too, but we really are past all that now and ready for the future."

Dad grins. "Oh, we're past it now too . . . after I had a little chat with your husband-to-be." My jaw drops in surprise. I hadn't known that Dad had talked to Aubrey. "Trey and me both had a little sit-down with Aubrey, and I think we're all in agreement. He keeps you happy, and everything will be just fine." I grin. The thought of my Dad, who's a rather average-sized man, doing anything to the mountain of a man that is Aubrey is a bit comical. But it's sweet. All of my boys are protective of me. A girl could do worse.

The music shifts, and I realize that's our cue. I take Dad's arm, trying to hold back the butterflies. I always heard that it's normal to be nervous on your wedding day, but I thought it was an exaggeration. Now, my legs quiver more than they ever did at the prom.

But there's something different this time. This time, standing at the front under a handcrafted woven-wood arch is Aubrey, looking so handsome in his black tux that I want to run to him. Far off to the side, and dressed in his own tux, is Rex, staring obediently at Aubrey. Rex looks sharp, and doesn't even seem to mind his human clothes. A fuzzy sensation courses through my chest at the sight and it's hard to hold in a grin as I float down the path.

Making it to the altar, I feel all my nervousness wash away as I take Aubrey's hand and our eyes meet. He mouths to me, "You look beautiful, baby." I beam, feeling the joy of the moment fill me. I'm marrying Aubrey, the way I always dreamed.

I'm surprised I'm not crying as I recite my vows, or as Aubrey says his, bonding us as husband and wife. There's no reason to. The tears are done. There's no need for them any longer. In fact, since the moment Aubrey proposed, upholding his promise of so long ago, I haven't cried a single tear of sadness. There's been plenty of laughter, and a few tears from that, and tears of happiness, but not a single tear of fear or sadness.

"And . . ." the priest says, smiling, "now you may kiss the bride."

Aubrey lifts my veil, smiling broadly as he cups my cheek. "My Sweet Ana. My wife."

I grin back, stepping closer and tilting my chin up. "Aubrey. My husband."

He pulls me in tight, kissing me long and hard. To hell with the standard wedding 'polite' kiss. We pull each other in for a deep, passionate kiss.

"Whoowhee, get it, girl!" I hear Brad hoot.

"That's my sister, asshole," Trey answers.

After another moment, Aubrey and I break our kiss, and he pulls me tight to his side, raising his other fist in victory.

Click. I hear a camera go off, catching the moment . . . the moment we begin our future. Our forever.

Aubrey

EVERYONE'S COMING UP TO US, SHAKING HANDS AND HUGGING US. I know they're family and friends, but it's taking all my self-control to not throw Ana over my shoulder caveman-style and run to the cabin with her. And not come out for days, maybe weeks. Maybe never. I could just live buried inside her, the two of us becoming one . . . forever. Figuratively, with the wedding, the symbolism of the rings weighs heavily on me, a welcome anchor keeping me on solid footing. But also, literally . . . I want to be one with Ana. Now.

But she's smiling, happily chatting with our guests, and I don't want her to miss out on this if it's what she wants. My goal in life is just to make her happy. Today and always.

She floats away, the conversation she's engaged in apparently needing to involve a nurse friend from the hospital. I'm alone for a moment when my parents come up. "Aubrey?" my dad asks hesitantly.

Ana had helped me reach out to my parents, had held my hand through the first tense conversations. The relationship with them is still awkward, but it's better than before. And I have hope that it will improve with time.

"Yeah, Dad?" I answer.

"Congratulations, Son. I hope you two have a long and happy marriage." It's maybe a bit of generic greeting card thing to say, but all things considered, I'll take the progress.

Mom is in tears. "It was a beautiful ceremony." She goes to give me a hug, then stops, freezing like she's unsure whether it's okay. I bend down, gently wrapping my arms around her like I did when I was a boy. I'm definitely bigger now, though, and her tiny arms barely reach up to my neck to hug me back.

"Thanks, Mom. I'm glad you're here," I tell them honestly. It's a start, something to build on, and I know we will.

They wander off, letting other guests come up to congratulate me. Finally, Carlotta approaches and I give her a big hug. "Thank you," I growl, but it's a happy one, maybe more of a purr.

Carlotta hugs me back, laughing. "You're definitely welcome if it gets me an Aubrey hug like this. Not to be dense, but what exactly are you thanking me for?"

I grin. "For everything. For putting up with me when I was a grumpy asshole, forcing me to rent out the cabin, yelling at me to go get Ana when I was moping around, and for the years of business stuff. Just thank you for everything."

She smiles back, teasing. "Oh, all that. Yeah, did I mention that my consulting fees have gone up considerably? You're gonna be indebted to me forever, big guy."

"Whatever you need, Car," I tell her.

"Oh, make sure you guys store the archway correctly when you take everything down. I've already got plans for a new brochure, highlighting the rental cabin as a combination wedding-honeymoon getaway. Folks can get married right here, full-service with food deliveries from town and you setting up the ceremony and reception spaces now that you have experience with it. And then after the wedding . . . right back to the cabin for the honeymoon. Boom. Gorgeous and done." She says it like I've already approved it. Hell, I don't know, maybe Ana did.

"Sounds good. We'll let you know," I hedge.

Carlotta laughs. "Oh, it's happening. The brochure is already done, just waiting for me to drop the pictures of your happy day into the predone spots. *That* is what you pay me for. And you're welcome."

I nod, smiling. I hear Brad has a no-bridezillas clause in his contract. We might need to get ahold of that too.

"Thanks again, Car. And when you're ready to have your own wedding out here, I'll even give you the friends and family discount," I joke, knowing that she's not dating anyone seriously but hopeful she'll find the love of her life soon. She deserves to be happy.

She flips me off, sticking her tongue out at the same time. Sassy but effective as she walks off.

I scan the clearing, looking for my bride, and find her making small talk with a few folks from the hospital. I make my way over, scooping her up from behind and carrying her toward the cabin, at my breaking point.

She lets out a big whoop, then hollers. "Aubrey, we haven't even cut the cake yet."

I yell over my shoulder, "Help yourselves to cake!" and keep going. I can hear the laughter behind us, but I don't care. My sole focus is on Ana . . . the connection we have, the commitment we made today, and the future before us.

Sitting her down on our bed, I drop to my knees and kiss her. I don't care about mussing her up anymore because I'm about to ravage her, so I run my fingers through her hair, releasing bobby pins as I find them and letting her hair fall down. I devour her mouth, not caring if her artfully applied lipstick rubs off. I hope it smears all over me. I'd wear it proudly as a badge of honor that she's marked me.

She's grinning at me, pink and flushed. "You are such a beast, Aubrey O'Day!" I think she means it to be scolding, but it comes out more as a compliment. To me, anyway.

"And you like me just like I am, a wild, untamed beast, but only for you," I say cockily.

She groans, the sound more of an agreement than any words could be.

"Ana, baby, I love you. But if you have anything on under this dress that you want to keep, you'd better take it off now, because I'm about to fuck you right here, right now, in this white dress. Ana O'Day, my wife. My Sweet Ana."

She's already scrambling to strip before I get the words out. Our future starts right now.

The End
Make sure to check out the other books in this series.
Irresistible Bachelor Series (Interconnecting standalones):
Anaconda || Mr. Fiance || Heartstopper
Stud Muffin || Mr. Fixit || Matchmaker
Motorhead || Baby Daddy

EXCERPT: MOTORHEAD

BY LAUREN LANDISH

MCKAYLA

Looking up at the neon sign that dominates the sunset sky, I whistle softly. Only one thought goes through my mind. *Ho-lee Shit! I can't believe I did it! Well,* **we** *did it.*

I'm standing in front of the Triple B Salon, in awe of the magic that Brad and I have been able to work in such a short period of time. When we took over this place, it had been sitting empty for almost a decade. The problem was that nobody really knew what to do with a former drive-in hamburger restaurant that someone stuck on the county register of historic landmarks because John Wayne used to be part-owner. You can't make a lot of changes to a place like that.

Then there's just the pure insanity of our idea. Most folks in the beauty industry flock to Hollywood, eager to work on celebrities and have their names in the rolling credits of a TV show. If you don't go there, you want to make it in New York, where the celebrities are just as numerous, but you also have a possibility at fashion industry fame. Getting your scissors on the locks of a supermodel is a lifetime achievement for some stylists.

Brad, my business partner and the funniest bitch I've ever known, and I both did that for years. We hooked up soon after he came to LA, our styles and personality just clicking fabulously. Brad mostly handled makeup, but he can snip a bang too. Meanwhile, I was the follicle genius, turning rat-nested, hungover A-list sluts into red carpet stunners. We worked the Hollywood scene doing movies, TV shows, awards shows, and more. I've had my fingers on more heads than a porn star gets her fingers around cocks. Name me a star who lives in Los Angeles, and I can probably tell you their hair care secrets— who's got gray hair, who needs some extra highlighting, and whose hair isn't even theirs. For quite a few years, I kept Hollywood's secrets and dealt with their bullshit quite nicely.

But last year, after a few things happened on a reality TV show that just left us feeling too creepy-crawly, the bug to settle and have something to call our own got its claws in us, and now, here we are. I was surprised when Brad agreed to come with me, actually. I thought that, coming from a rather hoity-toity East Coast background, he'd found heaven in Los Angeles. But here we are.

After some research, we couldn't really decide, so fate intervened. After a call from my friend Emily, who ironically triggered my sudden urge to get the fuck out of the California, we ran away from LA to Great Falls, a picturesque little town she'd told me about. It was where she and her now fiancé, Hayden, went the weekend after he asked her to marry him, and it's just north of where she lives now. It's a beautiful town, with a length of Main Street straight out of the 1950s, a brand-new luxury resort associated with the nearby ski area, and a vibrant arts scene that's been famous since Norman Rockwell was painting.

Ironically, we won't be giving up all of our Hollywood connections. The state has been doing a lot to try and get filmmakers to bring production to the state, and not just cable dramas or B-movie action flicks. There's been a ton of movies filmed out there over the past few years. Chances are, if you've seen a small town scene that was going for that American sense of nostalgia over the past few years, it was filmed somewhere in or around Great Falls. It's enough to give some people what my grandmother liked to call 'airs'. Still, there's a certain small town charm to Great Falls, and most people actually say hello to other locals they pass.

Talk about a change of pace! And that's why Brad and I chose this storefront. Sure, there were a ton of challenges with the historic landmark issue, but it's right in the middle of the main road leading up to the resort, where we can serve both the upper-crust tourists and the middle-class townies. And the landlord's been a sweet man, who told us, "As long as the county landmark people don't shit themselves, you're free to do whatever you want to fancy up the place."

When the landlord said that, I was a little terrified about what Brad would do. After all, I've seen some of his date photos. But I shouldn't have worried. Brad's always been artistic, even before he started focusing on makeup, and I have to admit that the result of his interior design vision is spectacular.

From the street, the big sign streetside has only been modified. The classic cowboy that has been there for fifty years now holds a pair of scissors instead of a Winchester, and the neon underneath reads *Triple B Salon* instead of *Duke's Drive In*. We've kept the old-fashioned pull-in spaces as parking, while the kitchen and sit-down diner area were gutted. Three black- and white-striped awnings catch your eye, drawing your eyes through the huge plate-glass windows to see the crisp white salon chairs and bubblegum-pink walls. The pink was my only demand . . . well, request, because demanding things with Brad is a surefire way to start a riot. And he fights dirty, too. He's not above taking a can of Aqua Net and using it like the LAPD uses pepper spray.

So pink had to be a suggestion. But it's my current favorite color, and the girliness of it contrasts perfectly with Brad's preppier style, giving the impression of chic extravagance. Besides, it gives the whole thing a sort of throwback vibe too. Clear out the salon chairs, and I could see someone doing a classic sock hop instead. We're just missing a baby-blue Chevy Bel-Air parked out front. I thought about it, but Brad and I both decided we weren't *that* throwback.

With a happy sigh, I look up and down the street for Brad, who was supposed to meet me here ten minutes ago. My best guess is that he's still working on making his eyebrows perfect. The man's got one flaw to him and that's eyebrows that would make Hepburn herself go running for a razor. But we've got to do our last walk-through to be ready for the grand opening this weekend. Getting the business license was harder than dealing with the historic landmark people. And we've still got some work to do, fucked up eyebrows or no fucked up eyebrows. It's why I'm dressed down right now in jeans and a t-shirt instead of my normal fabulousness. I've got fucking work to do.

As I scan, I spot a beautiful motorcycle parked outside the mechanic shop across the street. I know jack shit about bikes, but I know a work of art when I see one and have a momentary daydream about riding down the highway with that bad boy humming between my legs. Actually, the idea of any bad boy humming between my legs has me smirking a little. It's been too long since that's been a reality for me unless you count my favorite vibrator. Still, riding a bike like that, holding onto a warm hunk while the vibrations send ripples through my pussy, and wrapping my arms around his six-pack abs . . . sign me up!

My fantasy is cut short when I hear a little *ahem* behind me. Turning, I spot Brad, who looks like a walking fashion show, as always, with his slim khaki pants, plaid button-down shirt rolled to his elbows, and polka dot bowtie. And his eyebrows. Yep, I knew it. Freshly done behind his stylish bold black frames. "Glad to see you made it."

"Me? I wasn't the one spacing out!" Brad says with a laugh. He catches sight of the bike across the street and whistles. "I'd love to ride that hog!"

"The bike or the owner?" I ask, and Brad gives a smirk. "Gotcha. Doesn't make a difference. You'll just pick the hotter one."

"Damn right. So, honey, you ready for this? We're T minus forty-eight hours till the grand opening. I almost can't believe it! Who'd have thought we'd be out of Hollywood, in a little town, doing bridal hair and prom makeup again? Or more importantly, that we'd be so happy about it?"

I look at him carefully, evaluating because that sounded a little tight. Brad's always sarcastic, snarky, and hilarious, but that's a bit over-the-top even for him. "You okay? We've been planning this and busting our asses for months and you've been a hundred percent with me the whole time. You having last-minute second thoughts?"

Brad sighs as his eyes settle on the storefront's embossed nameplate that we put right next to the front door. "No, not second thoughts, just nerves I think. We're on our own, you know? It's always been someone else's risk and we just cash the checks. I'm a magician with a makeup brush, and you've definitely got a flair with hair, but business owners? I'm lucky if I remember to pay my own damn bills, and now we've got this too? Knowing my luck, we're going to be prepping some double-booked wedding because one of us brain farted, and that'll be the exact time that the power company cuts the damn juice just as we've got three harpy bitches with chemicals in their hair. Just . . . it's a lot of pressure and I want us to do well."

I have to hold back a smile at Brad's language. His flamboyancy isn't a put-upon act . . . well, most of it. Harpy bitches? Who else besides Brad would come up with that? Instead of smiling, I give him a light punch in the middle of his well-defined if skinny as hell chest.

"Do well? Fuck 'well', honey buns. We're going to *rock* this shit. We'll hire an office helper to do the bookings and pay the bills so we can do what we do best. If we do well enough, we can even make sure the office help is six foot two, styled like a mofo, with an eight-pack of abs and a big package for you to drool over. It's gonna be epic, Brad. You'll see."

"Oh, great," Brad mock-complains as I give him a huge smile, wrapping him up in a hug. I can feel the tension leave him, and he takes a big breath, hugging me back. "You're going to get us a lawsuit for sexual harassment."

"It's only harassment if it's unwanted," I joke back. "He's gonna love me, no doubt about it. You? We'll just have to wait and see."

Brad laughs, letting go of me and looking inside at the salon. He nods as if to himself and pats me on the back. "All right, let's check everything out so we're good to go for Saturday."

Unlocking and opening the door with a dramatic 'ta-da' from Brad, we step inside . . . and it's perfect. Even though we've been here off and on through the renovation process, it feels different to see it cleaned up and devoid of workers and realize just how fabulous of a job Brad has done. "So, what do you think?"

"I think if makeup ever falls through on you, you've got something hot waiting in interior design," I reply honestly. Walking through the reception area with throne-like hot pink leather chairs, I see that there are already magazines fanned out on the sleek metal tables. Further in, the black floor gleams under the spinning white chairs that face ornate mirrors that light up from behind, creating a shadow of lace on the pink walls. The hair wash station is set up with all of my favorite products, the same ones lined up perfectly on the shelves in reception to sell to customers. A lot of people would be surprised how much product sales can add to a salon's bottom line.

Brad's makeup station has quilted leather drawers to organize all of his products, with more hidden in cleverly disguised drawers around the station because he has so many doodads that he'd never find a way to look sleek if it were all visible. As I do a spin in the middle of the floor, I feel like I should be wearing a full skirt instead of jeans, letting it all twirl out and around like a Disney princess.

I'm so giddy that I squeal in delight. "Brad, it's so, so gorgeous and fancy and amazing and . . ." I'm rambling, trying to think of more adjectives, when I realize that he's staring at a wall in the reception area. Actually, as I freeze my spins, I see that he's ping-ponging his eyes from one wall to the opposite one, tapping a finger against his lips. "What's wrong?"

"Babycakes, we have a problem," he says, running a hand through his hair. "We need art. Here and here," he says as he points to one wall, then the other. I walk back toward him, eyes flicking back and forth like his did. The walls are bare, but I don't mind the minimalist nature of the reception area. I've done too many haircuts in crowded trailers or chaotic backstage areas with shit going off everywhere. A little minimalism sort of works for me.

"I think it's fine, but we can rush order some if you want. Just remember, we can't cover up the plaque from the county."

Brad hums, glancing over at the plaque, which we installed to note the historic nature of the salon building. "No problem, and I want. I definitely want. It'd be great if we could do black-and-white portrait shots of us, just a little mark of our style to give it a little personality."

I laugh, gesturing around me. "Uh, Brad, personality is in full effect here. But yeah, I'm never opposed to a little photo shoot." I fluff my big, juicy curls a bit, putting on a model's accent. "Just tell me where to stand and where to smile at the camera and we're good. But we probably can't get anything done for this weekend unless we did pictures right now. One thing, though."

"What?"

"This pink is too damn good to be kept black and white. I want the hair colorized."

Our eyes meet for a beat as our faces break into huge grins, and without a word, we both run for our stations to get prepped. Touching up my curls and adding a fresh pop of color to my lips and eyes, I ask, "Whatcha thinking for the shots?"

Brad looks thoughtful, then says, "I'm gonna grab a vest from my apartment first, but we'll need to head out to the woods. I want a nature shot, maybe take a stool to perch on, and get the sun behind me. You got any ideas what you want?"

With a flash in my brain like a lightning bolt being hurled into my head from Zeus himself, I know what I want. That motorcycle across the way is perfect, and in black and white, it would be all sexy curves, just like me. We could even colorize the chrome. It'd go with my hair in a great way. Grabbing the camera we use for before and after shots, we head outside into the bright morning light and walk across the street.

Brad sees the resting machine and agrees it's perfect. I knock on the door to the shop to see who the owner is, but there's no answer. Great. Find my dream, and nobody's home. Kind of like most of my dating life, actually.

I look over at Brad, who's admiring the curves but staying well away. To hell with it. I untuck my t-shirt and tie it tight under my boobs. I'll make this good. "All right, so I just won't touch it. I'll stand in front of it and the owner will be none the wiser. You good?"

Brad gives me a dip of his head, but I can tell he's not comfortable with this. "I'm not saying yes so that I can keep plausible deniability if the owner sees the pic and throws a shit fit, but you should definitely stand over there for the shot." He gestures toward the motorcycle, and I can't help it, I get into it. I've seen plenty of other women make love to the camera, and I decide to hell with it, I'm gonna do while the doing's good. I smile and begin posing, popping a hip out to face the camera full-on, turning and leaning forward to stick my ass out.

As I pose, I get caught up and lay one gentle hand on the handle-bars and the other on the seat. Brad continues clicking away, getting into his inner fashion photographer himself.

"Yesss, girl. Look here" —*click*— "and off toward the front tire" —*click*— "arch your back . . . that's it, now caress that chrome like it was the perfect cock."

I reach out, biting my lip and looking over my shoulder when suddenly, I hear a deep, sexy, but still furious growl. "What the fuck are you doing to my motorcycle?"

EVAN

I rub at my temples, washing down the second of the damn horse pills the VA gave me for bad times with a swig of coffee and wincing. It's already been a shitty day, and it's only eleven A.M. Even on good days, I'm getting no more than four hours of sleep a night, and I know my caffeine habit is getting the best of me. But I didn't sleep at all last night, not that that's anything new since I got back from my last tour and the nightmares started.

Well, nightmares might be putting it lightly since the dreams that plague me are more like sleeping reenactments of the worst moments of my life. I see them all the time, the ghostly images that I know are supposed to just be in my head but sometimes seem so damn real at two in the morning. I rolled out of bed at seven simply because I couldn't stand to lie around anymore. I felt like an extra in *The Walking Dead*, but I sucked it up and drove on, as we used to say. I took a shower, skipping the shave today because fuck it, and got ready to hit the day because that's what you do when you're responsible for helping out at a family business that provides both a needed distraction and the funds to survive.

What you don't do is what too many of my buddies have—fall into drinking, drugs, and for some of them, eating the end of a pistol barrel. I can't call them pussies. Some of those guys were the hardest-core motherfuckers any man could hope to meet. But that's not me. I'm not looking for congratulations, but damn if I couldn't use a little slack today.

Not that I've gotten any. As soon as I walked into the shop, my brother TJ started giving me shit about not pulling my weight when I drag-ass in an hour late and run off potential clients with my lack of customer service skills. "You can't just get by with being good with a wrench, goddammit!" he yelled at me. "You have to actually talk to people!"

He's probably right, but the last thing I need is my little brother telling me how to live, especially when he's had a cushy life here at home, never having to battle a damn thing other than some nerves when he asked his flavor of the week out for a drink or a fuck, her choice.

So I'm already near my boiling point when I walk outside to grab another coffee and a cigarette to clear my head so I can tackle the engine rebuild on my schedule today. It's not a bad one. Old GM small blocks are pieces of cake compared to European builds, but I want to be able to focus, and that means coffee. I just step out the door when I see some chick damn near lying on my bike.

Before I can even think, all of my anger from the morning boils over as I charge forward like a raging bull, exploding from deep in my chest. "What the fuck are you doing to my motorcycle?"

I see her jerk back, startled by the noise. Who does she think she is? Hands off my baby. I built this cycle from the frame up, and nobody, not even my brother, gets to touch it without my say-so.

The woman turns to face me, a placating smile already on her red-painted lips. "I'm so sorry! It's just such a gorgeous machine, I couldn't help myself." She dips her chin and pulls up one side of her smile a bit more, her head tilted slightly, and I can tell she's used the practiced pose to get her way more than once. Considering the smooth, creamy skin she's showing off under the tied-up t-shirt she's wearing, she probably doesn't have to ask twice either.

I huff, but that act isn't going to work on me. "It is gorgeous. Know what else it is?" I wait a half-beat, but before she can even open her mouth, I answer my own question. "Mine. Back. The. Fuck. Up."

She's taken aback by my vehemence, her eyes going wide as her full lips round, taking in a gasp of air. She is hot, not like most chicks I see around here. I mean, she's rocking metallic pink hair like it's nobody's business, and the jeans she's wearing do look natural on a bike like mine, but that's only if invited first. She stutters and swings off my bike, letting me see the rest of her, and she's no less hot in that tight t-shirt that shows off a front side nearly as curvy as her backside. "Again, I'm sorry. I knocked on the door to ask but nobody answered—"

"So you knew that it wasn't right but went ahead and touched my bike anyway? Yeah, you sound really sorry, Princess."

I can see the switch flip in her eyes instantly as she goes from nicely trying to apologize to nuclear. Guess she's got a button to push.

"I'm not a damn princess, asshole," she fires back, turning and jabbing a finger at me. "I just wanted to take a picture with your bike for our new salon. I'm sorry I touched it. Obviously, that's my bad. But you don't have to be so fucking rude."

As she rants, I'm suddenly struck by how the fire crackles in her wild eyes and the flush moves down her cheeks. She's gesturing all around with her hands like some caricature, pointing at me, the bike, and vaguely across the street. She's *cute* when she's pissed.

I can't help but laugh, but it's a snarky dark chuckle that she takes as my still being rude, though it wasn't really my intention. She plants her balled-up fists on her hips while the guy, who's looking like he wants to be anywhere *but* here, shakes in his overly tight khakis, holding his camera like a shield.

My eyes are mostly filled with the pixie in front of me that's about to go apeshit on me. "What? What the fuck are you laughing at?"

I can't help it, her boldness makes me laugh even harder. "Did you really just try to tell me that you're not a Princess? Have you seen yourself? Pink nails flicking all about, and makeup done like you're in a damn movie? And that hair? You look like a Powerpuff Girl or something. You're a walking, talking Pink Barbie Princess, honey."

Her voice drops to a throaty growl, and I know for sure that she doesn't appreciate being called Princess. A part of me that isn't pissed off and caught up in my throbbing headache sort of wonders why. "Don't call me Princess. If you want to address me, my name is McKayla, but I think we'd be better off if you just didn't call me anything, ever again. Sorry for touching your precious bike, asshole."

With a hair flip, McKayla pivots in her heels and stomps away. She's obviously pissed as fuck, flipping me off as she talks faintly to herself about what a jerk I am. But with every stomp, her ass bounces and sways, creating a sexy image if I ever saw one.

I cross my arms and watch her for a moment, one corner of my lips sneaking up just a bit until I feel eyes on me. I realize that the guy is still there, his polka-dot bowtie somehow adding that touch of absolute ridiculous unreality that makes me know for sure this isn't some waking nightmare. I'd never imagine this. He's watching me watch her, and I raise an eyebrow at him, not saying a word.

"So. That's McKayla and I'm Brad," he says in a lispy voice that certainly advertises which team he swings for. "We're the owners of the new Triple B Salon across the street. And who did we have the pleasure of meeting today?"

I nearly gape in disbelief. Shit. They're literally my new fucking neighbors. Of course they are, because that's how fucked up my life is. TJ's gonna kill me. With a hearty sigh, I look up to the sky, silently cursing whatever joke fate is trying to play on me.

Looking back at Brad, I relent and offer a hand. He shakes, and despite his effeminate aura, he's got a good grip to him. "I'm Evan Hardwick. My brother TJ and I own this garage. Looks like we're neighbors. Welcome to the neighborhood. But don't touch my bike."

Brad nods, taking his hand back. "Understood. Loud and clear. FYI, I'm the nice one. You've heard the expression 'a bark worse than the bite'?"

I nod, thinking I know where this is headed. "She's feisty but a little playful puppy inside?"

Brad shakes his head, surprising me. "McKayla's got a hell of a bark, but her bite is even worse."With a hum of disapproval, he gives me a look and then offers a little finger wave and sashays across the street toward the new storefront. I watch him walk in the door and then hop on my bike. I light it up with a grumble of the engine, the aggressive snarl mirroring my mood perfectly. I pull away from the shop, gunning it as I turn a half-circle and double-shift as I pass the salon window, the engine going from a howl to a full scream. Hidden behind sunglasses, I cut my eyes over to the salon. As I pass, I tell myself that I won that little battle of the day as I fly out to the highway, needing the wind in my face to let go of the shitty morning.

MCKAYLA

Brad and I stand in front of the small crowd, and when I say small, I mean like ten people and we're two of them. It's disappointing, to say the least, and I feel slightly ridiculous in my sexiest dress, petticoat, and heels. I spent at least an hour getting ready for this, and I've seen bigger crowds for a junior high school girls' volleyball game.

At least the guy from the newspaper is here. He said that we'll make tomorrow's weekly edition if I can give him a few good quotes. He's sort of cute, in a nerdy way, but he seriously needs some work on his hair. From the looks of it around here, dog clippers are considered a viable tool for hacking everything down to a quarter-inch buzz cut . . . but I can't do that.

Still, it's our grand opening, and Councilman Jaxson Kennedy, the suited representative from the city council, stands next to us as I thank everyone for coming and welcoming us to their town. "When Brad and I first decided on Great Falls, the first thing some of our friends said was 'Where?' But over the past few months, we've found ourselves welcomed warmly by this beautiful town, and I can say I understand why they call this place the friendliest town in the US. Thank you, and I hope everyone enjoys the Triple B!"

There's a round of light applause like it's a golf tournament, and then Jaxson hands us a laughably large pair of fake scissors. We pose for the local newspaper reporter to take a picture, and I remind myself that I need to deliver some better quotes than what my welcoming speech apparently was. Brad and I cut through the large ribbon in front of us, and we're officially open for business.

I take a moment as we step inside, deciding that ten people is enough. We've done it. I look over at Brad, and he's feeling the same way. Our smiles are huge, stretching across our faces in amazement at what we've already accomplished, so excited to get rolling with our new lives and new business in our new town. Setting the giant scissors behind the counter, I invite everyone into the salon and begin to mingle with the few folks present, introducing myself to what could be our first customers.

I approach a stunning blonde woman whose highlights make me wonder who I'm up against in town. She's seen someone with some good skills. Still, I know I can do better. I only hope that the people around Great Falls can tell the difference and be willing to pay for it too. I offer my hand and an introduction. "Hi! I'm McKayla, the Queen of Coifs, as my partner, Brad, calls me when he's in a good mood. Nice to meet you."

She shakes back, a polite smile warming her face. "Nice to meet you, McKayla. I'm Rose, your neighbor from a few doors down. I own the Mountain Rose Boutique store. Welcome to the 'hood!"

"Thanks for the warm welcome. I'll have to stop in to your store and see what you have. Admittedly, I get most of my stuff online, but it'd be great to get some things locally too."

"I'd love to have you come by. So, Brad's your partner?"

I laugh, glancing over my shoulder at Brad, who's being himself and already has a woman in his makeup chair doing a demon-stration of his skills. "Trust me, it's not *that* kind of partnership. Brad's not into women."

Rose chuckles. "So what does he call you when he's *not* in a good mood?"

I grin. "Let's just say that Triple B has different meanings. I like to say it stands for *Beautiful Badass Bitches*. When Brad's in a bad mood, the first two B's can change to *Basic Bossy Bitches*, which is funny because we're both anything *but* basic."

Rose giggles, and I feel that click that tells me I've made a friend. She smiles, and it's smooth conversation, putting me right at ease that I've done the right thing moving here and setting up shop, especially since her highlights are apparently natural. Not too many people are that lucky, that's for damn sure, and I'm doubly lucky that I don't have to worry about competition.

I shake hands with just about everyone, making sure I give the newspaper reporter plenty of good quotes. It's easier than I thought. Talking with Rose has relaxed me, and I'm able to be more of myself. I try to avoid namedropping too much, but let's face it, I'm trying to bring a little bit of Hollywood glamor, so I just try to be humble about it.

After the newspaper guy finishes up, snapping a pair picture with me and Brad, Jaxson comes over offering a pleased smile. "Well, Councilman," I say, grinning, "what do you think? Think we'll add something to Great Falls?"

"I'd say things look like they're going very well—maybe even get you some new business right off the bat. And please remember, just call me Jaxson. Maybe I can be your first customer."

I nod politely, feeling like he's being nice but getting a little tingle like he's flirting a bit with me too. Normally, I don't have a problem with it, but he just doesn't do it for me. "Sure thing, Jaxson. Don't want to steal you away from your current hair-dresser, but I'd be happy to give you a cut and let you decide from there. I appreciate the city council welcoming us to town."

"I don't think my current barber would be too upset since he cuts the hair of most of the guys in town," he says. Jaxson smiles, and again, there's something in that smile that ticks a little circuit in my brain. "But he's not nearly as pretty as you are, so I think I'd likely choose you even if you shaved me bald." He leans in to whisper conspiratorially, "But please don't."

Yep, he's definitely flirting with me now. I heard the compliment, but even as it's an ego boost to be noticed, he just doesn't light me up inside. No butterflies for the clean-cut guys. It's one of the first things I learned about myself in high school when all the other girls were swooning over jocks and big-man-on-campus types. Those guys don't do it for me.

Nope, I might be silly and I might be weird, but give me a rebel with—or without—a cause, a hellion, the brooding misfit who never walked the straight and narrow. Yeah, that's the guy who'll get me going, even when I know from experience that it's a bad fucking idea and only leads to heartbreak. But it gets me every time. At least they're usually honest about their fucked-uppedness.

My brain flips back to the asshole on the bike across the street. My eyes track over to the shop Brad told me he co-owns, but it's closed. I can see the lights are on inside, so they must be open for business, but the big bay doors are pulled down. Yeah, that's more my type of guy. Obviously, he's got issues, including a huge one about nobody touching his damn bike.

If only he weren't an asshole. I have a moment of disappointment, but before I can analyze it too much, I realize Jaxson is still talking. " . . . been on the council here for years, grew up down in the community college area, but came north after I graduated, and I never left. I'm hoping I can use my business degree and council experience for advantage and become mayor, then who knows? Maybe go bigger for a state rep seat."

I smile and nod, knowing that to most people, a sweet guy with ambition like Jaxson is a dream come true. He should be the type of guy every woman wants. He's a respectable adult and all, but even tuning out for half of his speech, I'm already a teensy bit bored, if I'm honest with myself. All I can think of is the fact that any haircut I give this guy is going to be over styled, totally conservative, and as boring as watching what little grass there is underneath the front windows grow. It'll be the kissing babies and shaking hands haircut, offensive to nobody except me and Brad.

Still, I want to be polite, and a customer is a customer. "That's quite a life plan you've got there, Jaxson. Sounds like you've got it all figured out."

Jaxson gives me another grin. "Yep, a one, five, and ten-year plan. Got to have both short-term and long-term goals and chase them with focused drive, sheer will, and hard work. It's all part of the secret, you know? You have to ask, then visualize and believe, and you'll receive it. Law of attraction and all, you know?"

I distractedly fidget with my necklace, knowing I've stepped in the deep end now. I realize I've made a mistake when Jaxson's eyes zoom in on the beads, just inches away from my cleavage. Shit, didn't mean to do that. I lower my hand, regretting my accidental signal. I get it. I've got some legit boobs . . . but not everyone gets to see them.

"How about lunch after everyone filters out?" Jaxson asks. I'm just about to apologize and say no when he continues. "We can go to the diner and I can introduce you to most everyone in town. It's a busy place for Saturday's lunch rush."

I so don't want to do this. I'd rather be in the salon, trying to make my impression the old-fashioned way, giving haircuts that'll leave people stunned and customer service that'll leave them wanting more. But looking around, I see no one waiting, and I know Brad can handle anything that happens. I sigh inside, knowing that I need to do this for the business connections.

I don't want to lead Jaxson on, but I do need to get out and get my face known. Suddenly, I'm struck with genius. To hell with it. We can officially open tomorrow. "You now what, Jaxson? That'd be great. Brad and I would really appreciate your introducing us to everyone. You really take your council role as welcome wagon seriously!"

Before he can correct me, I turn, hollering to Brad. "Hey, honeybuns!" I draw out the word to emphasize the endearment on purpose. "Jaxson offered to introduce us to some folks over lunch. Isn't that nice of him?"

Brad looks at me, immediately hearing our code word for "rescue me" that has come in handy more than once at a club when a guy wouldn't take the subtle hint and go away. It's a desperate plan, but hey, whatever works.

Brad straightens up, adding a little bit of bass to his voice. "Why yes, dear. That is rather nice." He looks at me with a shit-eating grin and I know he got the message.

I also know that once he and I get to hang out alone again, I'm so going to hear about this.

Want the rest? Get it here!

ABOUT THE AUTHOR

Other books by Lauren:

Irresistible Bachelor Series (Interconnecting standalones):

Anaconda || Mr. Fiance || Heartstopper

Stud Muffin || Mr. Fixit || Matchmaker

Motorhead || Baby Daddy

Get Dirty Series (Interconnecting standalones):

Dirty Talk || Dirty Laundry || Dirty Deeds

Connect with Lauren Landish
www.laurenlandish.com
admin@laurenlandish.com

Join my mailing list (www.laurenlandish.com) and receive 2 FREE ebooks! You'll also be the first to know of new releases, sales, and giveaways. If you're on Facebook, come join my Reader Group!

Made in the USA
Middletown, DE
22 February 2023